The Works of John Galt

Edited by D. S. Meldrum
and William Roughead

Volume Nine

THE LAST OF THE LAIRDS.
First Edition, published in One
Volume, post 8vo, 1826.

Throwing himself down on a sofa . . . said—
"I am all attention, Doctor"

Last of the Lairds]

[*Frontispiece*

The Last of the Lairds

By John Galt

With Introduction
by S. R. Crockett

Illustrated by C. E. Brock

Edinburgh : John Grant
31 George IV. Bridge
1936

Printed in Great Britain by
WILLIAM BLACKWOOD & SONS LTD.

ILLUSTRATIONS

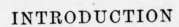

INTRODUCTION

INTRODUCTION

AT the beginning of the publication of this edition of Galt, I asked the Messrs. Blackwood to make "The Last of the Lairds" one of the volumes of the present edition of Galt. Kindly and readily, but somewhat wonderingly, they consented. And now I must pay for my whistle by writing a brief word of introduction to a book which few of this generation have ever heard of, and still fewer ever read.

"The Last of the Lairds" was not, I think, a favourite with the author. Like most of the rest of us, Galt was partial to the weaklings of the flock. He always considered "Ringhan Gilhaize"—a perfectly impossible historical puzzle—to be the best of his books, probably because the writing of it had cost him the most labour. On the other hand, he does not so much as refer to "The Last of the Lairds" in his curious and interesting Autobiography. It is throughout most suggestive to observe Galt's opinion of his own literary works. In his eyes they were mere recreations, the leisure studies of a man of action. All his references

to them do not occupy more than thirty or
forty pages out of the eight hundred of his
Autobiography. And, most curious of all, at
the close of the second volume of that work
Galt gives a list of " *all that he can remember* "
of his published works. He did not even take
the trouble to send to a library or to consult
a publisher's catalogue. Such scribblings were
evidently but " bairn's plaiks " to a man who
had subdued unmapped empires of virgin soil,
and striven unashamed with wild Indians and
the wilder Directors of Canada Companies.

But Galt's own standpoint is not necessarily
ours ; and, with all its imperfections, " The
Last of the Lairds " is a fine book—that is,
for those easily-pleased and happy persons who
can be amused and instructed by the rest of
the author's books. In this most characteristic
book there is no doubt a good deal of inferior
political economy and "gye dreich" talkee-
talkee. For instance, the Nabob and his gim-
crack palace of Nawaubpore are a pair of
unmitigated nuisances. Dr Lounlans is just
Sir Andrew Wylie turned wrong side up, and
deprived of wit in the process.

But then the book has two great merits.
The author's perfectly admirable descriptions
of old-fashioned things and old-fashioned
people, and the intimate knowledge he gives of

his favourite characters, would amply make up
to us for more dreary pages than exist between
the boards of " The Last of the Lairds."   I find
myself turning oftener to the description of the
mansion-house of Auldbiggings at the beginning
of the book, and to that of Mrs Soorocks' dining-
room show-cupboard, than to anything else in
Galt—except perhaps the ministerial trilogy
of wooings and wives described in the " Annals
of the Parish of Dalmailing."

Then how completely and intimately do we
become acquainted with the admirable Mistress
Soorocks!   We can almost tell what she will
say and do in different circumstances.   Then
the inseparable sisters, Miss Girzie and Miss
Shoosie, are altogether delightful, and the tale
waxes more pathetic when they are with difficulty led weeping apart on the bridal night of
the blushing elder maid.   The Laird himself is
almost as good as these three, when once his
utter futility is taken for granted.

It was a stroke of genius in Galt to make
Mr Malachi Mailings tolerable and even sympathetic, after telling us of the fatal " rouping
out of house and ha' " which he inflicted upon
his sometime light-footed sweetheart after the
death of his successful rival.   But Galt trium-
phantly does the seemingly impossible.   And
on the whole the Laird's adventures, matri-

monial and pecuniary, turn out far better than he had any right to expect.

But as Leddy Grippy remains the bright peculiar star of "The Entail," so Mrs Soorocks is the precious jewel carried in the head of one of Galt's most neglected books. She is perennially active with tongue and brain. She plots and counter-plots for the entire party. She cajoles, she scolds, she explains, yet is always ready and uniformly cheerful. And so this garrulous, intrepid Meddlesome Matty of a provincial Scotswoman forms an excellent foil to the decayed, futile, ignorant, obstinate, penniless old laird, who thought that, having done the world the honour to be born to the high dignity of Laird of Auldbiggings, nothing further could possibly be expected of him.

The whole mental attitude of such men—and they exist to this day in the corners of the land, specially in the south-west—is admirably expressed in that motto from "Sayings of the Laird's Jock" which the author prefixes to his book :

" What's the Laird doing, Jock ? "

" Doing ! What should he be doing, but sittin' on his ain louping-on stane and glowering frae him ? "

S. R. CROCKETT.

THE LAST OF THE LAIRDS

THE

LAST OF THE LAIRDS

CHAPTER I

THE Mailings have long occupied a distinguished
place in the laws and annals of Scotland. That
they were of Celtic origin many learned anti-
quaries shrewdly suspect, nor are we disposed
to controvert the opinion; although it must be
allowed they have never been without a taint
of Saxon blood in their veins, being from time
immemorial regarded as of intimate propinquity
with the Pedigrees, whose eminent merits and
great actions are so worthily celebrated in the
chronicles of venerable virginity.

In what part of the country they first struck
their inextricable roots would now be hard to
tell; but the forefathers of Malachi had, from
unrecorded epochs, flourished in the barony of
Killochen, a fertile and pleasant tract of Renfrewshire, and it is meet that we should describe
their habitation.

1   A

The mansion-house of Auldbiggings was a multiform aggregate of corners, and gables, and chimneys. In one respect it resembled the masterpiece of Inigo Jones—Heriot's Work—at Athens: no two windows were alike, and several of them, from the first enactment of the duty on light, had been closed up, save where here and there a peering hole with a single pane equivocated with the statute and the tax-gatherer. The pête-stones, or by whatever name the scalar ornaments of the gables may be known—those seeming stairs, collinear with the roof, peculiar to our national architecture—were frequented by numerous flocks of pigeons. The invention, indeed, of that species of ornament is a fine monumental trait of the hospïtality of our ancestors, who, while they were themselves revelling in the hall, after their Border joys of speed and spoil, thus kindly provided convenient places, where their doves, when returning home heavy and over-fed with foraging on their neighbours' cornfields, might repose, and fatten for spit or pie, in unmolested equanimity.

Appended to the mansion, but somewhat of lower and ruder structure, was a desultory mass of shapeless buildings—the stable, sty, barn, and byre, with all the appurtenances properly thereunto belonging, such as peat-stack, dunghill, and coal-heap, with a bivouacry of invalided utensils, such as bottomless boyns, headless barrels, and brushes maimed of their handles, to say nothing

of the body of the cat which the undealt-with
packman's cur worried on Saturday se'enight. At
the far end was the court-house, in which, when
the day happened to be wet, the poultry were
accustomed to murmur their sullen and envious
whiggery against the same weather which made
their friends the ducks as garrulous with enjoyment at the midden-hole as Tories in the pools
of corruption. But so it is with all of this world :
the good or evil of whatsoever comes to pass lieth
in the sense by which the accident affects us.

The garden was suitable to the offices and the
mansion. It was surrounded, but not enclosed,
by an undressed hedge, which in more than fifty
places offered tempting admission to the cows.
The luxuriant grass walks were never mowed but
just before haytime, and every stock of kail and
cabbage stood in its garmentry of curled blades,
like a new-made Glasgow bailie's wife on the first
Sunday after Michaelmas, dressed for the kirk in
the many plies of all her flounces. Clumps of
apple-ringie, daisies and Dutch-admirals, marigolds
and none-so-pretties, jonquils and gillyflowers,
with here and there a peony, a bunch of gardener's-
garters, a sunflower or an orange-lily, mingled
their elegant perfumes and delicate flourishes
along the borders. The fruit-trees were of old
renown ; none grew sweeter pears ; and if the
apples were not in co-rival estimation with the
palate, they were yet no less celebrated for the
rural beauty of their red cheeks. It is true that

the cherries were dukes, but the plums were magnum-bonums.

Where the walks met, stood a gnomonless dial; opposite to which, in a honeysuckle bower, a white-painted seat invited the Laird's visitors of a sentimental turn to read Hervey's "Meditations in a Flower-Garden;" and there, in the still moonlight nights, in the nightingale-singing season of southern climes, you might overhear one of the servant lasses keckling with her sweetheart. But it is time to approach the house, and make our way towards the inmates.

On approaching the door, and applying your hand to the knocker, you catch a broken key hanging by a string from the lion's mouth. The ring was wrenched away at the time of the auld laird's burial by Sparkinhawse, the drouthy portioner of Drycraigs, when he was coming out from the dirgie, to try if he could find the road to his own home; but, nevertheless, by the key, or your knuckle, you make a noise, which, after being repeated some three or four times, causes the door to open, when either one of the lasses looks from behind it, and says, "What's your wull and pleesure?" or Jock, the Laird's man, comes forth, and leaning his shoulder against the door-cheek, looks in your face till you have propounded your interrogation. On the present occasion it is Jenny Clatterpans, the kitchen-lass, and, as usual, snodless, snoodless, and shodless, who answers to the summons.

Jenny was not altogether just such an amiable
and nymphantine being as the moral master of
Lights and Shadows has discovered, glowing and
gleaming in the poetical regions of Scottish life,
but a substantial armful of those virtues and
graces which, in the shape of well-fleshed, clear-
skinned, sonsy, and hardy queans, may be seen,
with their legs bared above the knee, trampling
in washing-tubs at the open burn-side, or haply,
with the handle of an old spade, pursuing forth
from the kailyard a marauding cow, or engaged
in some of those other vocations of rural or
pastoral drudgery which are equally natural and
prosaical. In truth, Jenny had more of a thorough-
going haverelism about her than of that fond and
fine otherism, so interesting in the heroines of
romance. She was neither particular in her attire
nor methodical in her work, and her words were
unculled—in short, she was a wench likely to be
brought to book without much blushing. But
we forget our duty, and have not yet answered to
her "wull and pleesure," though she has opened
the door, and has dropped behind her the hearth-
brush she happened to have in her hand when our
summons was sounded.

Having inquired for the Laird, Jenny replies—
"Deed, sir, he's no right."

"Ay, Jenny, I'm sorry for that—what ails
him?"

"Ails! I canna say mickle's the matter wi' him,
poor bodie, but he's dwining, and he's no ill

either—trowth, ony ha'd o' health he has is aye
at meal-time, and yet he puts a' in an ill skin."

"Is he confined to his room, Jenny?"

"Room, sir! neither a doctor nor a dose o'
physic would keep him intil his room."

"Indeed! Then he must be greatly altered,
Jenny; for he was rather always of a sedentary
turn."

"That's a' ye ken about him; he's a busy
man."

"Busy, Jenny!"

"Ay, sir, dreadful! He's putting out a book.
Loke, sir, if he's no putting out a book! O that
wearyfu' jaunt to Embro' to see the King! It
has skail't the daunert wits o' the master—the
like o' you and the minister may put out books,
but surely the 'stated gentry hae come to a low
pass indeed when they would file their fingers
wi' ony sic black art!"

"And what is this book about, Jenny?"

"Na, that's a question amang divines, sir; ye
may speer, and I may say Yea or Nay, but what
will't make you the wiser?"

"True, Jenny, I'll never dispute that; but is
Mr Mailings not visible?"

"Veesible, sir!"

"May I not see him?"

"What for should ye no see him? At this
precious moment of God's time, ye may see him
writing his book through the keyhole."

"Through the keyhole, Jenny!—no possible?

I never heard of a man writing a book through a keyhole."

"Weel, weel, sir, no to summer and winter on idioticals, or sic like matters o' fact, the Laird told me that he wouldna be at hame to a living soul in the King's three kingdoms, 'cause he was inditing his book;—the which I thought was— I'll no just say it was a lee; but if it wasna a lee, it was surely very like it; and therefore, sir, though the master said it was an innocent deplomatical, I hae a notion that it was cousin and sib to the first-born of Satan, the whilk is Untruth."

This colloquy with Jenny greatly disturbed our wonted philosophical composure. The Laird, Malachi Mailings, writing a book, was a marvel most indigestible; for although he had become of late years somewhat addicted to reading, particularly of the newspapers, and the *Edinburgh Review*, which he borrowed from me, about a month after publication, the idea of the inspiring mantle dropping down about his shoulders surprised me as with the amazement of a new creation, and under the excitement of the moment, pushing Jenny aside, I hastened to his parlour.

CHAPTER II

On entering the Laird's apartment, I was struck
with several changes, additions, and improvements in the appearance of the room, the consequence of his visit to Edinburgh. For the old
map of Europe, which from the days of his grand-
sire had hung over the mantelpiece, and which
time had tarnished into a brown and yellow
illegibility, a new one of the two hemispheres
was exhibited, with a portrait of the King on the
one side, and of the Duke of Wellington on the
other. The most conspicuous object, however,
was a handsome leather-covered library chair, in
which he was sitting at a table with books and
papers and the other implements of writing
before him, like an Edinburgh advocate warsling
with the law.

He was apparelled in a dressing-gown, which
had evidently been economically made out of
two of his deceased lady's flagrant chintz gowns
of dissimilar patterns. His head was adorned
with a blue velvet cap, wadded and padded not
only to supersede the use of his wig, but even to
be warm enough to cause a germination of fancies,

8

if ideas could be raised by anything like the compost in which gardeners force exotics.

As I entered, he pushed up his spectacles upon his forehead, and raising his eyes from the paper on which he was writing, threw himself back in the chair, and looked not altogether quite satisfied at being so interrupted.

After the interchange of a few preliminary strictures on the weather on both sides, I began to inquire what he thought of the King, and how he had been pleased with his jaunt to Edinburgh.

" For the King," replied the Laird, " I never looked for a particular civility at his hands, though I have been a Justice of the Peace for the shire more than fifteen years, and was, moreover, of great service to his crown and dignity, as one of the officers of the first crop of volunteers. But yon's a pleasant place, yon toun of Embro' ; and the literawty are just real curiosities, and a' philosophers, the whole tot of them. I had an e'e in my neck when I was among them, and maybe some of them shall hear tell o't before long ;" and he glanced his eyes significantly towards the papers before him.

" Indeed, Laird ! and which of them have you seen ?" said I, desirous of hearing his opinion of persons so self-celebrated ; but instead of heeding my question, he continued—

" It's my persuasion, however, that there's a state o' matters yonder in great need of a reformation. But it's my intent and purpose to show the consequence of making men of family functy—offeeshy."

"What, Laird ? — making men of family, what ? "

"Cutting them off by sic legalities as writers to the signet, and advocates, and critics, frae the power of begetting a posterity."

The Laird was in this a little beyond my depth, and I could only rejoin somewhat simply, "And how is it, Laird, you intend to make out all that ? "

"Am I no writing my biography—my own life—wherein the grievance will be made most manifest ? "

"Your life, Laird ! What can there be in your life to record ? The holly-bush before the door has, I should think, had almost as many adventures."

He was plainly piqued at my remark ; but he replied, chuckling with the consciousness of being witty,—

"No man in his senses would ever expect to see an ignoramus bush, far less a doddered holly-bush, take up a pen to write a book. Branches are not hands—No, no—no, no."

To an observation at once so pertinent and unanswerable, I could only say, in a subdued tone, that I had no doubt his Memoirs would be highly instructive and interesting.

"It's to be a standard work," was his calm and

modestly expressed reply, "and the like o't has been long wanted; for if a stop is not soon put to the growth and increase of the conspiracy that I have discovered, there's no telling what our gentry will be brought to."

"Conspiracy, Laird! what conspiracy? And discovered by you! I should as soon have expected to hear you had discovered the longitude or the philosopher's stone, as anything of the sort."

"And is't no the proven fact that, what with the Government at the one end with the taxes, and the labourous folk at the other with their wages, the incomes of our 'stated gentry is just like a candle lighted at both ends?"

"I see, I see, Laird; you have been among the Political Economists, who have neither honour for the rich nor charity for the poor."

For the space of a minute or so he looked at me eagerly and suspiciously, and then, raising himself into an erect posture, said emphatically—

"No man stands in need of a reason to convince him of the animosity of a rhinoceros—do you admit that?"

"For the sake of argument," said I, "the proposition may be allowed."

"Na," said he, falling back in his chair, and spreading out his arms at the same time in the attitude of an astonishment in marble, "if ye deny a first principle, it is of no use to pursue the argument."

That the Laird had indeed been among the Athenian philosophers could no longer be doubted, and that he had in consequence suffered a material change in the habits of his mind was equally evident. Before the visit to Edinburgh, he was seemingly the easiest of mankind—more like a creature made of wool than of clay ; such, indeed, was the sleepy quietude of his nature, that, except when stirred by some compulsion of business or obligation, nothing seemed capable of molesting his tranquillity. 'But when molested —rare as were such occasions—he was testy, snappish, and self-willed ; and the little spurts of temper in which he then indulged betrayed the spirit of controversy which was slumbering within him, and which, in the vicissitudes of things, it was not improbable events might occur to rouse and call forth. I was, therefore, much less surprised at his propugnacity than at the course his opinions had taken ; and becoming more solicitous to see what he had written than to continue the controversy, I said—

"But in what manner, Laird, have you shown the existence of this alleged conspiracy between the Government and the people to overthrow the ancient gentry of his Majesty's hereditary kingdom ?"

"Isna there the changes in the value of money ? I can assure you that I have well considered this portion of the bullion question."

"I should like," said I, with all possible gravity,

"to hear your opinion of the bullion question;— of course, you examine the causes that affect the circulating medium and originate the agricultural distress?"

"The circulating curse—it's as clear a tax of five per cent. on our income as the five and ten deevelry of the war."

"But, no doubt, you have exposed it properly, and in its true colours. Will you have the goodness to read what you have said upon the subject? —for it is a subject which comes home to the business and bosoms of us all. Five per cent.! really, Laird, you surprise me—I never imagined it was so much."

"No man can maintain that it's one farthing less—for, since the coming out of the sovereigns, and the crying down of the old honest coin of the realm, both in the price of horse and horn-cattle a mulct of a full shilling in the pound has been inflicted on the whole agricultural interest."

"And where does that shilling go to, Laird?"

"Where, but to the bottomless pit, the pouch o' Government that they call the sinking fund? And is that no a depreciation?"

"Not to interrupt you, Laird," said I, "but how does the change in the money affect your income?"

"How! I'll show you how. Isna small coin the evidence of cheap labour; and when labour is cheap, has not a man of rental the mair to hain for lying money? But the sight o' a farthing now-a-days is good for sair een : it's no to be met wi', but now and then in the shape of a blot in a town-grocer's 'count, made out by his prentice in the first quarter of the school-laddie's time. It was a black day for Scotland that saw the Union signed, for on that day the pound sterling came in among our natural coin, and, like Moses' rod, swallow't up at ae gawpe, plack, bodle, mark, and bawbie, by the which mony a blithe ranting roaring rental of langsyne has dwinet and dwinlet into the hungry residue of a wadset."

"But, Laird, without calling in question the correctness of your historical observation, I am at some loss to understand how it happened you have been moved to write your life ? "

He made no immediate reply, but, leaning forward with a particularly knowing look, he said, in a half whisper,—

"I'll tell you a secret—it's to pay off one of my heritable bonds. That silly auld havering creature, Balwhidder o' Dalmailing, got a thousand pounds sterling, doun on Blackwood's counter, in red gold, for his clishmaclavers ; and Provost Pawkie's widow has had twice the dooble o't, they say, for the Provost's life. Now, if a minister got sae muckle for his life, and a provost twice the dooble for his, I'm thinking a 'stated gentleman should surely get a brave penny for the like wark."

"I will not dispute your logic, Laird; but

where are the materials for your life to be found?"

"Here and there," he exclaimed in exultation, striking at the same time his breast and forehead; adding, "No man, unless he writes from his own brains and his own bosom, need put pen to paper."

I assented to the justness of the observation; and, after ingratiating myself as well as I could into his confidence, he, in the end, invited me to stay dinner, and promised, as an indemnity for my consenting, that he would entertain me "with a feast of reason and a flow of saul"— a temptation too strong, and too exquisite, as served up by him, to be resisted.

CHAPTER III

THE Laird's work consisted of about half-a-dozen small copy-books, such as schoolboys are in the practice of using, two or three of them with marble covers; on one I observed a parrot, and on another the ruins of Palmyra. The penmanship was not very legible; it was narrow, cramped and dotty, and the orthography made me pause at the first sentence.

"Ye're troubled wi' my hand o' write," said he, "and deed I must own it's no a schoolmaister's, but wi' a thought o' pains ye'll soon be able to read it."

"I think, Laird, I could make my way with the writing, but the spelling is not for a man in haste."

"Ye may weel say that. No man can spell wi' Johnny Sellblethers the town-bookseller's pens—the bodie had ne'er a Christian-like ane in his aught; and I can assure you that an ill pen is baith a crabbit and a fashious implement —I now speak from experience; and I hae had words wi' him concerning his pens—but the creature has no a mouthfu' o' sense; he's a

thing that has nae mair sense nor that bottle
—that bottle did I say?—he has nae mair sense
nor that fender."

Upon some farther inspection of the manuscript, I saw, as the Laird had justly remarked,
that by-and-by, with some pains, I should be
able to make my way through it, in spite of the
penmanship, even too of the orthography; but
the matter was more difficult to manage than
either. It was not a continued and methodical
narrative, but consisted of detached notes and
memoranda, somewhat like Lord Byron's unpub-
lished Biographical Dictionary; instead, however,
of relating to things and accidents which had
befallen himself, they were entirely made up of
reflections on the price of grain and cattle—
denunciations against wages and taxes, ill-paid
rents, and all the other evils which agricultural
distress is heir to, with here and there an incidental note, such as " My mother died this year,
and her burial cost me a power of money—the
coffin was more than five pounds, but it was
very handsome;" or, " Obligated to roup out
John Lounlan's widow — a clamorous woman
that." Whether these were in the first or
second of his books, I do not exactly recollect;
but I could not help remarking that, although
the world would justly appreciate the value of
his information, I was yet apprehensive the critics
would expect some account of his family before
he entered on the matter of his own life and

B

opinions. His reason for having omitted it was most satisfactory.

"It would hae been a right down waistrie o' time and paper; and the need o' writing about my progenitors is not an indispensable. Hasna our family been a family o' note—that's an ocular fact in history—frae afore the Ragman's Roll? But if ye think the laws o' the Republic o' Letters call for an account at my hands, I'll no be weighed in the balance and found wanting."

"To be frank and friendly with you, Laird, the laws of the Republic of Letters certainly do require that your book should begin with some account of the family before you were born, and it should likewise tell us something of your mother's family. It was not, I believe, of the same degree as the Mailings?"

"It's no an easy task," replied the Laird, with a sigh, "to write a history book that will please everybody; but as to my mother, she was come o' pedigree blood, though, it may be said, no just the degree o' our family's."

"Who was she?" said I.

"Her father," resumed the Laird, "was Custocks of Kailyards, an ancient and as weel-kent a race as ony within the four quarters o' the realm; she was a coheiress, and her name was Barbara. Moss o' Peats was married intil her uterine sister, Martha, the other coheiress o' Kailyards, and they had issue a son, Ramplor Moss, begotten of her body, meaning the body o' Aunty Marthy; and he, being a captain in the king's army, gamblet his property wi' riotous living in foreign lands, till it came to be sold by a decreet o' court: and so through him there was an end o' that branch o' my mother's family——"

"All this, Laird," said I, "is most important and interesting. And so your father married one of the coheiresses o' Kailyards—and what then?"

"And what then!—am not I the fruit and issue o' that marriage in the male line? But, poor man, he wasna sparet to beget a better."

"That," replied I, "is much to be regretted, greatly, indeed; but I always heard he died early, and in very melancholy circumstances."

"As to his dying early, I'll no say it's a' truth, for he was weel stricken in the fifties before his espousal o' my mother; but his latter end was an event to be held in remembrance; oh, sir, it was a memento mori."

"Then you have neglected," said I, "by not describing it in your book, an occasion on which you might have given the world a fine impressive moral lesson."

"I am very sorry to hae been sae neglectfu', if ye think sae," replied the Laird.

"Indeed you have been much to blame; and, considering your talents, I must say you have hidden your candle under a bushel, Laird. How did your father happen to die?"

"It's a heavy tale, but it came to pass after this manner. Ye see he was ane of the Langsyne Club, that some threescore Yules bygane had its howff in a public in the town, keepit by a wife that was by name Luckie Gawsie, and he was a man (meaning my father) o' a pleasantrie in company, as I have often heard the late Sparkinhawse o' Drycraigs tell; mony a sooh and sappy night they had wi' ane anither; there wasna a blither bike o' drouthy neibours in a' the shire. Quaigh o' Plunkcorkie was the preses and Luggie o' Dramkeg the croupier. But mirth and melancholy are the twins o' mortality—walking hand in hand to and fro, roaring like lions seeking whom they may devour. Heh, sirs, that night they visited the public o' Luckie Gawsie— weel may I recollect what Sparkinhawse told me; it was wi' the tear in his e'e, for he was a warm-hearted bodie. We had been squeezing the sides o' the gardevin, and neither o' us were then fasting, but baith jocose, the whilk, as he said, put him in mind o' the auld langsyne. 'Laird,' quo' he, 'we were sitting in Luckie Gawsie's back-room, wi' her tappit hen o' claret wine on the table, according to the use and wont o' the club, and Luggie o' Dramkeg was singing the Gaberloonie like a nightingale—oh, he was a deacon at a pawky sang'—I use his ain words," said the Laird.

"And what happened?"

"What happened! Drycraigs, in the way of

a peradventure, some short time after the sang,
gied a glimpse out o'er the table at my father,
and, seeing something no canny in his glower,
said to the preses, ' Plunkcorkie,' said he, ' I'm
thinking Auldbiggings is looking unco gash.' [1]
'Gash !' quo' Plunkcorkie, 'nae wonder; he's
been dead this half-hour; his e'en flew up and
his lip fell down just as Dramkeg was singing the
verse about the courting at the fireside;—and
was I to spoil a gude sang for the likes o' him?—
so when it was done, through an accidence of
memory I forgot to tell you o' the 'poplexy. But,'
continued Plunkcorkie (as Drycraigs told me),
' now that it's noticed, we, for a decency, must get
the corpse ta'en hame to its ain house.' Whereupon they all raise frae their seats, said Drycraigs.

"Wasna that a moving sight? and they filled
lippies, and in solemn silence drank their auld
frien' for the last time; and Quaigh o' Plunkcorkie, the preses, held a glass to my father's
mouth, but he couldna taste, which was a sure
sign he was a dead man; whereupon they all fell
to the greeting with the hearts o' men mourning
in affliction."

I exerted myself to the utmost to sympathise
with the Laird during this affecting description
of the langsyne nights of claret in tappit hens,
and my endeavours were of necessity redoubled
by his moral reflections on the occasion.

"But," said he, " as one door steeks another

[1] *Gash.* With the under-jaw drooping.

opens, and my father's death brought me into the world mair than two moons afore the common course of nature—for, ye see, when my mother, through the mist o' a grey March morning, heard a sound coming towards the house, and lookit out at her window, she discern't the three fou lairds bringing her dead gudeman hame—Drycraigs and Dramkeg were harling [1] the body through the mire by the oxsters, his head dangling o'er his breast like an ill-sewed-on button—Plunkcorkie, the preses o' the club, was following in a sorrowfu' condition, carrying my father's wig and his hat, and one of his boots that had come off, no man could tell how, as they were hauling the corpse along the road; and Drycraigs told me that poor man, Plunkcorkie, was so demented wi' grief that when he came into the house he had the shank o' the very glass in his hand he had held to his old frien's lips, which you must allow was a very touching thing."

"And when they brought home the Laird, what was done?"

"Done! muckle was done—doesna everybody ken I'm a seven-months' bairn? the which is the cause of my weakliness, and has been o' the greatest detriment to me a' my days; because had I no been sae defective wi' infirmity, I might hae been walking the Parliament House o' Edinburgh, wi' a blue shaloon pock to haud fees— but a want is no a fault."

[1] *Harling.* Dragging.

"Very true, Laird," said I, "what you say is a most sagacious remark; but if by reason of any innate weakliness of faculty you have been kept from the bar, the world may have no cause to rue the loss of you as a lawyer, since we are so likely to profit by you as an author."

"No, man," was his emphatic answer—"no, man. I was going to make an observe in the way of philosophy, but let that pass, and do something for the good o' the house."

I had by this time sipped unconsciously the entire contents of my toddy tumbler, and accordingly, upon the Laird's suggestion, I began to replenish.

CHAPTER IV

AFTER the account which Malachi had given of his birth and parentage, I was curious to see what he had said of his education; but on lifting and opening the first volume, (for he dignified his books with that title), I found nothing whatever recorded respecting it, nor of anything which had befallen him till he reached his eighteenth year.

"Dear me, Laird," said I, "how is this? You have omitted what is even more important than the account of your family—all the happy days of your childhood."

"Happy days! that's a' ye ken o' them. Oh, if ye but knew what I suffered in the tender years of my childhood! I was persecuted like a martyr—the blains o' Dominie Skelp's tawse ye may yet discern by an inspection; a' the week there was nothing for me but read, read, read your lesson—write, write, write your copy—add, subtract, multiply, and divide; and on the Sabbath-day, when man and beast and spinning-wheel got leave to rest, I was buffeted by Satan ten times waur in the shape o' the Psalms o'

David. The deevil hae his will o' them, mony a
time thought I, that begat the Question-book."

"But, Laird, pains are pleasant in the recollection, and I should have expected, from the
manner in which you of course passed your youth,
that there would have been a vernal freshness in
the description, such a dewy blossoming in the
memory of your sports and recreations, as would
have moved the world to reveries of innocence
and delight."

"Poo, poo! what is't to be a slave, a nigger
slave, but to be flogged on the back wi' a whip!
Well do I know a tenderer part than the back,
and a whip has but ae scourge, our schoolmaister's
tawse had seven. Neither intemperance nor old
age hae in gout or rheumatic an agony to compare wi' a weel-laid-on whack o' the tawse on a
part that for manners shall be nameless."

"Well, Laird, though there is some truth in
what you say, yet I never should have thought
you were likely to have required any excessive
degree of admonition *a posteriori.*"

"But I was hated by the master—he had a
pleasure and satisfaction in gripping me by the
coat-neck and shaking me wi' a gurl,[1] because I
had no instinct for learning. It's my opinion,
had I been a Justice of the Peace at that time I
would hae prosecuted him to the utmost rigour
of the law. Do you know that once in his tan-
trams he flew on me like a mad dog, and nippit

[1] *Gurl.* Growl.

my twa lugs till he left the stedt[1] o' his fingers
as plainly upon them as the mark o' Peter's finger
and thumb can be seen on the haddock's back.
There wasna a day I didna get a pawmy but
ane, and on it I got twa, the whilk was ca'd in
derision a double morning."

"He appears to have been indeed a most
irascible dominie; but all was no doubt made up
to you when the blessed hours of play and sunshine came round—buoyant and bounding with
your school-fellows——"

"Haud your hand! nane o' your parleyvoo-
ing, ye loon that ye are," exclaimed the Laird,
half slyly, half earnestly, "for the laddies at our
school werena like ither laddies—the thought o'
the usage they gied me gars me grind my teeth
to this day. The master infectit them wi' his
hatred against me, and they never divaul't[2] wi'
their torments. Sure am I, if there be a deevil
that's called Legion, that deevil was the hundred
and thirteen laddies at Dominie Skelp's school—
for though many in number, they were but ane
in nature. Now just think o' what they did—
they ance liftit me o'er the minister's dyke and
gart me steal his apples?"

"But you were rewarded with a share of the
spoil?"

"Ay, yes—I was rewardit—that's nae lee—but
how? tell me that? They made me gie them my
hatfu', and when they got it, they a' set up a

---

[1] *Stedt.* Imprint.   [2] *Divaul't.* Ceased.

shout and a cry o' a thief in the yard, which brought
out Gilbert the minister's man like a raging bear.
He was a contemptuous wretch."

" What did he do to you ? "

" Do ! he laughed me to scorn wi' a guffaw,
and said he thought I had na spunk for sic a
spree ; and then out came Mrs Glebanteinds the
minister's wife, knocking her neives at me as if
I had been an unrighteous malefactor, till I was
sae terrify't that I terrify't them wi' my cries
o' dread. It has been said, indeed, I ne'er got
the better o' that fright ; and I hae some cause
to think no without reason, for I grue[1] wi' the
thought o' an apple to this day, like Adam and
Eve, when they had begotten their sons and
daughters. But I had my satisfaction o' that
finger o' scorn, Gilbert, though it was mair than
fifteen years after."

Well as I was aware of the Laird's disposition
to treasure and cherish resentment, this con-
fession of satisfaction at enjoying revenge so
many years after the schoolboy prank made me
say in a tone very different from that in which
I usually addressed him—

" Is it possible that a man could harbour
anger so long ? " My indignation was, however,
soon bridled, for I presently recollected to whom
I was speaking : his answer was characteristic.

" Had ye felt my provocation, ye would hae
been angry at him a' your days, though ye had

[1] *Grue.* Shudder.

lived to the age of Methusalem—and yet I was na very austere either."

" What did you to him ? "

" I'll tell you, if ye'll thole and listen like a man o' jurisprudence. Ye see, it came to pass that the minister, being weel stricken in years, stretched out his legs on the bed of sickness and departed this life; whereupon his wife, Mrs Gleb-anteinds, being sequestrated from the stipend, left the manse and went to live in the town on Sir Hairy's Fond,[1] which is, as you know, a grand provision for the like o' her. Thus it came to pass that auld Gilbert was ordained to earn his bread by the sweat of his brow, which is the portion of man that is born of a woman, and his lot was to howk[2] ditches. When he had laboured at that some dozen years or the like after the death of his master, he was afflicted wi' an income, and no being able to handle spade or pick, he was constrained to beggary; and so it happened that on the very first morning that he took up the meal-pock for eikrie o' life, as the folk called it, I was standing at the yett looking to see wha might be going to the town and wha coming frae't, when, lo and behold ! I saw an auld beggar-man, wi' a grey head and a cleaner pock than usual, and it was toom[3]—ye

1 The Laird would seem to have forgotten that the " Widows' Fund " was not, at the time of which he was speaking, under the able management of the Rev. Sir Harry Moncrieff. [Author's Note.]

2 *Howk*. Dig, delve.   *Toom*. Empty.

see it was his first morning at the trade—hirpling wi' a stilt towards the avenue; and so hirpling, when he saw me he stoppit, and swither't, and turned round, and was blate to come, the which made me wonder; but belyve, he took off his bonnet and cam to me wi't in his hand, wi' his bald head bare; and when I was marvelling wha this new-set-up beggar could be (for I had no thought o' Gilbert), he said, 'Laird, will ye hansel my pock?'—for he was aye a jocose body—'Will ye hansel my pock, for auld langsyne, Laird?' 'For auld langsyne!' quo' I, 'a hansel in the jougs would better serve you than an almous. Gae awa wi' you, ye fause loon! an ye come within the bounds o' Auldbiggings, I'll set the dog on you, for what ye did to me in the manse garden—that's the auld langsyne I keep in memento."

"And did he knock you down with his crutch?"

"Na, na, he durstna do that—but I trow he was dauntit, for he turn't on his heel and put on his bonnet wi' a splurt [1] like a Highlandman in a pet, and powled himsel awa wi' his stilt.[2]

"But," continued the Laird after a pause, during which he looked somewhat doubtfully at me—"but I see ye think I didna do right," adding, "I'm no, however, so hard-hearted as I let wot; for when I saw that I had made an impression, I ran after him and touched him on the shoulder, and putting my hand in my pouch,

---

[1] *Splurt.* Sudden start.   [2] Denoting ungainly speed.

I gave him a whole penny—twa new bawbees, gude weight, for it was then the days o' the tumbling Tams."

"And what said he?"

"Ye'll aiblins think he was full o' thanksgiving—nae sic thing, but as proud as when he was the minister's man. He took the penny—twa beautiful bawbees it was, and he looked at them, and what do you think he said?—'I'm a beggar noo, and I oughtna to refuse God's charity!' so, withouten a bethank, he hobbled on his way, leaving me standing in the middle of the road wi' my finger in my mouth."

There was something in this story which at the moment damped my curiosity, and, notwithstanding the Laird's earnest entreaties to prolong my visit, made me rise abruptly: a little more hastily, too, than was quite consistent with good manners, I bade him for that afternoon farewell. But as I walked homeward, I reflected on the singular circumstance of such a being attempting a history of himself, and soon settled it to my own contentment that if his book was not likely to furnish many materials for amusement, there was yet enough in his recollections and observations worthy of being a little further sifted. Accordingly, although I had left Auldbiggings half resolved never again to pass the threshold, it so happened that before I reached home my determination was formed to visit him again on the following day.

CHAPTER V

I HAVE a notion that the autobiography of an idiot might not only be interesting, but prove an acquisition of no inconsiderable value to the most philosophical thinkers ; and it seemed to me, upon reflection, that the Laird's undertaking was less preposterous than I had at first imagined. It was possible that although always regarded by the neighbours as a mere ruminating animal, he might yet, in the course of his time, have observed, in the passing current of things, something worthy of notice which had escaped the attention of men reputed wiser. This idea changed in some degree the estimation I had formed of his labour; I could not, indeed, refrain from thinking even of himself with feelings of augmented consideration.

In this speculative frame of mind I took my hat and stick next day, and walked saunteringly across the fields towards Auldbiggings, keeping a path which trended towards the house at some distance from the highroad, in order that I might not be disturbed in my reveries by any accidental encounter with those sort of friends who are ever socially disposed to inflict their company upon you, especially when you most desire to walk alone.

This path winded over the Whinny Knowes, an untenanted and unrentable portion of the Laird's domain, famed from time immemorial among the schoolboys of the town for nests and brambleberries, for which they, as regularly as the equinoctial gales, waged a vernal and autumnal war with Jock the Laird's man. For his master, by some peculiar and squire-like interpretation of the spirit and principles of the game laws, claimed and asserted a right of property over them, as sacred and lawful as that which he possessed to his own dovecot or the fruit of his garden. Accordingly, as soon as the gowans began to open the silvery lids of their golden eyes in the spring, Jock was posted among the blooming furze and broom, particularly on the Saturday's blessed afternoon, to herd the nests. And in like manner, and as periodically as the same play-hallowed day of the week returned, as soon as the celebrated ruddy apples began to blush on the boughs, he was again sent thither to defend the berries, nor were the oranges of the Hesperides guarded of old by a more indomitable griffon.

It happened that, on the occasion of which I am speaking, the warder had taken post for the first or second time for the season to watch the nests, (I am not sure if the day, however, was a Saturday, but if it was not, the weather was so bland and bright that it ought to have been). Jock was sitting in a niche of golden broom, and, inspirited by the influence of the birds and blossoms around him, was gaily whistling, it might be for the want of thought, or from the enjoyment of happiness, as he tapered a fishing-rod with an old table-knife of the true Margaret Nicholson edge and pattern. On seeing me approaching, he rose, leaving his task and implement on the grass, and, in a style I had never remarked in him before, he raised his hand to his hat, and held it there till I requested him to use no new ceremony. I said, however, to myself, "This is another effect of the King's visit;" but as Jock did not accompany the Laird on the occasion to Athens, I became a little pryish to ascertain whether this debonair touching of the hat was derived from the special tuition of his master, or had been acquired from some compeer's authority. Before I had time, however, to ask any question, Jock inquired if I was for "The Place," as the house of Auldbiggings was commonly called by the servants and villagers.

"Ye'll fin' the Laird," said he, "a busy man."

"Indeed! and what is he doing?"

"Doing? What should he be doing, but sitting on his ain louping-on stane,[1] glowring frae him?"

"And call ye that being busy, John?"

"And is't no sae? Isna idleset the wark o'

[1] *Louping-on stane.* Stirrup-stone.

C

a gentleman—and what more would ye hae him to be doing in that way ? what could he do more ? "

" Then he has given up writing his book, has he ? "

" He maun think o' what to put in't. King David made his Psalms in the watches of the night."

" 'Tis my opinion, John," said I, "that the Laird might do worse than consult you on the subject, considering how long and how well you have been acquainted with himself and all his family."

" I'm thinking," replied Jock, casting his eyes on the ground, " he would come but little speed without the help and counsel o' somebody, living sic a lonely life as he has done; till he gaed to the King's coming hame, it could na be said in a sense that he had cast an ee on the world."

" But your experience in that way, John, has been great ; and if he consults his own renown, he will take your advice in every sentence." I had in this my mind's eye on Molière's old woman.

" I'll no deny that I hae had a finger in the pie already ; but I was telling him yestreen, after ye went away, when he gied me an account of your applauses, that I thought the book would be better if he would saw it here and there wi' twa-three bonny kittle words out o' the dictioner. If it has a fault (and what hasna ?) it's a want o' gentility."

That Jock had long been viceroy over the Laird was well known to the whole parish; but that he was so deep in his literary counsels, and so participant in his lucubrations, I had not suspected. I felt, therefore, that to indulge curiosity further by leading him on to the unconscious disclosure of his master's secrets, would be as little consonant to gentility as the want of kittle words in the Memoirs. Accordingly, partly to appease my own compunctions, and partly to soothe him into an oblivion of the impertinence of which I had been so guilty, I complimented him on his long and faithful attachment to the Laird, and on the confidence which he enjoyed and which he merited.

"And he weel deserves to be weel servit," was the answer. "Isna he come o' a parentage o' pedigree, and born wi' a silver spoon in his mouth to an heritage o' parks and pastures, woods and waters, and a' the other commodities that mak blood gentle?"

Hitherto I had known little more of Jock than by sight; but I discovered by this accidental conversation that he was worthy of all the celebrity he enjoyed among the neighbours for the sagacity of his remarks and the singularity of his sayings,—many of the latter having acquired the currency of proverbs; but whether owing to the value of the bullion, or to the peculiarities of the mintage, might perhaps admit of some controversy. It was clear, however, that

Jock was worthy of his master; nor in the sequel will it be questioned that the Laird deserved such a man. But as it is both fit and expedient that the courteous reader should also become a little more acquainted with Jock, it may be as well to mention a few particulars of his personal history and character, while the scene of my own rôle in the drama is changing from the Whinny Knowes to the parlour of Auldbiggings.

Jock, or John Dabbler, as he ought to be called, when we quit the free vernacular of our colloquial pen and indite with the recondite dignity of history, was the son of one of the Laird's cotters. For some four or five years after his birth, it was the unshaken opinion of his mother that he was born to distinction, inasmuch as he had, according to her account of him, always showed a greater inclination to eat than to work; but increase of years, which expanded his capacity for the former, brought no compensating alacrity for the latter, and, in consequence, as he would neither learn a town-trade, nor help his father in the labour of dykes and ditches, she obtained for him, about the age of seven, a sort of ashypet office in the Laird's kitchen, where, in course of time, he acquired a grey duffle coat with a red collar, and was regarded as the helper and successor of an old man who had spent his whole life in the honourable vocation of flunkie to three generations of the Auldbiggings.

At the era of which we are treating, Jock, though far advanced into the wane of manhood, still retained the familiar callant abbreviation of his baptismal epithet, and still as devoutly believed as on the first day when he entered the house that the whole earth contained but two men worthy of worship—the King and the Laird ;—but to which the prime honour and the firstlings of homage were due, he had never determined to his own satisfaction. The leaning certainly, however, was in favour of the Laird; for, never having seen the King, he justly remarked, when sometimes drawn into controversy on the subject, that far-off fowls had fair feathers — thereby intimating that upon a nearer inspection and closer comparison, the difference would be found less between them than in the alleged disparity of the pomp and circumstance of their respective conditions.

Besides this personal opinion of the superiority of his master, Jock had as strong a feeling of property in everything belonging to the Laird as the Laird had himself, and probably considered himself as much an integral portion of the estate as the time-honoured holly-bush on the green, of which I have already spoken. But in this feeling there was none of that persuasion of a community of goods which is sometimes discovered among the domestics of the best-regulated families. On the contrary, Jock was as faithful to his menial trusts as the key or the mastiff; as true as the one, and not less vigilant than the other. It was owing to the impulse of this fidelity that our conversation on the Whinny Knowes was so suddenly interrupted, and the leisure afforded for this digression. For, just as I was on the point of sifting his opinion as to the constituents of gentle blood, he happened to discover a piquet of the schoolboys advancing towards the Knowes, and abruptly darted from me to challenge their intrusion.

CHAPTER VI

I DID not find the Laird, as Jock said I should, sitting busy with idleness on the louping-on stone at his gate, but in the parlour, and with the insignia of authorship arranged before him, installed in the library chair so particularly before described.

After the customary interchanges of visitation inquiries, he reverted to the subject of our yesterday's conversation.

"I hae been," said he, "a thought ravelled in mind wi' what ye were saying concerning the specialities o' my father and mother's kith and kin; but the book ye would hae me to make is no like what I mean to do—mine's to be a book o' soleedity, showing forth the wastrie of heritages by reason o' the ingrowth o' trade and taxes."

I was grieved to find the old gentleman really so much of a political economist; but as to have disputed with him would have served no purpose, I only replied—

"No doubt, Laird, any book you write will be well worthy of attention; and if it does not suit the plan of your present work to enter into those domestic details and circumstances of householdry, which none can describe better, perhaps you may favour the world with something of that sort hereafter."

"Ye're no without a nerve o' discernment—I can see that," was his self-complacent answer, "and I'll no say what's in the egg-bed o' my brain; but no to keckle ower soon, I hae been thinking a' this morning's meditation that if I get a satisfactory solacium for the turn in hand, I may be able belyve to pay off another o' the bonds, and so, by a graduality, clear the estate and die wi' a free income."

When he first told me that his motive in undertaking to write his life was to pay off one of the mortgages, the idea was too ludicrous to leave any serious impression; but this repetition of it made me suspect the debt lay more heavily upon him than I was aware of. I knew, indeed, that from the death of his wife his affairs had been ill managed, and that for many years the residue of his rental—that which remained after paying the interest on the heritable bonds—was scarcely sufficient for his thriftless expenditure; but that he felt anything like the actual pinchings of pecuniary difficulty had never occurred to me. I did not, however, then choose to ask him any direct question on the subject, but it was impossible not to pity the helplessness and infirmity of the poor old man, who could imagine that from any resource so ineffectual as his pen the means might be obtained to abate the pressure of embarrassment; nevertheless, I said to him half jocularly—

"But what can it signify to you, Laird, to die with a clear income, unless you intend to marry again, and mean to provide for a young family, seeing that at present you have no descendant, nor even an heir within the fifth degree of cousinship?"

He looked at me steadily askance for about the space of a minute, and then said with an accent in which there was a slight inflection of sadness—

"Ye're no acquaint wi' Hugh Caption, the writer?"

"I have heard of him; but I hope you have more sense, Laird, than to go to law?"

"So think I mysel," was his answer, expressed somewhat sedately; "but it's no the case wi' everybody."

"How, Laird!" cried I, startled by the import of the observation, and really feeling for him more anxiety than I affected; "blameless in walk and conversation as you have always been, is it possible that you can have fallen into the snares of Caption?"

"He's but the claw o' the case," replied the Laird, adding with a half-suppressed sigh, as it were in soliloquy, "and it's a claw that needs parin': an eagle's talons may tear the flesh frae the bone, but his grasping grip's enough to rive the seven senses out o' the soul.'

"I am grieved to hear you say so. How did you happen to fall into his clutches? By whom is he employed?"

"Stop, stop," interrupted the Laird; "the mair haste the waur speed—bridle the unicorn o' your impatience and I'll tell you all the outs and ins o't. Ye see, when Mr Rupees the Nawbub came hame frae Indy, and bought the Arunthrough property frae the Glaikies, who, like sae mony ithers o' the right stock o' legitimate gentry, hae been smothered out o' sight by the weed and nettle overgrowths o' merchandise and cotton-weavry, he would fain hae bought Auldbiggings likewise, and sent that get o' the de'il and the law, Caption, to make me an offer; but I was neither a prodigal son nor an Esau, to sell my patrimony for a mess o' pottage, so I gied him a flea in his lug, and bade him tell the Nawbub to chew the cud o' the sin o' covetousness, the whilk is disappointment."

"And from that I suppose, Laird, you and Mr Rupees quarrelled?"

"Oh no, it was the beginning to a great cordiality o' friendship, for he came o'er here the next day, and made a decent apology, inviting me in the civillest manner to dine wi' him, and was most enterteening about hoo they hunt elephants wi' tygers instead o' hounds; telling me, among ither news, o' the braw thing he did to a great Mogul, that was a Pishawa in Hydrobab, and had a Durbah. In short we came to an understanding, and ae night when we were sitting by oursels, drinking a bottle o' his best Madeira wine (that was eleven years in wood in Bengal before he bought it, and sixteen in the bottle after), he said that he had some spare money, which he would be glad to lend on easy terms, for seven years, or even a langer period, begging if I should hear of ony gentleman in want, to gie him an inkling."

It was not difficult to discern from this the machination of the Nabob's friendship for the innocent Laird, and I shook my head.

"Deed," said Malachi, "ye may weel shake your head, for his wine was a flee, and his money a hook, that I was a silly saumon to swallow. But he won upon me, so I told him o' the wadsets on Auldbiggings, and of the twa heritable bonds o' the doers [1] for the young leddies o' Hainings, the which might be called up in a day's notice, and thus it came to pass, frae less to mair, that I covenanted to take as meikle o' his siller as would pay off that precarious obligation, the thought of which was like guilt to my night's rest."

"And having so allured you to take his money," said I, "he now vexes you for repayment?"

"Na, he does far waur. He has gotten, the gude kens how, the right to the other wadsets, and put them intil the Nebuchadnezzar-like

---

[1] *Doers.* Trustees.

talons o' Caption, who has sent me word that if
the debt's no redeemed afore Whitsunday he's
instructed to proceed ; and he's, I needna tell
you, a sinner that skips, when he says the
Lord's Prayer, ' forgie our debts as we forgie our
debtors ; ' so ye see there is a needcessity for me
to do something—and books being in request, I
could think o' naething easier than making ane
to help me in the coming stress, money being
scarce to borrow, and land ill to sell."

By this disclosure it was evident that the poor
Laird's circumstances were much worse than I
had conjectured ; for, upon inquiring the amount
of the mortgages, I was grieved to find it almost
equal to the reputed value of his whole estate,
depreciated as the value of land was at that time.
I thought, however, that if the character of the
transaction was properly represented to the Nabob,
the apprehension of public odium might induce
him, if not to forego the prosecution entirely of
so harsh a suit, to mitigate the pressure of it by
some indulgence as to time, especially as, from
the date of his arrival in the neighbourhood, he
had cultivated popularity, and not by the least
ostentatious means.   Accordingly, I offered to
call on Dr Lounlans, the minister of the parish,
to beg his mediation in the business ; but on
mentioning his name, a change came over the
complexion of the Laird, and a slight convulsive
shudder of repugnance vibrated through his
whole frame.   He made no answer, but looked

at me suspiciously askance, and then taking off
his purple velvet cap, rubbed his bald head with
his hand, and fetched a deep breath which ter-
minated in something like a sigh.

" You do not seem," said I, " to approve of my
suggestion.   But a man of Dr Lounlans's personal character, with the great ascendency which
his eloquence gives him over the minds of all
who approach him, is in such an affair as yours,
Laird, the most likely to prove an effective
advocate."

" When that Neezam o' the Carnatic, Rupees,
offered me his money, he shook me by the hand
wi' meikle flattering confidentiality," replied the
Laird, after a pause of about the space of a
minute ; " but the thought o' his covetous de-
ceitfulness is neither sae sour nor sae bitter as
to think I would come under an obligation to the
like o' Dominie Lounlans."

The energy with which this was uttered had
more in it of alarm than of contempt.   The tone
was at variance with the language, and the look
was expressive of aversion rather than of dread.
It was evident, indeed, that some skinless feeling had been touched ; and that something had
occurred in the previous history of the Laird
regarding the amiable and eloquent preacher of
which I had not heard.   In that moment my
eye happened to glance towards one of the biographical copy-books on the table, and I suddenly recollected the note respecting the widow

Lounlans, whom the Laird had been obliged to roup out of the farm, and whose clamour on the occasion he had so emphatically recorded.

"Is Dr Lounlans," said I, "any relation to that widow who gave you so much trouble long ago?"

"Isna he her son? and didna he set himself in revenge against me to get the kirk? If he hadna been stirred up and egget on by a malice prepense, would he ever hae daur't to show his face in this parish, far less in our poopit, driven out o't as his mother and the rest o' them were, black wi' disgrace in my debt, that wasna pay't for ten years—though to be sure when it was pay't she alloo't interest on the interest; but that was only out o' a pridefu' spite to humble me, 'cause o' my justice, for there was no need o' sic payment, as I would hae been content wi' the single interest. But it's what we're to expec frae the upsetting o' the lower orders. It was the machinations o' thae very Lounlans that first opened my een to the conspiracy that's working the downfall and overthrow of sae mony birth-rights o' our national gentry. But if ye kent the original cause of their hatred to me, ye would be none surprised to see me sae grue at the thought of being behadin'[1] to ane o' them."

"Why, I think that's pretty well explained by what you have just told me. It was to be expected they would bear a resentful remembrance

[1] *Grue . . . behadin'.* So sick at the thought of being in-debted.

of the manner in which you drove them from the parish."

"They went of their own free wull," exclaimed the Laird eagerly, as if to defend himself from a reproach. "Had my rent been paid, I wouldna hae molested them, and they might have stayed in the parish for me, when I got them off the farm —but the woman had a hatred o' me lang afore a' that."

"And for what reason?"

"For no reason at a' but the very want o't; for when she was young she was a bonnie lassie, wi' blithe e'en and cheeks like a Flanders baby; and I would hae made her leddy of Auldbiggings. But I hae written a' the particulars about it here, the which ye may read, while I step to the Whinny Knowes to see what Jock's doing; and when ye're done ye can follow me."

As soon as the Laird left the room, I accordingly began to read; but I had not proceeded many sentences when I was tempted, of course by the Evil One, to copy the chapter verbatim. Whether, in doing so, I have been guilty of any breach of faith, the critic may determine for himself while the compositor is setting the extract.

CHAPTER VII

THE Laird began the record of his eighteenth year in these words :—

"There livt at this time, on ye fermsted of Broomlans, a pirson that was a woman, by calling a widow; and she and her husband, when he was in this lyf, had atween them, Annie Daisie, a dochter; very fair she was to look upon, cumly withal, and of a feeleeceety o' nature.

"This pretty Annie Daisie, I kno not hoo, found favor in my eyes, and I maid no scruppel of going to the kirk every Sabbatha day to see her, though Mr Glebantiends was, to a certentye, a vera maksleepie preecher. When I fore-gathered with her by accidence, I was all in a confewshon; and when I would hae spoken to her wi' kindly words, I coud but look in her cleer een and neigher like Willie Gouk, the haivrel laddie; the whutch maid her jeer me as if I had a want, and been daft likewyse; so that seeing I cam no speed in coorting for myself, I thocht o' telling my mother, but that was a kittle job—howsoever, I took heart, and said—

"' Mother——'

" ' Well, son,' she made answer, ' what woud ye ? '

" ' I'm going to be marriet,' quo' I.

" ' Marriet ! ' cried she, spredding oot her arms wi' a consternayshun—' and wha's the bride ? '

" I didna like just to gie her an even-down answer, but said I thought myselph old enough for a helpmeat to my table, whutch caused her to respond with a laff; whereupon I told her I was thinking of Annie Daisie.

" ' Ye'll shoorly ne'er marry the like o' her— she's only a gairner's dochter.'

" But I thocht of Adam and Eve, and said, 'We're a' come of a gairner.' The whutch to heer caused her presentlye to wax vera wroth with me ; and she stampit with her foot, and called me a blot on ye skutshon o' Auldbiggings ; then she sat doon, and began to reflek with herself ; and after a season, she spoke rawshonel about the connexion, saying she had a wife in her mind for me, far more to the purpose than sitch a cawsey danser as Annie Daisie.

" But I couldna bide to hear Annie Daisie mislikent,[1] and yet I was fear't to commit the sin of disobedience, for my mother had no mercy when she thocht I rebell't against her othority ; so I sat down, and was in treebolayshon, and then I speert with a flutter of affliction, who it was that she had will't to be my wyfe.

" ' Miss Betty Græme,' said she, ' if she can be persuaded to tak sic a headowit.'

[1] *Mislikent.* Miscalled.

D

"Now, this Miss Betty Græme was the tocher-less sixth dochter o' a broken Glasgow Provost, and made her leeving by seamstress-wark and floowring lawn; but she was come of gentle blood, and was herself a gentle creature, though no sae blithe as bonnie Annie Daisie; and for that I told my mother I would never take her, though it should be the death o' me. Accordingly I ran out of the hoos, and took to the hills, and wistna where I was, till I found myself at the door of the Broomlands, with Annie Daisie before me, singing like a laverock as she watered the yarn of her ain spinning on the green. On seeing me, however, she stoppit, and cried, 'Gude keep us a', Laird, what's frighten'd you to flee hither?'

"But I was desp'rate, and I ran till her, and fell on my knees in a lover-like fashion; but wha would hae thocht it? she dang me over on my back, and as I lay on the ground she watered me with her watering-can, and was like to dee with laffing: the which sign and manifestation of hatred on her part quencht the low o' love on mine; and I raise and went hame, drookit and dripping as I was, and told my mother I would be an obedient and dutiful son. Soon after this, Annie Daisie was marriet to John Lounlans; and there was a fulsome fraising[1] about them when they were kirkit, as the cumliest cupple in the parish. It was castor-oil to hear't; and I was determin't to be upsides with them, for the way she had jiltit me.

[1] *Fraising.* Phrasing, making a phrase of.

As I lay on the ground she watered me with
her watering-can

"In the meanwhile my mother, that never, when she had a turn in hand, alloo't the grass to grow in her path, invited Miss Betty Græme to stay a week with us; the which, as her father's family were in a straitened circumstance, she was glad to accep; and being come, and her mother with her, I could discern a confabling atween the twa auld leddies—Mrs Græme shaking the head of scroopolosity, and my mother laying doon the law and the gospel—all denoting a matter-o'-money plot for me and Miss Betty. At last it came to pass, on the morning of the third day, that Miss Betty did not rise to take her breakfast with us, but was indisposed; and when she came to her dinner, her een were blear't and begrutten. After dinner, however, my mother that day put down, what wasna common with her housewifery, a bottle o' port in a decanter, instead o' the gardevin for toddy, and made Miss Betty drink a glass to mak her better, and me to drink three, saying, 'Faint heart never won fair leddy.' Upon the whilk hint I took another myself, and drank a toast, for better acquaintance with Miss Betty. Then the twa matrons raise to leave the room, and Miss Betty was rising too; but her mother laid her hand upon her shoother, and said, 'It's our lot, my dear, and we maun bear with it.' Thus it came to pass that me and Miss Betty were left by ourselves in a very comical situation.

"There was silence for a space of time between us; at last she drew a deep sigh, and I responded, to the best of my ability, with another. Then she took out her pocket-napkin and began to wipe her eyes. This is something like serious coorting, thocht I to myself, for sighs and tears are the food of love; but I wasna yet just ready to weep; hoosever, I likewise took out my pocket-napkin, and made a sign o' sympathy by blowing my nose, and then I said—

"'Miss Betty Græme, how would ye like to be Leddy of Auldbiggings under my mother?'

"'O heavens!' cried she, in a voice that gart me a' dinle,[1] and she burst into a passion of tears; the whilk to see so affectit me that I couldna help greeting too—the sight whereof made her rise and walk the room like a dementit bedlamite.

"I was terrifyt, for her agitation wasna like the raptures I expectit; but I rose from my seat, and going round to the other side of the table where she was pacing the floor, I follow't her, and pulling her by the skirt, said, in a gallant way, to raise her spirits, 'Miss Betty Græme, will ye sit down on my knee?' I'll ne'er forget the look she gied for answer, but it raised my courage, and I said, 'E'en's ye like, Meg Dorts'—and with a flourish on my heel I left her to tune her pipes alane. This did the business, as I thocht; for though I saw her no more that night, yet the next morning she came to breakfast a subdued woman, and my mother, before the week was out, began to make preparations for the wedding.

[1] *Gart me dinle.* Caused me to thrill through and through.

"But, lo and behold! one afternoon, as Miss
Betty and me were taking a walk at her own
requeesht on the highroad, by came a whusky
with a young man in it, that had been a penny-
clerk to her father, and before you could say
Hey cockilorum! she was up in the gig, and
down at his side, and aff and away like the dust
in a whirlwind.

"I was very angry to be sae jiltit a second
time, but it wasna with an anger like the anger
I suffert for what I met with at the hands of
Annie Daisie. It was a real pawshon. I ran
hame like a clap o' thunder, and raged and rampaged till Mrs Græme was out of the house, bag
and baggage. My mother thought I was gane
wud, and stood and lookt at me, and didna daur
to say nay to my commands. Whereas, the
thocht o' the usage I had gottin frae Annie
Daisie bred a heart-sickness o' humiliation, and
I surely think that if she had not carried her
scorn o' me sae far as to prefer a bare farmer
lad like John Lounlans I wad hae sank into a
decline, and sought the grave with a broken
heart. But her marrying him roosed my corruption, and was as souring to the milk of my
nature. I could hae forgiven her the watering;
and had she gotten a gentleman of family, I
would not have been overly miscontented; but
to think, after the offer she had from a man of
my degree, that she should take up with a tiller
of the ground, a hewer of wood, and a drawer

of water, was gall and wormwood. Truly, it was
nothing less than a kithing of the evil spirit of
the democraws that sae withered the green bay-
trees of the world, when I was made a captain
in the volunteers, by order of the Lord-Lieutenant,
'cause, as his Lordship said, of my stake in the
country. But guilt and sin never thrive, and
she had her punishment."

Thus far had I proceeded with the extract,
when I heard the Laird's foot on the stair. I
knew it by the sound of his stick on the steps,
by which it was accompanied, and it made me
hastily, and, I must confess, not without something like the trepidation which is supposed to
attend the commission of a larceny, fold up the
paper, and hide it in my pocket, which I had
scarcely done and composed myself into a stu-
dious attitude, with the manuscript in my hand,
when the old gentleman entered the room.

CHAPTER VIII

WHEN the Laird had resumed his place in the library chair, I saw by his manner, and particularly by the peculiar askance look he gave me, which was only habitual to him while under the influence of jealousy or of apprehension, that something had occurred during his visit to the Whinny Knowes to ruffle his wonted equanimity; but as he evidently made an effort to conceal his perturbation, I abstained from saying anything which might lead him to suppose I observed it—on the contrary, I remarked, with reference to the treatment he had received in his courtships, that he certainly had suffered much from the cruel hands of womankind.

He again looked askance at me, and smiled for a moment, with a countenance as pleased and simple in its expression as the naif relaxation of sorrow on the features of a child, when indem-

nified with an apple or a toy for some heartfelt
affliction; he then said—

"But in those days, I was better able to
bear a' that and meikle mair, than within that
volume of the book it written is of me, as in
the words of King David, I may say, speaking
specially of that volume beneath the cuff of
your sleeve; for now I'm auld, and a wee blast
o' a blighting wind snools the pride o'[1] the doddered tree. What would ye think? There was
Caption, and Mr Angle the land-surveyor, wi'
brazen wheels within wheels, and the Nawbub
(Belzebub's ower gude a name for him) directing ane of his flunkies to run here wi' the chain,
and there wi' the mark. They were measuring
my lands—the lands o' my forefathers!"

"Not possible!" said I, unaffectedly partici-
pating in the feelings of the helpless and dispi-
rited old man. "If no better sentiment existed
among them, some deference to public decorum
might have restrained Rupees till the mortgages
were regularly foreclosed, or at least till he had
your permission."

"For the possibility of the trespass," replied
the Laird, "I'll no undertake to argue; but for
the fact, that has been proven a truth by deed
o' payment."

"Payment! to what do you allude?"

"I'll tell you. You see, when I beheld them
around the brazen racks and torments of valua-

[1] *Snools.* Breaks the pride of.

tion, I stood still, marvelling if I wasna dreaming the vision o' Ezekiel the prophet, and Jock, seeing me in that trance, came running in a splore o' wonder, crying, 'Odsake, Laird, if John Angle, the surveyor, hasna a loadstone watch in his curiosity, that tells the airts o' the wind!'"

The Laird's eyes at this crisis of his narrative kindled, and he became agitated with indignation. "My corruption rose," said he, "and stamping wi' my foot, I said to Jock, 'How durst you let the Boar into our vineyard? The bairns o' the town would tak but eggs, and birds, and blackberries, but Rupees and his rajahs are come to rob us o' home and ha'.' Whereupon Jock— he's as true's a dog—before the shape o' my breath was melted in the air, ran to them, and wi' the butt o' a fishing-rod he had in his hand smashed at ae blow a' their wheels o' evil prophecy into shivers, and told Caption that if he didna leave our land, he would mak sowther o' his harns¹ to mend them. Then there arose a sough and sound o' war, and rumours o' war, which caused me to walk towards them in my dignified capacity as one of his Majesty's Justices of the Peace, and I debarred them in the King's name, and with his royal authority, from trespassing on my ground—trampling the rising corn, doing detriment wi' their hooves to the herbage, and transgressing the bounds o' dyke and fence, to

¹ *Mak sowther o' his harns.* Make solder of his brains.

say nothing of yetts and ditches,—taking John
Angle to be a witness against Rupees, and lodg-
ing instruments o' protest, in the shape of a
shilling, in the hands of Caption himsel, 'cause
he's a notary public."

"And did he take them?" said I, not less surprised than astonished at such unwonted spirit
and decision on the part of the Laird.

"Tak them! he durstna refuse; for I told
him, if he did, his refusal was a thing that would
make the fifteen Lords o' Embro redden on their
benches."

"What then happened?"

"It would have done your heart gooa to see
what happened. There was Rupees slinking and
sidling awa' wi' his tail atween his legs, and
John Angle, wi' a rueful countenance, gathering
up the catastrophes of his oglet." [1]

"But what did Caption do?"

"He's the seventh son of Satan, and of course,
has by birth and instinct mair skill in deevilry
than his father. He stood looking at me wi' a
girn that was nothing short o' a smile o' destruction, and then he said, 'Laird,' quo' he, and
ye wouldna hae thought that honey could hae
melted in his mouth, 'I'll say nothing of this
here, but——' and wi' that he walked away.
Noo, what could he mean wi' that 'but'? I'm
frightened for that 'but.' 'But's' an oraculous
word frae the lips o' the law."

---

[1] *Oglct.* The Laird means "theodolite."

I could not but sympathise with the poor Laird's apprehensions. The character of Caption allowed of no doubt as to the persecution which would ensue, and it was not uncharitable to think that his malicious machinations would be supported by his rich and unprincipled client. Under these feelings and that impression I again said—

"You must indeed permit me to beg the mediation of Dr Lounlans. If any man can avert the trouble and vexation to which you are so unhappily exposed, he alone of all the parish——"

"Do you see that picture of the King on the wall?" replied the old man. "Bid it come out frae ahint the glass, and go to the Manse, and drink a glass o' wine wi' Dr Lounlans, and I'll be there when it does that, and beseech the Doctor to supplicate for me."

"Really, Mr Mailings, you surprise me. Forty years might have quenched the anger you felt against his mother for rejecting your suit, the proffer of your love."

"Oh, I was willing to forgie her for that—I had forgien her, and had amaist forgotten't; but when her gudeman dee't, and I was constrained by course o' law to roup her out o' the farm, I'll never forgie what she did then—no, no, never. She stir't the country like a wasp's byke about me—I durstna mudge[1] on the King's highway without meeting revile and molestation. It's no to be told what I suffer't. The cripple bodie, auld Gilbert, that was

[1] *Mudge.* Stir.

the minister's man, wudna tak an amous ae day
frae me—he ne'er got the offer o' another—'cause,
as he said, surely I was needfu' o't mysel. Heard
ye ever sic impiddence?—and a' this for acting
according to law, as if to do sae were a sin!"

There was enough in this statement to convince me that the conduct of the Laird towards
the widow and her children had not been exactly
in unison with public opinion, and I replied, "That
certainly, although to act according to law never
ought to be regarded as a sin, yet times and
occasions will sometimes arise when it may be
thought a shame—as, for instance, Laird, the
treatment you are now suffering from Rupees."

"But there's an unco difference atween the
like o' me and Mrs Lounlans," was his answer;
the force of which derived considerable emphasis
from his pettish and mortified accent. He added,
however, in a lowlier tone, "Rupees might hae
a decency for a neighbour that he was sae blithe
to mess and mell wi', either in his ain house or
here."

This egotism would perhaps have moved other
feelings than it did had it been said at another
time, and not so immediately in comparison with
his own harsh treatment of her on whom he
had been so willing to bestow his undiminished
fortune; but to have reminded him of any
similarity in the aspect of their respective impoverished circumstances, while he was sitting
in the defencelessness of age, and with such

evidence of effectless endeavour to avert inevitable ruin lying on his table, would have required the extenuation of some apology for myself. Guilt in fetters hath claims on Charity which Justice dare not forbid.

The reluctance of the old man to allow the mediation of Dr Lounlans was plainly to be ascribed to any sentiment but contrition. The paleness which overspread his countenance when I first suggested the expedient showed that his feelings had a deeper source than pride, and were mingled with recollections which awakened the associations of sensual repugnance, as well as those of moral antipathy. My curiosity, in consequence, became excited to hear something more of the history of Dr Lounlans's family; and as I was still desirous, notwithstanding the Laird's determination to the contrary, to procure the Doctor's good offices to mitigate the severity of the Nabob's proceedings, I resolved to call at the manse on my way home, partly to represent the unhappy state of the old man, and partly, if chance favoured, to obtain some further account of transactions so manifestly bitter in the remembrance. Accordingly, after a few general observations, chiefly of an admonitory cast, as to the caution requisite to be adopted in dealing with his adversaries, I bade the Laird good afternoon, with a promise to return next day.

CHAPTER IX

AFTER leaving the house, and having proceeded about half-way down the avenue towards the gate which opened upon the highway, I paused and looked back with a much greater disposition to indulge in an amicable sentimental vein than I had ever thought it possible for the mortgage-mouldered gables of Auldbiggings to have awakened. But in that same moment I was roused from the reverie into which I was falling by the pattering of footsteps nimbly approaching from the gate. I knew those footsteps by the sound of haste which was in them, and, could I have escaped unnoticed, I would have eschewed the evil of the owner's presence. I was grieved, indeed, to think that the Laird's impending fate had already become so publicly known as to call forth the afflicting commiseration of Mrs Soorocks, whose sole business and vocation in life consisted in visiting those among her neighbours who were suffering either under misfortune or anxiety, and feelingly, as she herself called it, "sympatheesing with their dispensation." But as it was impossible to retire without being observed, I went

forward with a quickened pace, in order that I
might not be detained by her.   In this, however,
I failed; for although I affected to be in quite
as much haste as herself, and on more urgent
business, she laid her hand upon my arm, and
entreated me to tell her all the particulars, and
if it was true that Mr Rupees had been knocked
down by the Laird; sedately, and with a sympathetic voice, asserting her perfect conviction
that the rumours in respect to that must be un-
worthy of credit.

"But," said she, "when the waur has come to
the warst, Auldbiggings has only to step o'er the
way to the house of Barenbraes, and make choice
of one of the sisters for his livelihood.   Poor
leddies, they hae lang waited for a man to speer
their price;[1] and in his state of the perils of
poverty, he needna be nice, and neither o' them
has any cause to be dorty."

Now it happened that the maiden sisters of
Barenbraes, Miss Shoosie and Miss Girzie Minnygaff, had long been the peculiar objects of Mrs
Soorocks' neighbourly anxieties, and the source
of her great interest in their fate and fortunes
requires that some account should be given of
their family and peculiar condition.

In the days of their youth they had never
been celebrated for any beauty.   Miss Shoosie
was at this time only in her fiftieth year, but so
mulcted of the few graces which niggard nature

[1] *Speer their price.*   Propose marriage to them.

had so stingily bestowed that she was seemingly already an aged creature. Her sister looked no younger, even although, as Mrs Soorocks often said, she had two years less of sin and misery to answer for.

Originally there had been three sisters ; but the eldest, during the life of their father, made what he called an imprudent marriage, at which he was irreconcilably indignant, because it did not suit the state of his means to give his daughter any dowry, an expedient not singular on similar occasions. Captain Chandos, the husband, an English officer of family and good prospects, was on his part no less offended at being so undervalued ; and in disgust carried his bride into Warwickshire, declaring his determination never to hold any communication or intercourse with her relations. Thus it happened that, when the old gentleman died, the two spinsters succeeded to the house and heritage—of course there was no money ; but the estate was entailed, and Mrs Chandos, as the first-born, was the heiress. Her sisters, however, never deemed it expedient to make any inquiry respecting her ; at the same time, they held and gathered as if they hourly expected she would revisit them as an avenger. This apprehension was accepted by their consciences for the enjoyment they derived from the indulgence of their natural avarice.

When they had been some four or five years in possession, a rumour reached the neighbourhood that Captain Chandos had succeeded to the title and estates of his uncle, a baronet; and Mrs Soorocks, being one of the first who chanced to hear the news, with all the Christian eagerness for which she was so justly celebrated lost no time in hastening to congratulate the sisters on the accession of dignity which had come to their family by that marriage, which they with their father had so expediently reviled.

After relating what she had heard, she added, in her most soothing manner, "The only thing, Miss Shoosie, the only thing that I'm grieved for is the thought of what will become of you and Miss Girzie in your auld days."

"Auld days!" exclaimed Miss Girzie.

"'Deed, Miss Girzie," resumed the sympathising visitor, "it's a vera melancholious thing; for, as ye are baith never likely to be married, it will come to pass in the course of nature that ye'll belyve be at a time o' life when ye can neither work nor want; and no doubt Sir Rupert and his leddy will call on you to count and reckon with them for every farthing ye hae gotten o' theirs. Nothing less can be expected from their hands, after the way they were driven, in a sense, from home and hall by your father. I hope it wasna true, though the fact has been so said, that ye were art and part in that unpardonable iniquity and crying sin against family affection. But for all that, as the English are well known to be a people of a turn o' mind for generosity, I would

E

be none surprised to hear that the baronet intends to be merciful. Surely, indeed, he'll never be so extortionate as to make you pay merchant's interest at the rate of five per cent., when it is well known ye have been getting no more than four from the bank; and as for the wadset o' your heritable bond on the lands of Auldbiggings, there will be room to show you great leniency, for I am creditably informed that if the estate were brought to sale the morn, it wouldna pay thirteen shillings and fourpence in the pound."

But notwithstanding these prophetic anticipations, the spinsters were not molested. It could not, however, be altogether said they were allowed unquestioned possession, for Mrs Soorocks never saw them, either at church or in her visitations, without obliging them to endure the kindest inquiries concerning Sir Rupert and Lady Chandos.

One morning she called on them at rather an unusual early hour with a newspaper in her hand, and a condoling spirit, most amiably expressive in the sad composure of a countenance evidently dressed for an occasion of great solemnity.

" I'm in a fear, leddies," said she, " that the papers hae gotten doleful news this day for you. Heh, sirs ! but life is a most uncertain possession, and so is all worldly substance. But maybe it's no just so dreadful as is herein set forth ; but if it should be the worst, you and Miss Girzie, Miss

Shoosie, are no destitute of a religious support;
and it never could be said that the baronet was a
kind brother, though, for that matter, it must be
alloo't no love was lost between you; nevertheless, decency will cause you to make an outlay for
mournings, and considering the use ye have had
of his money, ye oughtna to grudge it."

"And what's this Job's comforting ye hae
brought us the day?" said Miss Girzie, somewhat
tartly; but Mrs Soorocks, without answering her
pungent interrogation, gave the newspaper to
Miss Shoosie, saying—

"Ye'll find the accidence in the second claw
of the third page; see if ye think it's your gude-
brother that has broken his neck."

She then addressed Miss Girzie—

"And if it should be your gude-brother, Miss
Girzie, really ye have much cause for thanksgiving, for the papers say he has left a power of
money, over and forbye his great estates; and all
goes to his only surviving child and daughter,
Clara, 'ceps a jointure of three thousand pounds
to his disconsolate leddy. My word, your sister
has had her ain luck in this world! Little did
either o' you think, in the days o' your worthy
father's austerity, that a three thousand jointure
would blithen her widowhood. But I doubt, Miss
Girzie, ye'll no can expec her to domicile with
the like of you, now when she's come to such a
kingdom."

Miss Shoosie having in the meantime read the

paragraph, handed the paper to her sister, as she said—

" Really, sister, it's very like the death of a baronet; but I see no legality that he was our sister's."

" What ye observe," interposed Mrs Soorocks, " is no without sense, Miss Shoosie; and surely, if ye're treated by Lady Chandos just with a contempt, it's no to be thought that ye'll put more hypocrisy on your backs than ye hae in your bosoms. But, leddies, leddies, I see a jeopardie gathering over you. Miss Claurissie, your niece, she'll have doers; and though her mother, and her father, that the Lord has taken to himsell, scornt to molest you in this poor heritage o' Barenbraes, the doers will be constrained by law to do their duty as executioners—depend upon't, they will demand a restoration to the uttermost farthing. Maybe, and it's no unpossible, the doers may have heard of your narrow, contracted ways, and may think the money cannot be in closer hands; but for all that, be none surprised if they come upon you like a judgment. But even should they no disturb you, as maybe Sir Rupert may in his will have so ordered it, to show how little he regarded the beggarly inheritance of your family, ye yet daurna wile away ae plack, the which is a sore misfortune, for I doubt not, considering how light the beggar's pock returns from your gates, that both o' you have a kind intention to give the parish a mortification. But come what may, put

oil in your lamps, and be awake and ready, for
it will fare ill with you if ye are found not only
helpless old maids, but foolish virgins, when the
shouts of the bridegroom are heard—I mean,
when your niece comes to be married—for it's
very probable that she'll be the prey o' a spend-
thrift; and if such is the Lord's pleasure, think
what will become of you then !"

Such for many years had been the circumstances and situation of the maiden sisters of
Barenbraes; still they were unmolested by any
inquiry from England, and still, as often as the
various vocations of her neighbourliness permitted, they were as kindly reminded by Mrs
Soorocks of the audit to which they were liable
to be so suddenly summoned. Her idea, however, of counselling the Laird to pay his addresses to one of them, as an expedient to avert
the consequences of his impending misfortunes,
was not without a sufficient show of plausibility ;
although it might really seem to be only calculated to furnish herself with additional causes
for the afflicting sympathy she took in their
destinies, and to augment the pungency of her
condolence.

At this period more than thirty years had
elapsed since the elopement of Lady Chandos,
and still no intimation had been received, in
any shape or form, tending to verify the pre-
dictions of Mrs Soorocks; it was therefore not
altogether improbable that the martyrs of her

anxiety might be permitted the quiet enjoyment
of their possessions—at least so it appeared to
me at the time ; and accordingly, having wished
her all manner of success in her undertaking,
I pursued my own course towards the Manse,
while she posted on to Auldbiggings.

CHAPTER X

DR LOUNLANS was one of those modern
ornaments of the Scottish Church by whom her
dignity, as shown in the conduct and intelligence of her ministers, is maintained as venerable in public opinion as it was even when the
covenanted nation, for the sake of their apostolic
bravery and excellence, broke the iron arm both
of the Roman and of the Episcopal Pharaoh.
He was still a young man, being only in his
thirty-third year; but patient study, and the
gift of a discerning spirit, had enriched him
with a wisdom almost equal in value to the
precepts and knowledge of experience.

In his person, he affected somewhat more of
attention to appearance than is commonly observable in the habits of country pastors, the
effect of having had the good fortune to spend
several years as a tutor in a noble family, distinguished for their strict observance of those
courtesies and etiquettes which characterised the
aristocracy of the past age. His great superiority, however, consisted chiefly in the power
of his eloquence, and the serene and graceful

benignity of his manners, in which the calmness
of philosophy and the meekness of piety were
happily blended with the self-possession of
worldly affability.

He had at this time been only eighteen months
in the parish, and although the Manse, under
his superintendence, had received many embellish-
ments, yet traces of the ruder taste of his pre-
decessor were still evident in the house, the
offices, and the garden.   Mr Firlots belonged indeed to another age and generation—he was one
of those theological worthies who divided their
sermons into fifteen heads, and planted in the
same flower-bed cauliflowers and carnations.   The
pulpit became paralytic under his emphatic logo-
machies; and docks and nettles grew as rankly
in all his borders as epithets unpleasant to ears
polite flourished in the mazes of his doxology.
The docks and nettles, under the auspices of his
more refined successor, had now given place to
roses and lilies.   The pulpit was repaired, and
the desk thereof beautified with a new cover-
ing; the weedy pathway to the Manse door was
trimmed into a gravelled sweep edged with box,
and alternate tassels of red and white daisies,
interspersed with flowers of rarer name and richer
blossom, adorned the bed within.

On entering the house, I was shown into the
parlour, and obliged to wait some time before
the reverend young Doctor made his appearance.

I have always thought that the sitting-room

of a gentleman afforded no equivocal index to
his character, and certainly the parlour of Dr
Lounlans tended to confirm me in this notion.
It was in all respects well ordered—everything
was suitable, but a degree of taste pervaded alike
the distribution and the style of the furniture,
producing something like fashionable elegance
on the whole, notwithstanding the general Pres-
byterian simplicity of the details.

I observed some indications of preparation for
a journey—a portmanteau with the key in the
lock stood on one of the chairs, and near it on
another lay several articles of apparel, with a
pocket Bible in two volumes, very handsomely
bound in purple morocco, and apparently quite
new (indeed the paper, in which it would
seem the volumes had been wrapped, lay on the
floor)

When the Doctor came into the room, I could
not but apologise for having intruded upon him ;
for although dressed with his habitual neatness,
his complexion was flushed, and he had evidently
been interrupted in some exertion of strength
and labour.

" I am on the eve of going for some time from
home," said he, "and the fatigue of packing
obliged me to strip to the work."

Curiosity is the sin which most easily besets
me, and this intimation of a journey—a journey,
too, for which such packing and preparation were
requisite—produced the natural consequence.

" You are, then, to be absent for some considerable time ? " replied I.

" About three weeks, not longer."

" You do not, I hope, go soon ? "

" This evening, that I may be in time for the earliest steamboats from Greenock, in order to overtake the mail at Glasgow, in which I have secured a place."

" But you might as well stop till the morning, for the Edinburgh mail will be gone before you can possibly arrive at Glasgow by the steamboats."

" It is the London mail in which my place is secured."

" You surprise me. No one has heard of your intention of going to London."

The Doctor smiled, and replied a little, as I felt it, drily—he doubtless intended that it should be so felt—

" Nor am I going so far as London." He then added with his accustomed ease, " My journey is to Warwickshire, and I only take the mail to Carlisle."

To Warwickshire ! thought I : what can he have to do in Warwickshire ? It is very extraordinary that a minister of the Kirk of Scotland should be going to Warwickshire. In a word I was constrained to reply—

" I hope your journey, Doctor, is to bring home the only piece of furniture the Manse seems to want ? "

He blushed a little and said, " You are not far wrong; the object of my journey is indeed to bring home a wife; but whether she will become a fixture in this house is not yet determined."

" I regret to hear you say so : I had hoped you were among us for life. I have not heard of your call. Is it to Glasgow or Edinburgh ? Dr Chalmers is removed to St Andrews, and a new church is building in Edinburgh."

" If there be any call in my removal from this parish, I fear it may not be ascribed to the wonted inspiration which governs, as it is said, the translations of my brethren."

My curiosity was repressed by the cold propriety with which this was accentuated, and bethinking that the object of my visit was not to pry into the movements of the Doctor, but to procure his mediation with the Nabob in behalf of our defenceless neighbour, the Laird, I accordingly said—

" Dr Lounlans, I ask your pardon for the liberty I have taken; but in truth there is reason to lament your absence at this particular time, for your assistance is much wanted in a case that requires a charitable heart and a persuasive tongue, both of which you eminently possess : Mr Mailings has fallen into some difficulties with Mr Rupees."

" I have heard," replied the Doctor, " something of it; he has incurred debts to him, and to a large amount."

"Even so; and the Nabob, as he is called, threatens to foreclose the mortgage."

"In what way can I serve the old man?"

This was said with a peculiar look, as if there was a movement of some reluctant feeling awakened in his memory.

"By representing to Mr Rupees," said I, "the harshness of the proceedings in which he has embarked, and in what manner the effects will injure his own reputation amongst us. Without giving the poor Laird the slightest notice of his intentions, he is already surveying and valuing the estate."

"Indeed, indeed," replied the Doctor, "that is severe; almost as much so, to one so old and helpless, as it is to turn the widow and the fatherless out of doors. I am grieved to hear of Mr Mailings' misfortune, but my business does not admit of postponement. Did he request you to ask my interference?"

"I will be plain: he did not. I have heard something of the reason of his reluctance, but I am assured, from your character, that you will delight in returning good for evil."

"I cannot pay his debts," said the Doctor, after a short pause, "and Mr Rupees is not a man who will be persuaded to relent from his purpose by any other than the golden argument."

"Could you, however, try? He has but of late come among us, and is evidently ambitious of influence; you might represent to him the aversion which such indecent haste must universally provoke. He may yield to shame what he would refuse to virtue."

"Does the matter so press that it may not stand over till my return?"

"So special a question, Doctor, I cannot answer; I am not acquainted with the actual state of the poor old gentleman's circumstances. It is only notorious that he is in the power of his creditors, and that the Nabob shows no disposition to mitigate the severity which the law perhaps enables him to inflict."

The Doctor appeared to be somewhat embarrassed: he looked upon the floor; he felt if his neckcloth was in proper order; he bit his left thumb, and gathered his brows into a knot, which indicated the predominancy of the earthy portion of his nature in the oscillations of his religion, his reason, and his heart.

I looked at him steadily, but his eye was downcast, not shunning the inquisition of mine, but with that sort of fixedness which the outward organ assumes when the spirit looks inward. For some short space of time—it might be as long as it would take one to count a dozen—he remained thoughtful and austere. He then began to move his foot gently, and he glanced his eye aside towards me. There was sternness in the first glance; in the second the lustre of manly generosity, which in the third was dimmed with a Christian's tear, and he covered his face with his

hands as he said with emotion, "How true hath
been my mother's prophecy! The cruel, selfish,
arrogant man, whose all of worth lay in the earth
and turf of his inheritance, has—I forget myself,
no; he has not yet supplicated the help of those
in whose beggary he so exulted."

After a brief pause, and having wiped his eyes
and forehead, he turned round to me and said,
with a lighter tone,—

"I will postpone my journey for another day,
and take a pledge in doing so from good fortune
to provide me with a seat in the next mail. But
I fear you overrate my influence with Mr Rupees;
nevertheless, the task is one which I feel may
not be omitted, and I will do my best endeavour
to persuade him to pursue a course of mercy.
There have been things, sir, which make this
duty one hard to be undertaken; but, thank God,
the sense of what my character as a minister of
the Gospel requires is livelier in motive than the
resentful remembrance of early affliction."

It was accordingly agreed that he should visit
Mr Rupees in the morning, and I soon after took
my leave.

CHAPTER XI

AFTER quitting the Manse, I returned towards the path by which I had crossed the fields in the morning. This course led me to pass the gate of Auldbiggings, on approaching which, I observed Jock sitting on one of the globes which, some time during the last century, had surmounted the pillars of the gateway. He was busily employed in feeding a young hawk, which he held compressed between his left arm and his bosom.

At first I resolved to go by without speaking, my thoughts being engrossed with the retribution to which Dr Lounlans had alluded; but Jock himself, forgetful entirely of the ceremony which he endeavoured to practise when I met him on the Whinny Knowes, without rising or even suspending his occupation, looked askance from under the brim of his hat, and bade me come to him. There was something in this over-affectation of negligence which convinced me he was sitting at the gate not altogether at that time by accident, and I had indeed some reason to suspect that he had placed himself there on purpose to intercept me on my return home, for presently he began to sift me with a curious sinister subtlety peculiar to himself.

"This is fine weather for a sober dauner," said he, as I went up to him. "And whare will ye walk in a path o' mair pleasantness than the road atween your house and the Place? No that I would misliken the way to the Manse now and then, especially in the fall of the year, when the yellow leaf tells of our latter end, and the wind howls in the tree like a Burgher minister hallylooying about salvation."

"Upon my word, John, you spiritualise a walk to the Manse as ingeniously as the Doctor himself could do."

"Ah! isna Dr Lounlans a capital preacher?— isna he a great gun? He's the very Mons Meg o' the presbytery."

"And yet, John, I understand that the Laird has no particular esteem for the Doctor."

"Gentlemen are nae great judges o' preaching," said Jock; "it wouldna hae been fair o' Providence to hae allowt them both the blessings o' religion and the good things o' this world; and so the Laird, being a true gentleman by birth and breeding, is by course o' nature no a crowder o' kirks."

"But I should have expected that such a faithful servant as you are, John, would have been of the same way of thinking as your master."

"In temporalities — in temporalities I'm a passive obedient; but in the controversy with the auld tyrant that is called Diabolus, a name which the weighty Dr Drystoor says may be rendered into English by the word Belzebub, my soul is as a Cameronian, free upon the mountains, crying, Ha, ha! to the armed men.   But, sir, though I will allow that Dr Lounlans is in the poopit a bright and shining light, yet I hae my doots whether the mere man o' his nature hath undergone a right regeneration."

"Indeed! You do not call his piety in question?"

" No; but I dislike his pride. He has noo been the placed minister and present incumbent of our parish mair than a year and a half, and he has never paid his respecks at Auldbiggings.   I'm sure if I were the Laird I would ne'er do him the homage o' entering his kirk door—no, not even on a king's fast."

" John, there must be some reason for an exception so singular to the usual pastoral attentions which Dr Lounlans pays to all his parishioners. I have heard something o' the cause."

" Nae doot of that, for I see you are frae the Manse, and I'se warrant was treated there baith wi' toddy and jocosity, on account of our peradventure wi' John Angle's keeking wheels.   It would be mother's milk to the Doctor : weel kens he that there's no a claw the fifteen lords can put forth the whilk Caption will leave unhandled to rive the flesh frae the Laird's banes.   I'm speaking o' the Doctor in his capacity o' a mere man."

" Then, John, let me tell you you are very much

F

mistaken. Dr Lounlans feels for the situation of
your master as a gentleman and a Christian ought
to do."

" As a Christian—as a Christian he may ; but
will he pacify the Nabob ? "

It was plain from this incidental expression
that the cunning creature had been informed by
his master of the object of my visit to the Manse,
and that notwithstanding the repugnance shown
by the old gentleman at the idea of being obliged
to the Doctor, he was yet anxious to obtain his
mediation. It may be in supposing such mean-
ness I do him wrong, but that his servant had
no scruples on the subject was quite manifest,
for, in reply to my assurances that the Doctor was
not only distressed by what had taken place,
but had undertaken to interpose with Mr Rupees
to avert litigation and to suspend this annoying
survey of the estate, which I the more particularly explained, in order that it might be reported
to the Laird, he said—

" It would hae been an unco thing had he
refus't it, for he has baith the spiritual motives
of Christian duty and the carnal spite of upstart
pride to egg him on ;—but whether it be the
minister or the mere man that leads captive captivity, I'll sing with thankfulness—

' Behold how good a thing it is,
     And how becoming well,
  Together such as brethren are
     In unity to dwell.' "

" But, John," said I, " what is the true cause
of the animosity between the Laird and the
Doctor ? I cannot think that the rouping out of
Mrs Lounlans, though a very harsh proceeding,
could have occasioned feelings of such deep and
durable resentment. There must have been some
other cause."

" Cause, cause ! there was nae cause at a'. If
courting a young widow by lawful means be a
cause, that was the cause. Ye see, the short and
the lang o't is this, as no young gentleman's
education can be properly finished till he has
broken in on the ten commandments, the Laird,
after the burial of John Lounlans, threw a sheep's
e'e at the bonnie widow, as she was called, and
thought to win her love by course o' law, for her
gudeman died deep in his debt. But Whereas is
an ill-farr'd beginning to a billydoo ; so ye see,
Mrs Lounlans, instead o' being won to amorous
delights by multiplepoinding, grew demented ;
and taking the doctor-minister, who was then a
three-year auld bairn and orphan, by the hand,
she stood in the kirk-stile—the better day the
better deed—it was on a Sabbath—and there she
made sic a preaching and paternoster about a
defenceless widow and fatherless babies, that when
our Laird was seen coming to the kirk, soberly
and decently, linking wi' his leddy mother, the
weans in the crowd set up a shout ; and he was
torn frae her side, and harlt [1] through mire and

[1] *Harlt.* Drawn violently.

midden dub, to the great profanation of the Lord's day, and the imminent danger of his precious life. For mair than a month he was thought beyont the power o' a graduwa,[1] and his leddy mother, before the year was done, diet o' the tympathy or a broken heart. But how the Doctor should hate our Laird for that hobbleshaw, I ne'er could understand, for the Laird was the ill-used man."

Before I had time to make any comment on this affair, we were joined by the indefatigable Mrs Soorocks, returning from the Place. She did not appear, by the aspect of her countenance, to have been so successful in her voluntary mission as I had been in mine ; but I could nevertheless discover that she had not altogether failed, and that she had something to tell; for immediately on coming up, she took me by the arm and was leading me away, when she happened to observe the work in which Jock was employed.

"Goodness me!" she exclaimed, pausing and looking back at him, "no wonder poor feckless Auldbiggings is brought to a morsel—sic servants as he has! As I hae my een, the wasterfu' creature's feeding the bird wi' minched collops —worms are ower gude for't—and he's cramming them down its throat wi' his finger! For shame, ye cruel ne'er-do-weel—ye'll choke the puir beast."

What answer Mrs Soorocks got for her meddling it may not be fitting to place upon im-

---

[1] *Graduwa.* Graduate.

mortal record; but she observed, when she had
recovered her complexion and countenance, as
we were moving away, that Jock was a real curiosity. "He's just what Solomon would hae been
wi' a want, for his proverbs and parables are most
extraordinar!"

CHAPTER XII

Mrs SOOROCKS' road homeward lying aside
from the path across the fields, I was obliged in
civility to accompany her along the highway and
to forego my intention of taking the more seques-
tered course : not that she probably would have
scrupled to have gone with me in any direction
I might have proposed, but the public road was
the shortest way to her residence. When the
tasks of politeness are not agreeable, it is judicious
to abridge their duration—a philosophical maxim
worthy of particular attention whenever you undertake to see an afflicting old lady safely home.

When we had passed some twenty paces or so
from the entrance to the avenue of Auldbiggings,
my companion began to repeat the result of her
mission by complaining of the familiarity with
which the Laird allowed himself to be treated by
his man.

"When I went into the room, there was the
two," said she, "holding a controversy about your
mediation wi' Dr Lounlans, and Jock was argle-
bargling wi' his master, like one having authority
over him, the which to see and to hear was, to say

the least o't, a most seditious example to the natural audacity of servants. It's true that when Jock saw me he drew in his horns (for the creature's no without a sense o' discretion in its ain way), and left the chamber; but it's plain to me that yon is an ill-rulit household, and were it no a case of needcessity and mercy, I dinna think I ought to hae the conscience to advise the leddies o' Barenbraes to hae onything to say till't."

"Then you have made some progress with the Laird?"

"I hae made an inceesion, but no to a great length. For what do you think is the auld fool's objection? He's in a doot if either o' the leddies be likely to bring him a posterity."

"A very grave and serious objection indeed; considering the motive by which you have been so kindly actuated, it could not but surprise you."

"Surprise! na, I was confounded, and said to him, 'Mr Mailings,' quo' I, 'my purpose o' marriage for you, at your time o' life and in your straitened circumstances, ought to hae something more rational in view than the thoughts of a posterity.' But Miss Shoosie's no past the power o' a miracle even in that respeck; for Sarah, ye ken, was fourscore before she had wee Isaac, and the twa-and-fifty mystery o' the Douglas Cause should teach you to hae some faith in the ability of Miss Girzie, who to my certain knowledge was only out of her forties last Januar, for I saw their genealogy in their big Bible. It was lying on the table when

I called at Barenbraes on Sabbath, and neither o'
the leddies being in the room, I just happened to
observe that twa leaves at the beginning were
pinned thegither, nae doot to hide some few o'
the family secrets. Gude forgie me! I couldna
but tak out the prin, and you may depend upon
it that Miss Girzie was just nine-and-forty last
Januar. But I couldna advise him to hae onything to say to Miss Girzie, and so I told him."

"What do you mean? I have never heard of
aught to her prejudice—I have always, indeed,
understood that she was the most amiable of the
two."

"Nae great sang in her praise. But amiable
here or amiable there is no a thing to be thocht
o', for it's no a marriage o' felicity that we're to
speed, but a prudent marriage; and would it no
be the height o' imprudence for a man to lay
hands on the wally draig [1] when he has it in his
power to catch a better bird?"

"I do not exactly understand you, Mrs Soorocks, for if there is any superiority possessed
by the one sister over the other, you allow that
Miss Girzie has it."

"I alloo of no such thing—and were the Laird
to marry her, what's to prevent some other needfu'
gentleman (and when were they plentier?) frae
making up to Miss Shoosie—she is the old
sister, ye forget that—wouldna deil-be-lickit be
the portion o' the younger couple? No, no, if

[1] *Wally draig.* The youngest bird in the nest.

Auldbiggings is to marry any o' them, it shall be
Miss Shoosie. It would be a tempting o' Providence if he did otherwise."

" But, my dear madam, are you not proceeding
a little too fast in thus disposing of the leddies
without consulting them ? Should you not ascertain how far either of them may be inclined to
encourage the Laird's addresses ? "

" What can it signify to consult them, if it be
ordained that the marriage is to take place ? But
if I hadna seen the auld idiot so set upon a posterity, it was my intent and purpose to have gane
ower to Barenbraes the morn's morning, and given
Miss Shoosie an inkling of what was in store for
her. But the matter's no ripe enough yet for
that."

" The growth, however, has been abundantly
rapid ; and I am sure, Mrs Soorocks, that whatever
may be the upshot, the whole business hitherto
does equal credit to your zeal and intrepidity."

" It is our duty," replied the worthy lady
seriously, " to help ane anither in this howling
wilderness. And noo may I speer what speed ye
hae come wi' Doctor Lounlans ? for Auldbiggings
told me that he had debarred you from going
near him, the which, of course, could only serve
to make you the mair in earnest wi' the wark.
I'm shure a debarring would hae done so to me,
though ye're no maybe the fittest person that
might hae undertaken it. But weakly agents
aften thrive in the management of great affairs,

and if ye hae succeeded with the Doctor, I hope
ye'll be sensible of the help that must have been
with you—not that your task was either a hard
or a heavy ane, for the Doctor is a past ordinar
young man—but there's a way of conciliation very
requisite on such occasions. Howsomever, no doot
ye did your best, and I hope the Doctor has consented to pacify the Nabob."

"Whether he may be able to succeed is perhaps
doubtful," said I.

"And if he should fail," cried the lady, interrupting me, "I'll then try what I can do mysell;
in the meantime, it's a comfort to think he has
promised, for really the circumstances o' poor Auldbiggings require a helping hand;—weel indeed
may I call him poor, for it's my opinion he hasna
ae bawbee left to rub upon anither."

"But the promise," said I, "was given under
circumstances which make it doubly valuable.
You are probably aware, though I had not heard
of it before, that the Doctor is on the eve of
marriage?"

"Going to be married, and none of his parish
ever to have heard a word about it! I think it's a
very clandestine-like thing o' him. And whare is
he going, and wha's he to marry? She canna be
a woman o' a solid principle to be woo'd and won
as it were under the clouds o' the night."

"The Doctor and the lady, madam, I am persuaded have been long acquainted."

"I dinna doot that, and intimately too," replied

Mrs Soorocks insinuatingly. "But whatna corner o' the earth is he bringing her frae? We'll a' be scrupulous about her till we ken what she is."

"I do not question the prudence of the parish in that respect; but, if I understood him right, she resides in Warwickshire."

"In Warwickshire! that's a heathenish part o' England. And so Madam o' the Manse to be is an Englishwoman, and of course o' a light morality, especially for a minister's wife. She'll be a calamity to the neighbourhood, for it will be seen that she'll bring English servant lasses among us to make apple-pies and wash the doorsteps on the Lord's day, as I am creditably told a' the English do. But did ye say Warwickshire? Lady Chandos and her dochter, the heiress by right o' Barenbraes, they live in Warwickshire; oughtna we to get her sisters, the leddies, to open a correspondence wi' her concerning the minister's prelatical bride—for she canna be otherwise than o' the delusion o' the English liturgy and prelacy; and if neither o' them will write, I'll write mysell, for it's a duty incumbent on us all to search into the hiddenness of this ministerial mystery. Warwickshire! I canna away wi't—the very sound o't flew through the open o' my head like a vapour. Weel indeed may I say that it's a mystery, for noo when I think o't, the vera first time that Dr Lounlans drank his tea wi' me—it was the afternoon o' the third day after his placing—he speer't in a most particular manner about the leddies of

Barenbraes, and how it came to pass that they keepit no intercourse by correspondence wi' Lady Chandos. But is't no wonderfu' that I never thought, then nor since syne, o' speering at him about what he ken't o' her leddyship? Surely I hae been bewitched, and mine eyes blinded with glamour, for I sat listening to him like an innocent lamb hearkening to the shepherd's whistle. But I hae always thought there was a providence in that marriage of Lady Chandos, for she was an excellent and sweet lassie; and now it has come to pass that she may be a mean to guard her native land, and her heritage too, against the consequence of the manifest indiscretion o' Dr Lounlans' never-to-be-heard-tell-o' connection."

During this harangue, I endeavoured several times to arrest the progress of the good lady's suspicion and the growth of her conviction that the Doctor's marriage must be in some way derogatory to his character and pestilent to his parish; but it was all in vain: my arguments only riveted her opinion more and more, until, wearied with the controversy, I bade her adieu, ungallantly leaving her to find the path to Barenbraes alone, whither she determined forthwith to proceed, "before it might be too late."

CHAPTER XIII

ALTHOUGH I did not expect to see Dr Lounlans until after his interview with the Nabob, nor
was under any apprehension of a visitation from
Mrs Soorocks, and had predetermined not to call
on the Laird without being able to carry with me
some consolatory tidings, I yet rose an hour earlier
than usual next morning, and felt very much as
those feel who have many purposes to perform.

This particular activity was ingeniously ac-
counted for by Mr Tansie, the parish schoolmaster,
who in passing by happened to observe me at
breakfast an hour before my accustomed time ;
and the parlour window being open that I might
enjoy the fragrance of the sweetbriar which grows
beneath it, he came forward and complimented
me on the good health which such solacious par-
ticipation in the influences of the season (as he
called it) assuredly indicated.

The worthy dominie was generally known
among us as the Philo, a title bestowed on him
by one of his own pupils, which, not inaptly,
described about as much of the philosophical
character as he really possessed.   I was no stranger

to his peculiar notions, for we have often had
many arguments together, and in reply to his
observation on the source of my enjoyment of a
spring morning, I said, after telling him something of what was impending over the Laird,
"But whether the impulses of activity by which
I am so unwontedly stirred, arise from any benevolent desire to lighten the misfortunes of the
old gentleman, or come from the spirit of the
vernal season, it would not be easy to determine."

"Not at all," said he, "they are emanations
of the same genial power, which prompteth un-
vocable as well as intelligent nature to bloom
and rejoice in the spring. It were easier indeed
to explain the motives of the breast, by considering the signs of the zodiac under which each pro-
pelleth action, than by the help and means of
metaphysical philosophy. Are not all things around
us luxuriating in the blandishments of the spring?
—the buds are expanding, the trees are holding
out their blossomy hands to welcome the coming
on of abundance, juvenility is leaping forth with a
bound and a cheer, and there is gladness and
singing, and the sound of a great joy throughout
the whole earth : universal nature overflows with
kindness, and therefore the heart of man is melted
to charity and love. The germinative influences
of Taurus and Gemini are now mingled, and good
deeds and pleasant doings among men have their
seasonable signs in the green fields, the musical
bowers, and the promises of the rising corn."

" You explain to me, Mr Tansie, what I never before rightly understood, namely, why primroses and public dinners come into season together, and how it happened that lamb and eleemosynary subscriptions at the same time adorn the tavern altars of charity ; but now I see how it is—they are all the progeny of the same solar instincts."

" Can you doubt it ? Why in summer are we less active ? Do not the feelings of the heart then, like the brooks, run low and small ? No fruit tempteth the hand to gather ; the heat is too great for hard labour, and the bosom wills to no action; while we lighten the burden of our own raiment, who, beneath the dazzle of a burning noon, would think for merciful pity of clothing the nude and those who are needful of drapery ? "

" But how does it come to pass in autumn, Mr Tansie, when Nature may be said to stand in vitingly by the wayside, holding out her apron filled with all manner of good things, that man is then of a churlish humour, and delights in the destruction of innocent life ? "

" It is indeed," replied the dominie, " a marvellous contrariety ; but the sign of the scrupulous balance is a token of the disposition of the genius of the season : were we not moved by its avaricious influence, should we so toil to fill the garnels of gregarious winter ? "

" Then according to your doctrine, Mr Tansie, it must be fortunate for the Laird that his rupture with the Nabob has not happened under the aspect of Libra, and there may be some chance at this genial season of Dr Lounlans succeeding in his mediation."

"Therein, sir, you but show how slightly you have examined the abysms of that true astrology. Though the time serves, and all humane sympathies are at present disposed to cherish and to give confidence, yet are there things on which the sweet influences of the spring shed bale and woe; for the energy which it awakeneth on the doddard and the old is as a vigour put forth in age and infirmity, causing weakness while it seemeth to strengthen. Mr Mailings is of those whose berth and office have become as it were rubbish in the highway of events. The day of the removal cannot be afar off."

In this crisis of our conversation, and while Mr Tansie was thus expounding his philosophy, leaning over the sweetbriar with his arms resting on the sill of the window, on which he had spread his handkerchief to save the sleeves of his coat, I saw Mrs Soorocks coming across the fields. That some special cause had moved her to be abroad so early admitted of no doubt; but whether her visit should relate to the minister's marriage or to the misfortunes of our neighbour, it gave me pleasure at the moment; for the imagination of the ingenious dominie was mounted in its cloudy car, and so mending its speed that I began to feel a growing inclination to follow in the misty voyage, notwithstanding my long-determined resolution never to engage in any sort of ratiocination in the forenoon, a space of the day, however well calculated for special pleading, particularly unsuitable for theoretical disquisition, as every lawyer and legislator must have often remarked.

On hearing the indefatigable lady's steps, the dominie rose from his inclined position, and gathering up his handkerchief from the sill of the window, replaced it in his pocket; but she had more serious business in hand than afforded time for any sort of talk with him. She came straight up to the door, and announced herself by knock and ring, without appearing to notice him, though he stood with his hat off and was ready to do her all proper homage.

While the servant admitted her, the dominie turned round again to the window, and said to me before there was time to show her into the parlour,—

"She hath had an incubus;" and placing his hat somewhat tartly—doubtless displeased that she should have passed him unnoticed—he immediately retired, evidently piqued at being so slightingly considered, forgetting entirely the immeasurable difference of rank between the relict of a laird of a house with a single lum, herself the coheiress of what Gilbert Stuart calls "the harvest of half a sheaf," and a modest and learned man, on whose originality and worth the world's negligence had allowed a few cobwebs—the reveries of solitary rumination—to hang with impunity—

G

more to the dishonour of those who observed them than to the deterioration of the material with which they were connected. I saw the good man's mortification, and, although almost as eager to hear what the lady had to tell as she herself was evidently anxious to communicate, I started abruptly from my chair, and, going hastily to the door, cried out, "Show Mrs Soorocks into the library, and I shall be with her immediately."

"No ceremony wi' me—I'm no a ceremonious woman, as you may well know," was the answer I received; and, in the same moment, brushing past the servant at the door, she came into the room, and, looking me steadily in the face for the space of some four or five seconds, portentously shook her head, and, unrequested, walking to an elbow-chair, seated herself in it emphatically, with a sigh.

I have never felt much alarm from any demonstration of that inordinate dread which Mrs Soorocks, and her numerous kith and kin in the general world, and in our particular environs and vicinity, are in the habit of displaying on occasions which do not at all concern themselves; but the threefold case of anxiety created by the Laird's misfortunes, the minister's marriage, and the intended co-operation with Providence to raise up a husband for one of the spinsters of Barenbraes, presented a claim to attention which I could not but at once both admit and acknowledge, by inquiring, in the most sympathetic manner, what had happened to discompose her?

CHAPTER XIV

WHEN Mrs Soorocks had fanned herself with her handkerchief, and had some four or five times during the operation puffed her breath with a sough somewhat between the sound of a blast and a sigh, she looked for her pocket-hole, replaced the handkerchief in its proper depository, then stroking down her petticoat and settling herself into order, thus began—

"It's a great misfortune to be of a Christian nature, for it makes us sharers in a' the ills that befall our frien's. I'm sure, for my part, had I broken Mr Rupees' head with my own nieve, and crushed Angle the land-surveyor's commodity in the hollow of my hand, I could not hae suffert more anxiety than I do in the way o' sympathy at this present time, on account o' the enormities of the law, which Caption, the ettercap, is mustering, like an host for battle, against our poor auld doited and defenceless neighbour. But a' that is nothing to the vexation I'm obliged to endure frae the contumacity o' yon twa wizzent and gaizent [1] penure pigs o' Barenbraes."

[1] *Wizzent and gaizent.* Withered and dried-up.

" You have perhaps yourself, madam, to blame a little for that: you need not, I should think, meddle quite so much in their concerns."

" But I cannot help it—it's my duty. I find myself as it were constrained by a sense of grace to do what I do. Far indeed it is frae my heart and inclination to scald my lips in other folks' kail—and why should I? Is there any homage frae the warld as my reward? Let your own hearts answer that. And as for gratitude frae those I sae toil to serve, the huff o' Miss Shoosie Minnygaff is a vera gracious speciment."

From the tenor of these observations, and particularly from the manner in which they were uttered, I began to divine that the worthy lady had not been altogether so successful in her matrimonial project with the maiden sisters as she had been with Auldbiggings, and I expressed my regret accordingly.

" 'Deed," replied she, " ye were ne'er farther wrang in your life, great as your errors both in precept and in practice may hae been. But no to mind an ill-speaking world on that head, what would ye think I hae gotten for my pains frae the twa, Hunger and Starvation, as I canna but call them?"

" It is impossible for me to imagine—they are strange creatures; I should be none surprised if they were unreasonable in their expectations as to the jointure which Auldbiggings may be able to afford. Poor man! I fear he has nothing in his power."

" Guess again, and if ye hope to succeed, guess an impossibility."

" Pin money."

" Pin snuffy ! They too hae their doubts if the Laird will connive at a right way o' education for their children ! Did ye ever hear the like o' that ? And wha do you think the objection first came frae ? Miss Shoosie—auld Miss Shoosie : the sight o' her wi' a child in her arms would be like a lang-neckit heron wi' a lamb in its neb, or a kitty-langlegs dan'ling a bumbee—the thing's an utter incapability o' nature, and so I said to her."

" That explains her ingratitude. I certainly, my dear Mrs Soorocks, cannot approve of throwing cold water on her hopes of a posterity, especially as the only objection which the Laird made to the ladies was an apprehension of disappointment in that respect."

" Sir, the thing is no to be dooted ; but I should tell you her speech o' folly on the occasion. 'To be sure, sister,' said she, speaking to Miss Girzie, when I had broken the ice, ' Mr Mailings is a man o' family ; and though in his younger years he did marry below his degree, yet noo that his wife is dead, she can never be a blot in a second marriage. But then he's a most stiff-neckit man in the way of opinion, and I doot, if ever him and me were married, that we would agree about the way o' bringing up our children; for if I were to hae a dochter,' quo' she, ' and wha knows if ever I shall—— ' "

"I could thole this no longer," exclaimed Mrs Soorocks, "and so, as plainly as I was pleasant, I said, 'Everybody kens weel eneugh, Miss Shoosie, that ye'll never hae a dochter.' And what think you got I for telling her the true even-doun fact?"

"Probably whatever she had in her hand."

"Oh, ye're a saterical man!—to judicate that leddies would be flinging householdry at ane anither's heads! But she did far waur. I never beheld such a phantasie. She rose from her chair, her een like as they would hae kindled candles, though her mouth was as mim as a May puddock, and crossing her fingers daintily on her busk, she made me a ceremonious curtsey, like a maid of honour dancing a minaway[1] wi' the Lord Chancellor, and said, 'Mrs Soorocks, I thank you.' I was so provoked by her solemnity that I couldna but make an observe on't, saying, 'Hech, sirs, Miss Shoosie, it must be a great while since ye were at a practeesing, for really ye're very stiff in the joints. I hae lang kent ye were auld, but I didna think you were sae aged. I canna, therefore, be surprised at your loss o' temper, for when folks lose their teeth, we needna look for meikle temper amang them; the which causes me to understand what Mr Mailings meant when he said that between defects and infirmities ye were a woman past bearing. But, Miss Shoosie, no to exasperate you beyond what is needful in

---

[1] *Minaway.* Minuet.

the way o' chastisement, ye'll just sit doun in your chair and compose yourself; for ye'll no mak your plack a bawbee in striving wi' me in satericals, the more especially as, by what I hae seen o' your dispositions this day, I canna marvel at your being rejected o' men—na, but rue wi' a contrite spirit that I should ever hae been so far left to mysell as to even sic a weak veshel to a gentleman of good account—as they say in the Babes in the Wood—like that most excellent man Mr Mailings, who, if he were to lift the like o' you wi' a pair o' tangs, ye might account yourself honoured;—and yet I was proposing him for a purpose o' marriage ! But, Miss Shoosie, I'll be merciful, and treat you wi' the compashion that is due to a sinful creature;' and then I kittled her curiosity concerning the minister's marriage wi' a leddy in Warwickshire; so ye see she's no a match for me, as I could make her know, feel, and understand, but for the restraining hand o' grace that is upon me."

" On the topic of Dr Lounlans' marriage, Mrs Soorocks, how did you handle that?"

" Weel may ye speer, and the gude forgie me if I wasna tempted to dunkle [1] the side o' truth ; for I said, ' Leddies, what I hae been saying about the sheep's ee that the Laird would be casting at you is a matter for deep consideration. Be nane surprist if ye hear o' very extraordinar news frae Warwickshire. I'll no venture to guess what's

[1] *Dunkle.* To dint, as you might a can with a blow.

coming out o' that country, but I hae had a
dream and a vision of a fair lady dressed in bridal
attire—look you to what blood's in her veins."

" How, Mrs Soorocks! did you say that the
Doctor is going to marry their niece ? "

" I said nae sic a thing—and I request that
ye'll cleck no scandal wi' me ;—but, knowing
what I do know, and that's what you yoursell
taught me, could I omit a seasonable opportunity
for touching them on the part of soreness, in the
way of letting them know that riches make to
themselves wings and flee away to the uttermost
ends of the earth ? 'Be none astounded,' said I,
'leddies, if ye look forth some morning from your
casements, and behold all your hainings[1] and
gatherings, your pinchings, your priggings,[2] your
counts and reckonings, fleeing away to Warwickshire like ravens and crows, and other fowls o'
uncanny feather ; or maybe the avenger, in the
shape of a sound young minister of the Gospel
o' peace, coming to herry you out o' house and
home.' "

" But, my good madam, how can you reconcile
all these innuendoes with that strict regard to
truth which you so very properly on most occasions profess ? These unhappy ladies cannot but
imagine that Dr Lounlans is going to marry their
niece—a circumstance which you have not had
from me the slightest reason to imagine."

---

[1] *Hainings.* Savings.
[2] *Priggings.* Beatings down in bargains.

" Is't a thing impossible ? " cried Mrs Soorocks;
" answer me that.   And if it's no impossible, why
may it not be ?   I'm sure Providence couldna gie
a finer moral lesson than by making it come to
pass."

" Am I to understand, then, from all this, that
there is no great likelihood of Mr Mailings being
extricated from his difficulties by marriage with
either of the sisters ? "

" It's no yet to be looked upon as a case o'
desperation, for, handlet wi' discretion, I think
the weakness on both sides concerning the education o' their posterity—really the very words
would provoke a saint—but, as I was saying, if
we can overcome that weakness, a change may
be brought about."

" But, my dear madam, is there no other among
our friends and neighbours whom you might
propose to the Laird ?   Considering the precarious situation of the ladies of Barenbraes, there is
some risk, you know, of his condition being made
much worse, should a demand for restitution come
upon them.   I have been much struck, Mrs Soor
ocks, with the kind interest which you take in
the old gentleman's affairs ; might I suggest——"

" Would ye even me [1] to him ! " cried the lady,
raising her hands and throwing herself back in
her chair ; " and do you think that I would ever
submit to be a sacrifice on the altar o' poverty for
a peace-offering to the creditors of Auldbiggings !

[1] *Even me.*   Compare, with a view to marriage.

No: gude be thankit, and my marriage articles, I'm no just sae forlorn. It's vera true that, in the way of neighbourliness, I hae a great regard for Mr Mailings, and that the twa innocent auld damsels are far-off connections of mine, with whom I hae lived on the best o' terms; but regard's no affection, and connections are neither flesh nor blood: moreover, there's an unco odds atween doing a service and becoming a slave, as the blithe days that I spent with my dear deceased husband have well instructed me to know. I own we had our differences like other happy couples, for Mr Soorocks had a particular temper; but knowing what I know, it would be a temptation indeed that would bribe me to ware my widowhood on another man, especially one of an ineffectual character, like the helpless bodie that's sae driven to the wall."

At this crisis of our conversation we were interrupted by one of the Nabob's servants with a note, requesting, in the most urgent manner, to see me. However ill-timed, as Mrs Soorocks said it was, I was yet glad at the message, and indeed feigned more alacrity than I felt in obeying it and in wishing her good morning.

CHAPTER XV

IT was a sunny and a hot rather than a sultry day when I approached Nawaubpore, the newly-erected mansion of the Nabob, around which everything displayed the wealth and taste of the owner.

The lodges at the gate were built in the style of pagodas. It was intended that they should represent the Grand Taj or Targe of Agra; but some of those defects inherent in all copies made them, in many respects, essentially different from their model—the minarets performing the functions of chimneys, and the cupolas those of dovecots. The gate itself was a closer imitation of the Fakeer-gate of Delhi.

The avenue from this gorgeous Durwaja consisted of two rows of newly-transplanted lime-trees, shorn of their tops and branches, each bound with straw ropes, and propped by three-forked sticks, to keep them in a perpendicular position, until their truncated roots, as the botanists express it, should have again fastened themselves in the earth. In the park groups of trees were placed similarly circumstanced, pro-

tected from the inroads of the cattle by palisades
of split Scotch fir, connected by new rough-sawn
rafters of the same material. In the distance, notwithstanding the metamorphoses which the moss
had undergone, I recognised my old acquaintances
the venerable ash-trees, which had surrounded
and overshadowed the ancestral cottage of the
Burrah Sahib, now serving as a screen to a rid-
ing-house, framed of timber, and tinted with a
mixture of tar and ochre into a mulligatawny
complexion.

The court of offices occupied the foreground
between the Hippodrome and the Burrah-ghur.
They were in the purest style of classic architecture. Whether the plan was suggested to the
Nabob by that delicate discrimination, and that
exquisite feeling of propriety in art, for which
Mr Threeper of Athens, his legal adviser, is so
justly celebrated, or was procured for him by
his maternal relative, a prosperous gentleman,
Archibald Thrum, Esq., of Yarns, and manufacturer in Glasgow, from the Palladio of the
northern Venice, I have never been able satis-
factorily to ascertain; but the pile was worthy
alike of this Venice and of that Athens, for in
looking in at the gate, a copy of the triumphal
Arch of Constantine, you beheld the cows tied
to Corinthian pillars, looking out of Venetian
windows.

The Burrah-ghur, or mansion of the Burrah
Sahib, was a splendid compilation of whatever

has been deemed elegant in antique, curious in
Gothic, or gorgeous in Oriental architecture.   It
was a volume of Elegant Extracts, a bouquet of
the art as rich and various as those hospitable
hecatombs of the cities on the banks of Clutha,
amidst which, according to the veracious descriptions of Dr Peter Morris of Aberystwith, the
haggis and blanc-mange are seen shuddering at
each other.   There a young artist might have
nourished his genius with a greater variety of
styles and combinations than the grand tour,
with an excursion to Greece and Stamboul, could
have supplied.   Instead of a knocker or bell, a
gong of the Celestial Empire hung in a niche
within the verandah, at the sound of which, the
folding doors

——" self opened,
On golden hinges turning."

On entering the vestibule, a Kitmagar, who
was squatted on his hams in a corner on a mat,
rose to receive me : he placed his palms together,
touching his forehead three times with his thumbs,
bowed to the ground, and then standing upright,
pronounced in a voice of homage, " Salaam Sahib."

He was habited in a kind of shirt of blue
cloth, with long open sleeves, and bound round
the loins with a blue and yellow rope.   On his
head he wore a turban shaped like a puddock-
stool, and trimmed with yellow cloth and gold
lace.   His wide silk drawers hung down to the

ground, and his slippers, embroidered with silver, looked up in the toes, like other vain things in the pride of splendour.

I inquired for his master, and with a second salutation as solemn as the first, he replied, " Hah Sahib," and showed me into a room, one entire end of which was occupied with a picture representing a tiger-hunt, in the foreground of which, seated on the back of an elephant, I discovered a juvenile likeness of Mr Rupees ; and in the background an enormous tiger, almost as big as a Kilkenny cat, was returning into the jungle with a delicate and dandyish officer of the Governor's guard in his mouth.

When I had some time admired this historical limning, another Oriental conducted me to the library door, where, taking off his slippers, he ushered me into the presence of the Burrah Sahib. The room was darkened according to the Indian dhustoor, and from the upper end, by the bubbling of a hookah, I was apprised that there the revelation was to take place.

On approaching the shrine, I beheld the Vishnu of Nawaubpore, garmented in a jacket, waistcoat, and trousers of white muslin, with nankeen shoes—his head was bald to the crown, but the most was made of what little grey hair remained on his temples by combing it out ; that which covered the back of his head was tied in a long slender tapering tail. He lolled in an elbow-chair, his feet supported on the back of another, before which stood his Punkah-wallah, cooling his lower regions with a gigantic palm-leaf fan, while the Hookah-burdhar was trimming the seerpoos in the rear.

On hearing me announced, the Nabob started to his feet, and shook me in the most cordial manner by the hand, thanked me for my alacrity in attending his summons, and "before tiffin" proposed to conduct me in person through his ghur, modestly intimating that he did not expect me altogether to approve of the prodigality of his tradesmen; at the same time insinuating that, for himself, he was a man of plain habits and particularly fond of old-fashioned simplicity.

CHAPTER XVI

HAVING perambulated the magnificent intricacies and chambers of Nawaubpore, praising, of course, to the utmost all I saw—for which may God forgive me; but this is an age much addicted to hypocrisy, and the purest minds are necessarily tainted by the spirit of the times.

Carving and gilding everywhere appeared in such profusion that no room was left for taste. The furniture was numerous, cumbrous, and excessive, and interspersed with it, above, below, and all around lay a miscellaneous assemblage of splendid nicknackery, like those relics and remnants of curiosities which remain in the hands of an auctioneer after he has disposed of whatever is valuable or really curious in the executor-ordered sale of a virtuoso's collection. Pictures by such artists as Zoffani covered the walls, purchased, however, at Tulloh's saleroom in Calcutta, at a price which, if told to Mr Peele, would make him chuckle at the bargain he got of the Chapeau Paille; Derbyshire-spar vases, plaster busts, French clocks, interestingly ornamental, but deranged in their horal faculties;

Dresden china swains and shepherdesses; models, by Hindoo artists, of gates and pagodas; two verd antique pillars on castors in the dining-room atoned for supporting nothing by being hollow, and containing within post-cœnobitical utensils; feather fans, Pekin mandarins, Flemish brooms, musical snuff-boxes, large china jars, japanned cabinets, spacious mirrors, and icicled lustres : all so disposed to produce the utmost quantum of confusion with the least possible contribution to comfort.

Tiffin was served in the breakfast-room. It consisted of cold meats, hot curries, mulligatawny soup, kabobs, pillaws, and a fowl fried with onions to a cinder, bearing the brave name of country captain; ale (Hodson's of course), claret, genuine from the vaults of Carbonelle, and the far-famed Madeira, so fatal to the poor Laird, which, according to his account, had been sixteen years in a wood in the Bay of Bengal.

Our conversation in the meantime was various and desultory, so much so that I began to wonder for what purpose my presence had been so urgently requested at Nawaubpore, and for what object I was treated with such distinguished consideration, till I happened to fill myself a glass of Madeira while partaking of the currie.

" My good friend," said the Nabob in a tone of alarm, placing his hand on my arm to restrain me, " do you mean to make a suttee of yourself ? But I need not be surprised at you doing such a thing, for I have seen a candidate for the Direc-

H

tion, and a successful one too, do the very same thing. Need we wonder at the blunders in the government of India when we meet with such ignorance of Indian affairs among the ghuddahs of Leadenhall Street? The Paugul was a Cockney banker; do you know, he was so absurd as to ask me across the table—it was in the London Tavern —his Majesty's Ministers were present—whether the Coolies carried the Dhoolies, or the Dhoolies the Coolies! One of the Ministers looked significantly at me, and said that he believed it was a doubtful question; but another who sat next me whispered that if, like the Court of Directors, they got on in any way, it mattered little which was beast and which burden. By-the-bye, it was on the same occasion that the pious member of the Durbah stated, and to me too, the singular progress and great fruits which had blessed the labours of the missionaries in the East. 'D—n the blessing,' said I — I begged his lordship's pardon for the damn—'they have only taught a dozen or two pariah soors to eat beef and drink as much rum as they can steal.'—'That, however,' said another Minister, whom I observed particularly attentive to my remark, 'that, however, is a step in the progress of wants;' and he added, 'having once acquired a desire for beef and rum, their industry will thence be stimulated to obtain these luxuries, and a superior morality will be gradually evolved by the consequent cultivation of industry.'—'The stealing of which you speak,

is something like the turbidness of fermentation,
a natural and necessary stage in the process of
refinement, which will produce wine or vinegar,
as the case may be,' replied I ; upon which another
of them interposed mildly, saying, 'I am quite
sure that by the late reduction of the duty on
wine, a reduction in the consumption of ardent
spirits must supervene, and that the change will
be salutary to the best interests of our Indian
population.' "

By this time the Nabob had bestowed so much
of his tediousness upon me that I here attempted
to break the thread of his discourse ; but although
I did so with all my wonted address, he was on a
subject congenial to the Indian temperament—
the sayings and doings of great men—and he
would not be interrupted, for, without noticing
my impatience, which he ought to have done, he
continued—

" There was another Peshwa, who had particular views of his own for what he called the
amelioration of Indian society ; the principle of
his plan was by a transfusion of a portion of the
redundant piety of the United Kingdom into what
he called the arterial ramifications of Oriental
mythology——"

At this crisis one of the servants entered with
the customary salaam, and said something in his
own language to the Burrah Sahib, who answered
him abruptly, " Hemera bhot bhot salaam do
doosera kummera reedo bolo ;" and turning to

me, he added, "Padre Lounlans sent a chit this
morning to say he would call on me about the
affairs of that d—d sirdar Paugul the Laird, and
I wish to consult you before seeing him. The
murderous old dacoit and his Jungle-wallah of a
servant, while I was only ascertaining whether or
not he had cheated me in the extent of his estate,
on which I, like a fool, have advanced twice as
much money as I dare say it is worth, charged
upon me like a brace of Mahrattas, and with a
lump of a lattee smashed my surveyor's theodolite.
Mr Caption, my vakeel, is ready to take his oath
before a magistrate (if he has not done it already)
that they were guilty of assault and battery,
against the laws of this and every other well-
governed realm; inasmuch as, on the 19th of the
present month of June, or on some day or night
of that month, or on some day or night of the
month of May preceding, or of July following,
they did, with malice aforethought, thump, beat,
batter, bruise, smash, break, and otherwise inflict
grievous bodily injury on one theodolite. But not
to waste our time now on the law of the case, I
have no doubt that the Padre is sent to negotiate
a treaty. Now, do you think that where a Rajah
has an undisputable right to a Zemindary, and
the Kilhdar resists his authority in the persons of
his army and artillery (I mean Caption, Angle,
and his theodolite), the Rajah ought not to tuck
him up, as was done at Faluari in the business of
the Deccan? By-the-bye, the delay in the payment

of the Deccan prize-money is too bad; had my
friend old Frank suspected such proceedings, he
would have made a drum-head division of the
loot. I remember when I was attached to the Residency at Rumbledroog, about thirty years ago, a
detachment, under the command of my friend
Jack Smith, stormed a hill-fort where he found
considerable treasure; so he told the paymaster
to make out a scale, and all the coined money
was first divided, and then the bullion and jewels
were weighed and measured out. Jack got two
quarts of rings, which were picked off by the
drum-boys from the toes of the ladies of the
Zenana in the glorious moment of victory; but
the d—d lootwallah of a paymaster slyly cribbed
a large diamond, which immediately touched him
I suppose with the liver complaint, for he soon
after gave in his resignation on that pretext, and
sailed for Europe. On reaching London, he went
immediately into Parliament, and has ever since
been presiding at missionary meetings and Bible
societies, and be d—d to him!"

At this pause I interposed and reminded the
Nabob that Dr Lounlans was waiting.

"True, true," said he, "I had forgotten him;
but old stories, and anything like fraud or oppression, make me forget myself and neglect my own
affairs. Had it not been for the warmth and generosity of my feelings in that way when I was at—
Devil take it! I am at it again; let us go at once
and hear what the Padre has got to say."

CHAPTER XVII

THE Nabob bustled on before me to the room where Dr Lounlans was waiting, and leaving me to follow, went forward and received the reverend gentleman with a hearty jocular urbanity.

"Warm weather, Doctor, this," said he; "never felt the heat more oppressive in Bengal, except a day or two during the hot winds, but even there you can keep it out by means of tatties, you know. Here, in Europe, we are still very far behind. Houses are very good for winter and wet weather, not at all adapted for the summer climate; but when I have once got Nawaubpore in proper order, I'll make my own climate, as the Nawaub of Lucknow told Lord Wellesley—I'll have a subterranean parlour for the hot season. But hadn't you better take some sherbet or a glass of sangaree, after your walk? My aubdaar will cool it for you with a whole seer of saltpetre; for my icehouse has gone wrong, you know, by the mason leading the drain of the washhouse through it, like a d—d old fool as he was.—I beg your pardon, Doctor."

Dr Lounlans had evidently prepared himself

for the interview: his manner was dry, cold, and almost repulsive, as he said, "No offence to me," dwelling emphatically on the last word, and adding—

"The business, Mr Rupees, which has induced me to postpone a journey until I could see yourself is very urgent, and I hope it is convenient to let me proceed with it."

The Nabob was somewhat taken aback at the abruptness of this commencement; but, significantly winking to me, requested the Doctor to be seated; and, throwing himself down on a sofa, he lifted up one of his legs upon it, and said, "I am all attention, Doctor."

Prepared as the young pastor was for his undertaking, this nonchalance somewhat disconcerted him, but he soon recovered his self-possession, and replied—

"When I came into this parish, I understood that Mr Mailings, your neighbour, was one of your most particular friends."

"Well, and what of that?"

"And now I understand," resumed the minister, "that without any fault on his side, but only the misfortune of having borrowed your money, you have instituted proceedings against him of unusual severity."

"Well, and what then?" responded the Nabob, winking at me.

"Such rigour, in such a case," replied the Doctor, "cannot, Mr Rupees, have proceeded from the dictates of your own feelings, but must be the effect of advice, in which your long absence from the usages of your native land has been employed as much to the disparagement of the goodness of your own heart, as to the prejudice of the solitary old man, your unfortunate debtor."

The Nabob, putting down his foot, and assuming an erect posture, looked a little more respectfully towards the Doctor, as he said with cordiality—

"I suppose, Doctor, you think that the people of India are less liberal than those of Europe, but they are a d—d sight more so—I beg your pardon, Doctor. For myself, I never pretended to be a philanthropist, but I have often given fifty gold mohurs to an officer's widow, when people of the same rank in Europe would have thought a guinea prodigal. In this very case, did not I lend the old Guddah £3000 at four per cent. when Consols were at 73, and when I might have had ten in Calcutta from my friend David, bear as he is?"

"Your kindness in that respect, certainly," replied Dr Lounlans, "is not to be disputed; but to exact a repayment at this particular time is turning your former favour into a misfortune."

"Who says so?" exclaimed the Nabob, resuming his recumbent posture on the sofa. "I have not yet asked for my money, though the last half-year's interest has not been paid."

"Then you are unjustly suffering in public opinion, for it is universally reported that you have given instructions to your man of business to demand repayment, and in the event of refusal—the poor debtor must of necessity refuse —it is also reported that you have ordered every measure of law to bring his estate to sale at this time, when it is morall certain that it will not sell for half its worth."

"Dr Lounlans," said the Nabob, looking loungingly over his shoulder, and then winking at me,

 "The worth of anything
Is just whatever it will bring."

The Doctor turned to me with dismay in his countenance. He was conscious that argument could make no impression, and apprehensive that entreaty would prove equally ineffectual; but nevertheless he again addressed the Nabob, in a firmer tone, however, than he had hitherto employed,—

"Sir, such proceedings are not in unison with the feelings of this country. Mr Mailings is the representative of an ancient family; the habits and affections of the people of Scotland are still strongly disposed to take the part of a man of his condition when he suffers from oppression."

"They were," replied the Nabob drily; "but now, I suspect, they are quite as well disposed to esteem those who, by their own merits, have made their own fortunes, and have brought home from other countries the means of improving their native land. I have myself spent more money here, Dr Lounlans, on Nawaubpore, than all that the Mailings, since the Ragman's Roll, have had to spend, whether got by thieving in days of yore, or by rack-rents and borrowing in our own time."

" But, sir," replied the young minister fervently, "the day is yet far distant, and I hope will long remain so, when the honest people of Scotland will look tamely on and see mere wealth and ostentation treading down their ancient gentry."

"Ay, honest! Ah! that's but a small portion of the nation, even including the General Assembly of the Church and the College of Justice. But if they were as numerous as the daft and the imbecile, who, you will allow, are not to seek among gentry of the landed interest, as, indeed, in my opinion, they constitute the majority of the nation at large ; for you know that every man of sense and talent seeks his fortune abroad, and leaves only the incapable and those who are conscious of their deficiencies at home——"

Apprehensive that the conversation might become a little too eagerly pointed, I here interposed, and said, to turn aside the sarcasm which I saw Dr Lounlans was preparing to launch, "Your observation, Mr Rupees, explains to me why it is so difficult to give any correct exhibition of Scottish manners without bringing Tom o' Bedlams on the stage. In the Parliament House of Edinburgh you may see——"

Made them tottle out of the room . . . as if some horrid
monster was bellowing at their heels

"I beg, sir," said Dr Lounlans, interrupting me, "I beg your pardon. Am I then to understand, Mr Rupees, that you are determined to persevere in your rigorous proceedings?"

"I intend to do no more than the law permits me to do. I will do nothing contrary to law; and if there is any rigour in the case, the fault is in the law, not in me."

"But," replied the Doctor, "consider public opinion."

"D—n public opinion," responded the Nabob —"I beg your pardon, Doctor."

"But, Mr Rupees, reflect on the prosperity with which it has pleased Heaven to crown your endeavours."

"Well, sir."

A short pause here intervened, as if the Doctor felt in some degree deterred from proceeding; but presently he rallied and replied, "The same Power that has filled your cup to overflowing, hath seen meet to empty that of your ill-fated neighbour, and you should——"

"Should!" interrupted the Nabob sharply; "would you have me fly in the teeth of Providence?"

It was now evident that, notwithstanding the popular eloquence and many excellent qualities of the Rev. Doctor, he was not possessed of stamina sufficient to stand a contest with a character of so much energy as the Nabob, whose original strength of mind had been case-hardened in the fiery trials of Indian emulation and ambition, and whose occasional liberality sprung more from ostentation and the feeling of the moment than from any regulated generosity or sense of duty.

The Doctor rose somewhat flushed, and coldly wishing the Nabob good morning, immediately left the room. I also rose and followed him. The Nabob at the same time had likewise risen, and as I was going out at the door, patted me on the shoulder, and, chuckling with triumph, said in a whisper, " Haven't I done for him; did you ever hear such a fellow ? Canning, I'm told, calls my friend Sir John, Bahaddar Jaw, but our worthy Padre would better merit the title."

CHAPTER XVIII

ON leaving Nawaubpore, having bid adieu to Dr Lounlans at the gate, I walked leisurely, in a mood of moral rumination, towards Auldbiggings.

It seemed to me that there was no chance of mitigating the dispositions of Rupees, nor any mode by which the old Laird could be extricated from his unhappy situation, save only that which Mrs Soorocks had, as I thought, so impertinently suggested. The more, however, that I reflected on her suggestion, ridiculous as it had appeared in the first instance, the more I became persuaded that it was not only plausible, but judicious; and accordingly, before I reached the avenue of the Place, I was resolved to do all in my power to further and promote the marriage. Fortune favoured the benevolent intention.

On approaching the house, I discovered the old man seated, as his custom was about that time of day, on his own louping-on stane. He seemed more thoughtful than usual; instead of looking anxiously towards the highroad to see who was going to, and who coming from the town, his head hung dejectedly drooping, his hands, the one within the other, rested on his knees. He was indeed so rapt in the matter of his own thoughts that he did not observe me until I was close upon him.

After the customary interchange of morning civilities, I told him that I had been with the Nabob, whom, with a prospective view to the matrimonial proposition which I had determined to urge, I described with lineaments certainly as harsh as those which he had shown in the conversation with Dr Lounlans.

"'Deed, sir," replied the Laird with a sigh, "it's a' true that ye say: he's as boss[1] in the heart, and as hard, as a bamboo cane; but what can ye expect frae the like o' him, or o' them, as the worthy Mr Firlot used to say, 'beggars whom the Lord had raised from the dunghill, to set among the princes of his people'? Set him up indeed! Before his mother's brother sent him to Indy, I mind him weel, a dirty, duddy do-nae-guid, that couldna even tak care o' his father's kye; for ae day he was sae taen up on the brae wi' getten the multiplication-table by heart—weel has it taught him baith to increase and to multiply!— that he left the puir dumb brutes to tak care o' themselves, and ane o' them, a silly stirk, daunert o'er the quarry-craig and was brained. But what am I to do? To fight in law wi' this Great Mogul wud, wi' my light purse, be as the sound o' the echo to the pith o' the cannon-ball. Gude help

---

[1] *Boss.* Hollow.

me, I maun submit! And what's to become o'
me, wi' thae feckless auld hands, unhardened by
work, and the book o' my life but half written?
I may sing wi' Jenny in the sang—

> 'I wish that I was dead,
> But I'm no like to dee.'"

To such despondency it was not easy to offer
any immediate consolation, but I said, "It is
much to be regretted, Mr Mailings, that at your
time of life you have not the comfort of an agreeable companion to cheer you. A man of your
respectability, I think, might do worse than look
out for a helpmate to lighten these cares that
have fallen in evil days on your old age."

"I have had my thochts o' that," replied he,
"but I fear I'm tyke auld,[1] and November's no
a time to saw seed. But between ourselves,
I'm no overly fond o' the rule and austerity o' a
wife, after the experience that I hae had o' the
juggs o' matrimony that Mr Firlot set me in for
the business o' Babby Cowcaddens, 'cause she had
got an injury and wyted me."[2]

"You don't mean to say that the late Mrs Mailings was a woman of that description? I always
heard her spoken of as one to whom you were
greatly indebted for the order and frugality with
which she managed your domestic concerns."

"It would hae been an unco thing an she

---

[1] *Tyke auld.* Dog old, very old.
[2] *Wyted me.* Blamed me.

had been in a faut," replied the Laird. "Nae dout she rampaged up and down the house frae Monday morning till Saturday night like a roaring lion, cowing the lasses, and dinging me about as if I had been nae better than a broom besom, by the whilk we grew rich in napry and blankets. But O she made dreadfu' saut kail on Sunday!"

"But, Mr Mailings, is it the case that you had been gallant to her before marriage?"

"I canna deny but I might hae been, but she was leed on if she wasna thranger wi' a Captain Gorget that was recruiting in the toun."

"Who was she?"

"Oh, she was weel eneugh in respec of connections, for she was the only daughter o' Cow-caddens of Grumphyloan. She had lost her mither vera young, and so, being edicated amang the giglin hizzies and rampler lads o' the nee-bouring farms, she was—But, to make a lang tale short, Mr Firlot said that if I didna marry her, she being o' sae respected a family, he wad gar me repent in the bitterest manner he could; so that rather than be sae disgraced, o' the twa evils I chose the least. But she's quiet noo, and her bairn lies by her side, and has, I trust, found a Father on high, though its parent, by the father's side, in this world, sure am I, must hae been a matter o' doot when it was laid to my door."

"Well, but, Mr Mailings, though your first marriage was not a happy one, might you not now, in your maturer years and riper judgment, choose for yourself? There, for example now, are the ladies of Barenbraes, excellent gentle-women, rich, and of the purest character;— could you, Mr Mailings, do better than make up to one of them, and thereby obtain a careful and kind companion, and free yourself from the thraldom of the Nabob's oppression?"

"That meddling woman Mrs Soorocks was here yestreen, on ane o' her sympatheezing visitations, and really spoke sensible on the vera same head; but ye know that baith the sisters are past the power o' posterity, which is an ob-jection, even if my heart didna tell me that I ne'er could like either the tane nor the tither o' them: they're no for a man that likes a free house and a fu' measure; a' might be pushon that's aboon the plook wi' them,[1] and that, ye ken, wad never do for the hospitable doings o' the house o' Auldbiggings."

"Laird, better small measure than no drink."

"That's a gude truth; but Miss Shoosie's very ordinar, and Miss Girzie ne'er was bonnie—I grue at the thochts o' either o' them."

[1] Scotch pint-stoups, before the reformation of the imperial measure, were made to hold something more than the standard quantity; but at the point of the true measure a small *papilla* or plook projected, the space between which and the brim was left for an *ad libitum*, an exercise of liberality on the part of vintners and other ministers to haustation. When, however, measure was regulated by the *scrimp* rule, it was said prover-bially of those who did so, "that of their liquors all was poison abune the plook."—*Author's note.*

I

"Mr Mailings, take the serious advice of a friend who feels for your situation, and do not allow the fancies that may be pardonable in a young head to bring your grey hairs down with sorrow to the grave."

At this moment Jock came running towards us with a paper in his hand, crying—

"Laird, Laird, here's news; the king's greetin."

"What's he greetin' for?" said the Laird; "I'm sure I hae mair cause, and it'll be lang or ye'll see me greet."

I took the paper from the servant's hand, and saw that it was a summons raised at the instance of Hugh Caption, notary public, for an assault.

"This," said I, "Mr Mailings, should put an end to any scruples that you may have to the ladies of Barenbraes; and therefore, with your permission, I will go to them before returning home, and declare your desire to throw yourself at the feet of one of them. If you would take my advice, your affections should be set on Miss Shoosie, for she's the eldest sister."

"If I maun consent, I maun—there's nae help for't; and so ye may just choose for me. It's a sore thing for a man to be frightened into his first marriage by the bow-wow o' a kirk session, and driven into a second by a coorse o' law."

CHAPTER XIX

ON arriving at the house of Barenbraes, I could not help feeling that my mission was one of peculiar delicacy. It required, indeed, all the consciousness of the benevolence and rectitude of my intentions to reconcile me to the task of confidant (or blackfoot, as it is called in classic Scotch) to such a "braw wooer" as the Laird.

I hesitated before entering at the dial on the green—took out my watch, saw that there was a difference of several minutes between the time of the gnomon and the chronometer—adjusted the latter—placed it to my ear to hear if it was going; not that my resolution to perform the duty I had undertaken was in any degree weakened—I only doubted as to the manner and terms in which I should, as proxy, declare a passion at once so ardent and refined.

As I was leaning against the dial, I overheard the voice of Mrs Soorocks with the sisters resounding from the parlour. I went forward to the door, which was open. I again halted there, for the ladies were engaged in a vehement controversy on the very subject of my mission. No member of the *corps diplomatique* would lose the opportunity of listening to the cabinet councils of the court with which he was to negotiate, if he had it in his power ; and therefore I stood still.

The first words I distinctly made out were from Miss Girzie.

" 'Deed, mem," said she, addressing, as it would seem, Mrs Soorocks, "the old gentleman has his failings, that ye must alloo."

"Failings !" replied Mrs Soorocks, " havena we a' our failings ? and between friends, Miss Girzie, ye hae your ain infirmities likewise."

Here Miss Shoosie interposed with a declaration to the effect that Mr Mailings would never be the husband of her choice.

" Choice, Miss Shoosie !" exclaimed the Laird's advocate. " Choice! mony a far better woman than ye were in your best days never had a choice. Really, at your time o' life, Miss Shoosie—ye ken ye're aulder than your sister—you ought to accept wi' a gratefu' heart, and be thankfu' to Providence if onything in the shape o' a man is evened to you."

The widow made nothing by this taunt, for the indignant spinster retorted—

" It would be gude for us a' if we saw oursells as ithers see us ; but if I could hae demeaned mysell to tak' up wi' sic men as some folk were glad to loup at, I might noo hae been in my widowhood. Oh, but ye hae been lang obliged to thole that dispensation, Mrs Soorocks—that was your ain choice, nae doot."

"Sister," said Miss Girzie, "surely ye forget that Mrs Soorocks has aye been vera obliging to a' kinds o' wanters suitable to her years."

"O ay," replied Miss Shoosie, "we hae baith heard o' mair than ae instance o' her condescension."

"There was Dr Pestle," said Miss Girzie, "hi! hi! hi!"

"And Mr Grave, the Relief minister, ha! ha! ha!" responded Miss Shoosie.

"It was said you were particular to auld Captain Hawser o' the press-gang," added Miss Girzie.

"Was that true, mem?" subjoined her sister; "I'm sure ony woman maun hae had a cheap conceit o' hersell that would hae thought o' sic an objik—and only three parts o' a man too, for he had a timmer leg."

To all this Mrs Soorocks replied with her wonted candour and suavity.

"It's very true that there was a time when I was inclined to have changed my condition—I'll ne'er deny't; but no one could ever impute to me a breach o' discretion. We live, however, in an ill-speaking warld, Miss Shoosie; and wasna there a time, my dear, when folks werena slack—they ought to have been punished, Miss Shoosie, for cooming [1] your character in the way they did—but ye had great credit for your bravery. I didna think it was in the power o' woman to

[1] *Cooming.* Blackening.

have sae face't it out.   I allow frankly and freely
that it was a maist improbable thing that a young
woman o' a genteel family should hae foregathered
in a glen by appointment wi' a blackavised, pockyawr'd,[1] knock-kneed, potato-bogle o' a dominie.
Ithers had their cracks, as wha can stop the
mouths o' a scandaleezing warld ? but, for my
part, I aye thocht and upheld the meeting for an
accidental ane, and so I said at the time to Mr
Firlot, when he was bent on sending the elder
to test the fact and mak peremptory investigation.
It's no to be tell'd to what a bonnie pass matters
might have been brought, for the session were a'
on the scent, and the daughter o' an heritor was
game no every day to be hunted after.   But, as I
aye observed, it wad be mair candid and Christian-
like to let the thing drap; for, in the first place,
it mightna be, and I houpit wasna true; and in
the next place, couldna be proven, which was the
best thing that could happen for baith parties,
there being nae leeving witness, at least that
either the members or me ever heard tell o'."

Here a yell so alarmed me that I could not
resist rushing into the room, where the amiable
disputants, in the warmth of argument, had
started from their seats, and were standing in
the middle of the floor.

The aspect of Mrs Soorocks indicated the most
resolute calmness, and a sweet smile played round
her lips, and no one could have traced the storm

---

[1] *Pockyawr'd* (pockarred).   Marked from the smallpox.

of passion raging within but by the lightning that flashed from her eyes.

Miss Shoosie, a tall, meagre, heron-necked anatomy of womankind, was standing as stiff as Dr Gaubins, of Glasgow, of whom Beeny Hamilton said that he looked as if he had swallowed a decoction of ramrods. Her hands were fiercely clenched, her cheeks pale, and her lips quivering, her teeth grinding, and her small greenish-grey eyes sparkling as if they emitted, not constellations of fire only, but visible needles and pins.

Miss Girzie had thrown herself between them, and was pushing her sister back by the shoulders, evidently to prevent her from fixing her ten bloodthirsty talons in the imperturbable tranquillity of her antagonist's countenance.

On my appearance the storm was instantly hushed, the sisters hastily resumed their seats, and Mrs Soorocks, with ineffable composure, addressed herself to me.

"How do you do, sir? Me and the leddies hae been just diverting ourselves, talking o'er auld stories, till we hae been a' like to dee of laughin. Miss Shoosie there ye see hasna got the better o't yet. O Miss Grizzy! but ye're gude at a guffaw; as for your sister, I'll no forget the way she would joke wi' me. I hope ye havena taen't ill, Miss Shoosie? I was just reminding her, sir, o' a wee bit daffin in the days o' her youthfu' thochtlessness."

The insulted virgin could stand no more.

Bouncing on her feet, she gave a stamp that shook the aged mansion from roof to foundation, and raising her clenched hands aloft, she screamed through the throttlings of rage—

" It's false—it's false—as false as hell ! "

And so in verity it was, for the whole insinuation, with all details and particulars, was only an invention got up by the ingenious Mrs Soorocks, on the spur o' the occasion, having no other material wherewithal to parry the cutting innuendoes of her acrimonious adversaries. The widow, however, took no notice of the judge-like energy of the denial, but said—

" Good day, my old friends, and tak an advice from me : Put a bridle on the neck of your terrible tempers. Miss Girzie, I may say to you, as Leddy Law said to ane like you, 'Maybe if you would shave your beard, it would help to cool your head.' "

With these words she swirled meteor-like out of the room, with a magnificent undulation or curtseying motion, before Miss Girzie could discharge the bomb of her retort. That it might not, however, be lost, but strike, as the artillery-men say, by *ricochet*, the infuriated virgin turned sharply to me, and said—

" She's ane, indeed, to speak o' shaving faces— she ought to be taught to scrape her ain tongue. But it's beneath me to discompose myself for sic a clash-clecking clypen [1] kennawhat. She's just a midwife to ill-speaking."

[1] *Clash-clecking clypen.* Scandal-hatching, tale-bearing.

Miss Shoosie, who had by this time in some degree rallied, exclaimed—

"Sister—I beg, sister, ye'll say no more about her, for I'm determined to take the law;" and with these words she burst into tears.

CHAPTER XX

WHEN, after some desultory conversation, in
which, with all my usual tact and suavity, I had
in a great measure succeeded in soothing the
irritated feelings of the ladies, Miss Girzie, "on
household cares intent," had left the room; and
finding myself on the sofa beside her sister, I
began to throw out my feelers with a view to
ascertain in what manner the negotiation should
be opened.

"Miss Shoosie," said I gravely, "it is the misfortune of your sex to stand in need of a protec-
tor. Without some one of ours being interested
in your happiness, the variety of insults and vexa-
tions to which you are hourly exposed—to say
nothing of the value of a male friend in affairs of
business—renders it the duty of every prudent
woman, at some time of her life, to clothe herself
with a husband."

In saying this, I laid my hand upon hers, to
give the greater emphasis to my persuasion ; but
the look with which she considered the movement
was to me truly alarming.

"'Tis a very just observe, sir," replied she,

sighing and endeavouring to look amiable. Such
particular manifestations brought me at once to
the point, and I resumed—

" You are sensible, Miss Shoosie, that no man
can take a deeper interest in the happiness of his
friends than I do; and, as you are a lady of
sense and knowledge of the world, I acknowledge
to you that my visit this day is for a very special
purpose."

Here I felt her thumb, as it were, fondly disposed to turn up and embrace mine ; and I was
therefore obliged to be quick with the declaration,
for I saw that we were running the risk of coming
into what the Laird would have called a comical
situation ; so I added—

" I have been this morning with our friend
Auldbiggings, and have had a very earnest conversation with him on this very subject."

Miss Shoosie withdrew her hand, and taking
hold of her elbows, she erected her person and
said drily—

" Well ? "

" He spoke of you with great tenderness, lament-
ing that the circumstances of his first marriage
had prevented him, in the ardour of youthful
passion, from throwing himself at your feet."

" Did he really say so ? "

" Nay, I assure you, that it would offend your
delicacy were I to repeat the half of what he
said; but I can assure you that his youthful feelings towards you have undergone no change."

"No possible !" said Miss Shoosie, relaxing from her stiffness.

"It is, however, true, my dear madam; and surely it is much to be deplored that two persons so well calculated to endear themselves to each other should by the malice of Fortune have been so long kept asunder. What is your opinion, Miss Shoosie, of Mr Mailings?"

But instead of answering the question, she said—

"Do you know, sir, that Mrs Soorocks, when ye came in, was talking in very high terms of him? And certainly I never heard that he was guilty o' ony indiscreetness, 'cept in the misfortune o' his marriage; but in sic things the woman is aye mair to blame than the man, and there have been folk that said Mr Firlot the minister ought not on that occasion to have, in a manner, as they said, forced the marriage. But ever since Mr Mailings has been a widower, he has conducted himsell, I will allow, wi' the height o' discretion."

"But how does it happen, Miss Shoosie, that you and him never meet?"

"It's no my fau't," said she; "for ye ken that my sister and I are very retired; it's no our custom to wear other folk's snecks and hinges, like Mrs Soorocks; nor wou'd it become women in our situation to be visiting a wanting man."

"Upon my word, Miss Shoosie, I do not see that there would be the least indecorum in your asking Mr Mailings and myself on a Sunday afternoon to a sober cup of tea."

" I wou'd have nae objection," was the answer ; "but what way could it be brought about wi' propriety ? "

" 'Tis quite refreshing," replied I, " to converse with a sensible woman. Had you been Mrs Soorocks, Miss Shoosie, the chance is that, instead of the refinement and sensibility with which you have accepted the offer of my worthy friend the Laird's hand——"

" Offer, sir ! I never have had an offer."

" O Miss Shoosie ! what then is the purpose of my being here but to make you an offer ? "

" You don't say so ! " said she with a simper, looking away from me, and turning down the side of her head as if she was hiding blushes.

" I do, Miss Shoosie, and I think you most singularly fortunate in receiving such an offer from the man on whom your affections have been so long placed."

" Are you really sincere, sir ? Because if you are, I'll ne'er deny that I have long thocht that, with proper management, Mr Mailings might make an excellent husband."

" Then, Miss Shoosie, why delay your felicity and the felicity of the man of your choice ? "

" O sir, you would never advise me to take such a rash step as to change my condition without consulting my friends. Our sister Lady Chandos is at a distance——"

"I hope her ladyship is very well," said I, imitating the humour of Mrs Soorocks. "When did you hear from her last?"

"My sister was never gude at the writing."

"But her man of business, when he draws on you for the rents, surely lets you know of the welfare of her ladyship and the young heiress, who, I understand, is about coming of age? It will be a most fortunate thing, Miss Shoosie, both for you and Miss Grizil to have the assistance of a husband like Mr Mailings when you come to settle accounts with the executors of your brother-in-law."

"To be sure, there is no needcessity that I should consult Lady Chandos, for when she was married she never consulted me; but I can give no answer to the proposal till I have conferred wi' Girzie."

"Then let us call her into the room and settle the business at once. I shall return to Auld-biggings wi' a light heart, conscious that I have this day been instrumental in establishing the happiness of two persons worthy of one another."

"But, sir," replied Miss Shoosie with solemnity, "is there no glammoury in what you hae been saying, for ye ken it would be thocht a most extraordinar thing were I to confess a preference for Mr Mailings, and nothing to come o't?"

I assured her that I was fully accredited to make the proposal, adding—

"Indeed, Miss Shoosie, you are highly hon-

oured, and your marriage cannot fail to be a
happy one, since, like a princess, you are courted
by proxy. Let us call in Miss Girzie, and as the
day is warm and I am tired with my walk, I
hope on such a blythe occasion you will not refuse
me a glass of your delicious currant wine and
water."

"That you shall have, sir, without delay—but
you must leave me and my sister to confer in
private."

" Am I then to give my friend any hopes ? "

" I dare say you may say he needna despair."

" Miss Shoosie," I exclaimed, " you are a pattern
to your whole sex, and I cannot but envy my
friend that the disparity of our years, and the
fidelity of your affections to him, would, even if
I were willing, allow me no hope of success as
his rival."

" O sir ! O sir ! " said she, with a self-congratulat-
ing titter, " ye gar me doot—I wish ye may hae
a' this time been o' a true sincerity."

" Miss Shoosie, a marriage made up without
jocularity was never a happy one ; 'a dull bridal
and a scrimp infore,' as the old proverb says,
' bodes quench'd love or toom pantries.' Bring
in the wine and let us drink—may there ne'er be
waur amang us.'

CHAPTER XXI

W HEN I returned home in the evening, I sat down to the full enjoyment of those agreeable reflections which are sometimes all the reward that kind-hearted people like me receive in this world for the trouble of doing good and charitable actions.

The day, as I have already mentioned, had been uncommonly warm, but the twilight was cool, calm, and clear. The moon was just above the horizon, and so directly behind the high church and steeple of "the canny town," as King James the Sixth used to call Paisley, that they appeared like an apocalyptical vision dimly on her disc. I heard the faint far-off sound of the bell at intervals — now and then the bleating of the sheep on the Whinny Knowes, accompanied with the occasional bark of their guardian collie— while the sound of a flute from a neighbouring grove, as Harvey says in his "Meditations," came upon the ear with "auricular fragrance," or as a Lake poet describes the dashing of oars during the night on the bosom of Windermere in his amiable poem of the "Hoxter."

As I was sitting by the open window of my study, tasting the freshness of the evening air and listening to the soothing harmony of those mingled sounds, I observed the shadow of a man on the moonlight wall of the garden, coming by the footpath towards the house; and presently Mr Tansy, the schoolmaster, emerged upon the lawn from behind the shrubbery. I immediately ordered candles, and by the time they were lighted he was admitted.

"You have come in a happy moment," said I to him. "I have been enjoying the delicious tranquillity of this still and fragrant night. The spirit of contentment is abroad, and there is a pleasing augury of peace and repose in the aspect of universal nature."

I knew that these euphonious phrases, imitated from the style of that mysterious little work, *The Omen*, in which the cabalistic sentimentality of our Northern neighbours has been so prominently brought out, would act as ignited touch-paper on the dominie's inflammable enthusiasm; and so it happened.

"Call you it a happy time when everything indicates a crisis? The sun hath for the season reached the maturity of his power; he sent forth a heat which the memory of the oldest person in the parish cannot parallel, and from this day his glory will begin to decline into the ineffectual lustre which illuminates but warms not the dreariness of winter. The moon is in this very

K

hour at the full, and already hath begun to dwindle and to wane. The grass hath been cut down, the sheep are shorn of their fleeces, the sweet influences of the spring are over and gone, and the summer pauses in the weaving of her garlands, as if she had twined enough for the use of the year—all gives the sign of mutation, and the fortunes of men are in unison with the condition of things. We shall hear rumours of strange matters that will speedily ensue. The green boughs of prosperity will soon be seen with the sere and yellow leaf; tidings of change and decay will come among us, and proud hearts will be moved with disastrous fears."

This sort of almanack prognostication of the good and simple man derived an impressive emphasis in its meaning from the events of the day; insomuch that, although I had set him off in the mere playfulness of the moment, it had yet considerable effect upon my feelings, and I replied—

"There is something of a vague and hazy truth in your observations; but I have heard as yet of no particular occurrence to convince me of the existence of that astrological reciprocity between the course of moral actions and celestial signs which you so often maintain. On the contrary, I have this day myself sown the seeds of an event which cannot fail to be of prosperous issue."

The philosopher looked serious, and said—

"Modesty requires that you should add to the
bravery of such a boast an 'if likeas,' if no un-
foreseen accident comes forth to blight it ; but
whatever experience, sir, you think you have had
of a contrariety to my doctrines, I myself have
met with a wonderful instance of their truth.
This very day, a man and a child have come to
Renfrew, and are abiding at the public there.
What I have heard of them, and of the jeopardies
they have come through, convinces me that they
are unconscious agents to bring about some singular mutation that is ordained to come to pass
in this country-side.   They have come here, as I
am told, from a foreign land, in quest of great
wealth that appertains to the child, whose parentage was burned at sea.   More I have not heard ;
but hearing this much, I could do no less than
come to tell you ; for knowing how well gifted
you are wi' the faculty o' curiosity, I am sure that
you can lose no time in going to Renfrew the
morn's morning, to satisfy yourself by sifting all
the particulars, and doing your utmost to help the
friendless in this, to them, strange land."

"I beg your pardon, Mr Tansy, I am not a
man of such curiosity as you seem to think, but
only actuated by a liberal spirit of inquiry, the
love of truth, and a constitutional penchant for
facts."

I was indeed not quite pleased to hear myself
so considered, notwithstanding the compensation
in the just acknowledgment of my benevolence.

Our conversation was here interrupted by the arrival of a messenger from Mrs Soorocks in " the form and pressure " of one of her servant lasses. That lady was always particular in the choice of her handmaids, both as to character and personal appearance, and therefore I desired Leezy, as the girl was called, to be sent into the room, that I might hear the message from her own lips; at the same time, I requested the dominie to sup with me, begging him to have the goodness, for a minute, to take one of the lights and go into the dining-room, giving as my reason that I knew the business to which Mrs Soorocks was desirous I should attend was private and confidential.

The dominie accordingly left the room, and Leezy came forward.

She was of the better order of Scottish housemaids—a ruddy lively girl of twenty, and habited as befitted her condition. Her ankles, which is the next thing one is apt to look to in a woman after her face, were well turned, stockingless it is true, but, even by candlelight, of a fresh pink colour, which finely contrasted with her neat black shoes; her petticoat was of chocolate-coloured calimanco, and of an engaging brevity, and she wore a white dimity jupe, with a many-coloured silk handkerchief over her full bosom; her hair, saving the front locks in ringlets, was closely smoothed back and gathered within a kipplin comb.

"Weel, Leezy," said I, "which o' your sweet-hearts has led ye sae far a-field to-night?"

"Sweethearts! The last sweetheart I had was a gingerbread faring, and I eat it."

"Oh, had I been made o' gingerbread, and in such lips!" replied I, in the tone of Romeo wishing himself a glove.

"Ye would hae been o' some use," retorted Leezy; "but I have nae time the night to haver wi' you, for my mistress tell'd me to come straight back, and she aye threeps that I lose her time when I foregather wi' you—she's just been wud wi' a passion o' haste the night."

The spirit of inquiry was roused within me by this remark, and I exclaimed—

"What has happened?"

"How can I tell? Ye ken best what trafeckin has been between you and her; but she bade me gi' you her compliments, and to say that she wished ye would come the morn after breakfast, and convoy her to Mr Roopy's, on the business that ye ken o'."

At that moment, Mr Tansy, with the candle in his hand, looked in at the door, and said—

"I thought she was away."

"Ah! Mr Tansy," cried I, "just busy yourself for half-a-minute more in thoughts of adverbs, prepositions and conjunctions, and I'll be with you immediately."

Then turning to Leezy, I added—

"Give my compliments to your mistress, and say

I'll wait upon her; but take care of yourself with the young lad that's waiting at the gate."

"He'll wait lang that I care for," replied Leezy, slily adding, as she passed the dominie in quitting the room, "Whan, Mr Tansy, are ye to make anither 'clipse o' the moon?"

CHAPTER XXII

ACCORDING to appointment, I went over immediately after breakfast to Keckleton, the residence of Mrs Soorocks, whom I found sitting with her pelisse and bonnet on, waiting for my coming. The instant I entered her neat well-ordered parlour, she, snatching her gloves and parasol from one of the shining mahogany tables, said, "I'm ready, and hae been expecting you, for I fear that, if we dinna mak haste, the ill you and Dr Lounlans hae done will be past reparation. Bonnie ambassadors ye hae shown yourselves! But come awa."

With that she took my arm and hurried me out of the house.

"My dear ma'am," cried I, "but tell me first how you intend to proceed?"

"Dinna ye fash your thumb about that; ye'll see that I'll no let a wark o' needcessity slip through my fingers like a knotless thread."

The rest of our conversation till we reached the verandah of Nawaubpore was not worthy of particular preservation, although pertinent enough to the matter in hand, namely, the concerns and character of our neighbours.

Our reception by the Nabob was particularly courteous; to the lady he was indeed all smiles and gallantry.

After we had been seated a few minutes, he shouted with a voice that made us both start, "Q'hy," which brought into the room one of his Indian servants, to whom he said something in his own language touching tiffin.

"What an elegant creature that is!" said my companion; "for though his face is the colour o' a brass jeely-pan, and his dress like a man's on a tea-cup, hasna he a genteel manner about him?"

By this I discovered to what key she had modulated her meditated performance.

"Your remark is perfectly just, madam," said the Nabob; "there is a natural grace even amongst the lowest of the Asiatics, which no European, unless he has been very long in the country, can acquire. I have seen a Metranie throw on her capra in a style that an English princess, whom you would call here the ornament of society, would have given half her dignity to be able to imitate."

"O Mr Roopy!—Nawaubpore, as I should rather ca' you—I always heard that ye gaed very young to Indy."

"Yes, ma'am, I certainly did; but besides that, I had the good fortune to be early attached to our Residency at the court of Delhi, where I had an opportunity of frequently associating not only

with the first native society in India, but with the
princes of the blood of Timour."

"Nae wonder that, wi' such advantages of education, you hae the fine taste that everybody's
speakin about. Oh, but that's a lovely picture !
And what a handsome young gentleman that is
there, on the back o' that elephant ! Weel, I
never thocht that an elephant was just a pig grown
out o' the bounds o' moderation ; but, dear me,
Mr Roopy—Nawaubpore, I should say—I think
that bonnie lad on the beast's back must hae been
a relation o' yours, for he's really very like you ;
it's weel seen that he has been amang superior
folk—nane o' our hamewart gentry cou'd sit wi'
sic an air o' composity in the middle o' a stramash
like that. Did the teegur there really rin awa
wi' the blackamoor ? "

"He would have done so," replied the Nabob,
"had it not been for the trueness of my aim,
for I'm the young man in the houdah that
you have been pleased to compliment, and
it was considered in those days a very good
likeness."

"In those days, Nawaubpore ? That canna hae
been vera lang ago ; but I have heard that you
hae a wonderfu' fine collection o' pictures.   I
hae a great inclination that way, ever since I saw
Daniel in the Lion's Den in Hamilton Palace,
and that was on my marriage jaunt to the Falls
o' Clyde. It's an auld story, Nawaubpore ; ye
were then a young man, making conquests o' the

yellow ladies, I dootna, in that great Mogul toon, where ye learnt manners."

I had begun at this to be afraid that the lady's curry would prove too rich even for the Oriental palate of the Nabob; but the complacent smile which played over his turmeric-coloured countenance soon convinced me of the capacity of the Indian temperament for adulation. But it would seem that there is something in the influences of the sacred Ganges that generates an inordinate craving for flattery, as well as the hepatic maladies; there have been cases of this disease even late in life, a noble instance of it very recently, where the symptoms, so insatiable in India, are said scarcely to have been mitigated by empirical doses of the *Leadenhall* faculty.

"My pictures," said the Nabob, "are not very remarkable (some people, however, have tho't well of them), but, ma'am, allow me the gratification to show them to you, such as they are."

"Na!" said Mrs Soorocks, taking his offered arm, "this is politeness;" and as they walked out of the room I followed them.

All she beheld filled her apparently with the most extraordinary delight. On entering the principal drawing-room she exclaimed—

"O Mr Roopy!—Nawaubpore, as I should weel ca' ye—you and me are just like King Solomon and the Queen of Sheba, when he was showing her all his wisdom, and the house that he had built, and the meat of his table."

" That you shall see presently," said the Nabob, laughing, " for I have ordered tiffin in the dining-room."

" And I see, like him, ye hae sitting servants too," rejoined the lady ; " all this must hae cost a power o' money, Nawaubpore."

" It did cost a few lacs, and a great deal more than I could well afford."

" Weel, I'm vera sorry indeed to hear that— it accounts for what I have heard : for sure am I, a gentleman o' your extraordinar liberality, had ye no straitened yoursell wi' this grandeur, would never hae thocht of molesting that poor silly doited do-naething Auldbiggings about his wadset."

" Oh, not quite so bad as that neither, ma'am ; for all his debt would be but a drop in the bucket in my affairs," said the Nabob.

" Weel, I was sure o' that, and I so said to them that told me ; and I said, likewise, that you had been very ill-used, for if Auldbiggings didna insult you himsell, he egget on the misleart creature his servant-man to break your land surveyor's implement ; and that it wasna the worth o' the money that gar't you persecute him, if it were sae, for that ye were a man far aboon heedin' whether ye were pay'd at this time or seven years hence, especially as you could not but know that the property would come vera soon to you in a natural way—the feckless body being in a deep decline, wi' a great hoast, and a sore defluction o' the chest."

"I have long known," said the Nabob, laughing, "that his *chest* was out of order."

Here the lady burst into a most immoderate guffaw, in which the Nabob heartily joined. At the conclusion, she exclaimed—

"Really, Nawaubpore, ye're as funny as ye're wise; but it's no Christian-like for you and me to be gambollin o'er the weak man's infirmities. Couldna ye just let him be? I'm sure, if I had but the tenth part o' your fortun, and no the half o' your generosity, rather than hear the clash that's bizzin' about a' the kintra-side concerning you and Auldbiggings, I would put his heritable bond in a blank cover—I wouldna demean myself to write the body—and send it to him wi' my contempts."

I thought Mrs Soorocks truly like the Queen of Sheba for her management in this instance, especially when the Nabob, with a slight shade of thoughtfulness, replied he was sorry to hear that there was so bad an account of himself in the country.

"But," replied she, "I never believed it; and ye needna fash yourself, as ye ken it's no true—it's a soogh that'll soon be ower."

"Everything, my dear madam," said the Nabob, "is in this world misrepresented and much exaggerated—that hectoring, lecturing prig of a fellow, Padre Lounlans, came here dictating to me what I should do."

"He's a self-conceited man, Dr Lounlans,"

interrupted the lady, "he would rule the wisest in the parish if he could, and for your own dignity, Nawaubpore, you who have seen so much o' the great world, couldna suffer yoursell to be governed by the likes o' him. It will, however, be a pity if you let your scorn o' a meddlin minister hurt your ain character. If I was in your place, noo that the Doctor's awa to be married, I would show the world that I would do muckle mair o' my ain free will than I wad do either for fleechin or preachin."

The Nabob was now evidently thawed, and said—

"You think my own tho'ts, ma'am. I have been for some time intending to stop the proceedings which my man of business had advised me to institute."

"But," said Mrs Soorocks, "if ye stop the proceedings, which is as much as can be expected of you, I wouldna advise ye to gie up your heritable bond; for if ye didna get the property at his death, somebody less deserving will."

"I'm sure, Mrs Soorocks," said the Nabob, "I shall do anything you like in the matter; I am too happy in having made the acquaintance of a lady so judicious to refuse her any wish in so trifling a matter. Allow me the honour to show you the way to the dining-room."

CHAPTER XXIII

HAVING bid adieu to the Nabob at the Fakeer gate, or, as Mrs Soorocks called it, "the Beautiful Gate," to which he had accompanied us, we walked on together, congratulating each other on the success of our undertaking.

"Weel," said the lady, "ye see how a thing may be done, if folk kent how to set rightly about it. To be sure, considering that Dr Loun-lans is a young man no experienced in the ways o' the world, and that ye're but an authour, which, in a certain sense, is only a something between a dominie and a bookseller ; and that Nawaubpore is a man o' abilities (though a thocht vain o' them, that maun be allow't), it was none surprising that ye baith cam sae little speed. Folks say that the Nabob's proud, but, for my part, I think he's a man o' condescension ;—and hasna he a fine style o' manners ? It will be lang in the day or ye'll see ane o' our stirks o' country gentlemen linking a leddy about his house, and showing her his plenishing and other curiosities. Poor bodies ! they ne'er hae a greater curiosity than themselves. He maun indeed be a rich man yon. I said he was like King Solomon in all his glory, and, like Solomon, he has his weak side too; but I couldna help thinking, as he showed me his gold and his silver and his precious stones—didna ye think the big chiny jars maist handsome?—that he was mair like Hezekiah showing the men that brought him the present, after he was no weel, from Berodoch-Beladin, the son of Beladin, king of Babylon. It's surely a neglect in the Scriptures no to tell us what the present was, for no doot it was some very fine thing. I hope, however, that what Nawaubpore has shown to us this day of his precious things, his spices and his ointments— there was rather an overly ostentation of spice in yon mugglecatauny soup; but we shouldna look a gien horse in the mouth, so I hope that the pride of the Nabob's heart is no to be dismayed wi' the sight o' his veshels o' gold and his veshels o' silver carried away captive, as it were, to the Babylon o' Glasgow, to be put in the fiery furnace o' William Gray's melting-pot."

This speech, dishevelled and ravelled as it was, reminded me of the schoolmaster's prediction, and I told Mrs Soorocks of the strangers who had come to Renfrew, and of my intention of then going there to see them; advising her, at the same time, to proceed to Auldbiggings to comfort the Laird with the tidings of our achievements.

She was greatly struck with the coincidence of the strangers' arrival at the time of what she

called the Nebuchadnezzar vanity of the Nabob
about the great Babylon he had built; and she
would willingly have accompanied me to see the
bottom of such "a judgment-timed event," using
many ejaculatory terms concerning what might
come to pass. I had, however, enjoyed enough
of her company for one morning, and shook her
off with as much civility as possible, promising to
call on her as I returned home to tell her all the
particulars.   We accordingly separated where the
roads diverged—I for the royal burgh and she
for the Laird.

I had not parted from her more than two or
three hundred yards, when I met Jock, the Laird's
man, coming leisurely from the town.

"Where have you been this morning, John?"
said I; "and how is your master?"

"He's like a lying-in wife," replied Jock, "as
weel as can be expecket, and I hae been getting
for him a cordial o' mair efficacy for his state than
a' the drogues o' a doctor's bottle."

"Indeed! and what may that be?"

"What may that be? I'm sure ye ken that the
malady wherewi' he's afflicted is a sair disease."

"The want of money, do you mean? What's
your remedy, John?"

"I had hain'd three-and-twenty shillings and
fivepence hapeny out o' the wage that was pay'd
me twa year bygane, and I barrow'd four shillings
and sixpence from Jenny Clatterpans—ye'll ken
her—she's ane o' our lasses. Wi' that, and a

bawbee that I saved out o' twopence that the
Laird sent me to waster on snuff for him—isn't a
daft-like thing for a man to create an appetite in
his nose, when he's sae fash'd to get the wherewithal to satisfy his mouth?—wi' the aught-and
twenty shillings I hae bought a sixteenth, and
when it comes up a prize o' therty thousan pounds,
me and the Laird intend to go o'er the knowes to
the Great Mogul, and pay him his wadset, plack
and bawbee, sine snap our fingers in his face.
But oh! sir, sic a stramash is in the toun o'
Arenthrou! The bailies are rinning about hither
and thither like dogs wi' pans tied to their tails;
for some Paisley hempies that cam doun to the
fishing, it being their fast-day, have gotten themselves fou, and mortally affronted the toun by
miscaaing the gude steeple. The folk wadna
thol't, and coudna stand it; so, weel-a-wat, they
hae gotten sic quarters in the stane chaummer as
they richly deserve. If ye want to see the tail o'
the business, I wad advise ye to muve on a thocht
brisker, so I wish ye a very guid morning."

With this scrap of provincial intelligence, as
big with importance to Jock as the mutiny at
the Nore was to the British Government, the
Laird's man sauntered home to Auldbiggings,
and I onwards to Renfrew.

CHAPTER XXIV

I FOUND the stranger with his young ward in
" the inn," and, upon requesting to see them,
was shown into " the best room up the stair,"
where they were then sitting.

Mr Coball, for so the stranger was called, was
a plain but respectable elderly person, of a tropical
appearance ; the little boy wore also the impress
of the Indian clime, for though in voracious
health, his face was colourless, and though his
eyes sparkled with the morning light of life,
his cheeks were untinged with any of its vernal
bloom.

It was not easy to explain the motives of my
intrusion, but I got through the ceremony of
self-introduction tolerably well, and without much
embarrassment, for instead of affecting to offer
any apology, I professed to offer my services, at
the same time assuring Mr Coball that, although
I should have much pleasure in showing him
everything interesting in the town, there was in
fact nothing worthy of a traveller's notice in it.

" I'm not here," he replied, " in quest of those
things which attract travellers, but, as it were,

by accident ; yesterday I was landed at Greenock
from America, and was on my way to Edinburgh,
for the purpose of instituting some inquiry to
discover the relations of that poor child, when I
happened to hear the name of a gentleman mentioned, who is probably the chief person I am so
anxious to find. He left India two or three years
ago, that is, if the same whom I believe he is,
and I have halted here to call on him, which I
propose to do in the course of the day."

But not to dwell on uninteresting particulars,
it proved that the gentleman in question was the
Nabob, and that he was supposed to be either
nearly related to the boy, or acquainted with his
friends ; if he had not been executor to his father,
who died about five years before, leaving a wife
and three children.

"They were coming home," said Mr Coball,
"in the same ship with me, but by the terrific
calamity that befell us, and our subsequent dis-
asters, all the evidences (with the exception of a
few seemingly unimportant letters) have been lost,
by which the unfortunate child may be identified
to his relations."

He was too much moved by the recollection
which this incidental allusion to his misfortunes
recalled for me to interpose any question ; but as
his emotion subsided, he began to describe his
sufferings, till he insensibly came to talk of the
catastrophe of the ship.

" It happened," said he, " on a Saturday night

—we had been all merry, according to the custom at sea, and had retired to our respective cabins and berths, in the hope of making the Cape in the course of a day or two. I had just fallen asleep, when a sudden and strange noise roused me from my pillow. I listened, and a wild cry of fire was instantly echoed by many voices. I started up and ran on deck—I could see nothing, but only a steamy white smoke issuing from the fore-hatchway. In a moment every soul on board was around me.

"The captain with undismayed coolness ordered all to prepare for the worst, and the other officers with their trumpets were immediately at their posts, directing the crew in the attempt to extinguish the flames. The night was calm, the heavens above were all serene, and the sea lay so still around that the ship appeared to hang in the centre of a vast starry sphere, so beautiful and bright was the reflection of the skies in the unbounded ocean.

"I may not describe the dreadful contrast which the scene on board presented to that holy tranquillity. There were distraction, and horror, and wild cries, and fearful screams, and hideous bursts of delirious laughter. Then there was a crash below, and silence for a moment—and then the busy troubled sound of the consuming destruction, felt as well as heard, gnawing and devouring the inward frame and beams of the ship, still growing louder and fiercer.

" In the meantime the boats were lowering—the first that floated was instantly overloaded, and sank with a horrible startling cry—every soul who had so wildly leapt on board perished.

" The rage of the burning still increased—it was no longer possible to go below, without the risk of suffocation.

" Another boat was launched—one of the officers leaped on board, and, sword in hand, shoving her from the ship's side, suffered none to follow until water and provisions were handed in ; but notwithstanding his prudent endeavours she was soon filled both with the sailors and the passengers. The mother of this orphan was standing on the gangway with her three children ; she looked as if she too would have leapt into the boat, but the babies clung to her, and so hung upon her arms that she could not disentangle herself from their fond and frantic embraces.

" I tore this poor boy from off her—she cried, 'O save him if you can !'—the third boat was by this time in the water—I flung him to a sailor on board ; she snatched up the other two beneath her arms, and with a shrill dismal shuddering shriek, which made every one that hung clustering about the shrouds and gangway look round, she rushed into the smouldering cabin and shut the door.

" Her madness infected all who witnessed it —the boat was pushing off—there was no other chance for me—I leapt into the water and was taken on board. Many followed me, but the officer, with a terrible compassion for those who might be saved, hewed off their hands with his cutlass as they laid hold of the gunwale. 'Row,' he cried to the sailors who had seized the oars; 'the fire is making towards the magazine. Row off, or we shall be blown to pieces.'

"The sailors rowed with their utmost vigour. As we left the ship a cry arose from all the unfortunate wretches who were abandoned to their doom—so frantic, so full of woe and despair, that it made even the firm-minded officer exclaim, 'Good God! what is that?'

"I covered my ears with my hands, and bent my forehead to my knees, that I might neither hear nor see.

"When we had rowed to some distance, the men at the oars paused. I uncovered my ears and looked up—a deep, low, hoarse, murmuring and crackling noise came from the ship, and now and then a human cry. As yet the flames had not appeared; but all around us, save where those dread and dismal sounds arose, was stillness and solemnity—and the smoke from the devoted vessel appeared like the shrouded form of some incomprehensible and tremendous phantasma, ascending from the sepulchres of the ocean to the dominions of omens and powers.

"We looked at the spectral sight with terror and in silence. The orphan was clinging to my knees. At last the fire began to break out. The

flames first showed themselves at the cabin windows
—in a moment they whirled up the rigging—the
sails blazed, and the ship was for the space of a
minute like some unblest apparitional creation of
sorcery.

"'It is all over,' said the officer, and his voice
sounded hollowly over the mute and echoless
ocean.   'The fire is in the gunroom !   Ha !'

"At that instant a vast sheet of flame filled
the whole air, and like an angry demon unfurling
his wings, scattered meteors and malignant fires
against the stars.   The black forms of many things
hovered like motes in the sunbeam for a moment
in the blaze.   I distinctly saw an anchor, and many
like men with outspread arms.

"That momentary and indescribable vision of
fires and fragments was succeeded by a booming
roar, as if an earthquake had raised its voice from
the abysses of the silent waters, and then there
was a numerous plashing noise of many things
falling around us into the sea ; but that too soon
passed, and then there was darkness and silence.

"At that moment a cold wet hand caught hold
of mine, which was hanging over the boat's side;
and a man from the sea cried in a homely
Aberdonian voice : 'For Christianity, will ye no
tak me up ?'   The officer heard him, and relent-
ing from his firm and merciful purpose, ordered
him to be taken on board.   'Na, na," cried the
Scotchman, 'tak my bag first,' and he held up
to me a small haversack, which I grasped and

lifted in ; but in the same instant an undulation of the sea came rolling from the whirlpool where the ship had sunk, the boat rose on the swell, the fated wretch lost his hold, and sank beneath her for ever ! ''

After a short pause Mr Coball added : " It pleased Providence to rescue us next morning from our perilous situation. A ship bound for the Isle of France had seen the glare of the burning during the night, and steering towards it when the wind freshened, came up to us by daybreak and took us all on board. As the orphan (whose name is Charles Bayfield) still hung about me, I undertook, if possible, to return him to his friends. He is a singularly sharp boy for his years, and in the Aberdonian who had so strangely preferred a bag to his life, he had recognised one of his mother's servants. The contents of the bag were in consequence adjudged to belong to him, and assigned to my custody. They con- sisted of the letters I have mentioned—besides several packets of valuable pearls and other costly trinkets, which may help me to discover his friends. But I hope the Mr Rupees of this neighbourhood is the same gentleman of that name, who by the letters appears to have been the executor of the deceased Colonel Bayfield, the child's father.''

Our conversation after this became general. Mr Coball mentioned several things, the know- ledge of which he had acquired from the letters in the bag, which convinced me that the Mr

Rupees he was in search of could be no other
than our Nabob. But I became uneasy when he
stated that by some of the letters it appeared
Colonel Bayfield had died very rich, and that the
bulk of his fortune was in the hands of his executor, from whom his widow had not been able
to obtain any satisfactory information concerning
it. I did not, however, divulge what I feared,
but only advised Mr Coball to see the Nabob as
soon as possible, adding: "If you   the assistance of any friend necessary, make no scruple
of calling on me, for you have both interested my
feelings and awakened my curiosity." I then
took my leave.

Thus it came to pass that, what with the Laird's
affairs and this new adventure, I, good easy man,
who never meddled with any other body's business
—for my innocent curiosity can never be called
meddling—had as much toil for my feet, work
for my hands, and talk for my tongue as Mrs
Soorocks herself. Mine, however, was owing to
the purest and most disinterested motives, while
her visitations sprung from a prying disposition
and an unaccountable desire to have a finger in
every pie baked in the neighbourhood—the neighbourhood, did I say !—I might well say the country.
I have indeed often wondered that she did not
remove herself to the multifarious field of Glasgow;
but her reason was excellent: "Because," said
she, "nobody in a populous town cares for one
another, and I would die if I did not ken some-

thing about my neighbours. It's no a field for dispensing the workings of grace or the exercise of a mind void of offence, for I love to do good, especially to my friends in affliction." How blind some people are to their most obvious defects !

CHAPTER XXV

Fatigued with my long walk, the heat of the day, and the influence of my dinner, I had thrown myself on the sofa to indulge in a short siesta, before going, as I had promised, to tell Mrs Soorocks the result of my journey to Renfrew. I had not, however, stretched out my limbs many minutes when that indefatigable personage herself was announced.

"I thought," said she, as soon as she had entered the room, "I would spare you the trouble of coming to me, for although I was just curious to hear the discoveries that ye hae made, I could better spare hearin o' them than refrain frae telling you o' the tribulation we are baith likely to be put in for the pains we hae taken, out o' a sense o' religion, to help the Laird in his jepordies."

"What tribulation? What has happened?"

"Oh, the swine's run thro't!" exclaimed she; "no sooner had I told the auld gaumeril that Nawaubpore was a perfec gentleman, and was disposed not only to treat him with mitigation, but to allow him to live on the estate upon easy

terms for the remainder of his life, than he began
to hum and haw, and to wish that he hadna
geen authority to you to bespeak ane o' the Miss
Minnygaffs to marry him. Did ye ever experience
such black ingratitude?"

"You do not say so? My dear madam, if he
draws back, what shall I do? I have pledged
my honour for him to Miss Shoosie."

"I see nothing for it but to tak her yoursell,"
said Mrs Soorocks, laughing.

"It is no laughing matter to me, Mrs Soorocks,
after the praises I have bestowed on Miss Shoosie,
which, though they carried no offer, might yet
perhaps, by the help of Edinburgh advocacy, be
screwed into as much as, if it did not draw
damages, would draw from my pockets the fees
both of advocate and writer, and worse than all,
make me be talked of as a perjured wretch in
all the boarding-schools of Athens; even though
the case should happen to be accurately reported
in that amusing periodical, Shaw and Dunlop's
Decisions of the Court of Session."

We were here interrupted by my servant
coming into the room, saying that the ladies of
Barenbraes wanted to speak a word wi' myself
in private.

"They'll be comin to consult you anent takin
the law o' me," said my visitor, endeavouring to
smile; and she added, "Oh, but this is a treacher-
ous warld! Howsoever, ye can go, sir, and see
what they daur to say, and I'll bide till ye're

done wi' them. I redd ye, sir, tak tent that ye say naething to put up their birses, for when angered they are perfect wild-cats."

I accordingly left her and went to the ladies, who had been shown into the drawing-room, and were sitting on the sofa, with pink silk scarfs, like twin cherries on one stalk. Miss Shoosie was doing amiable with bridelike bashfulness, her eyes perusing the carpet, while she played with her shoe-toe with the point of her parasol. Miss Girzie had less of downcast modesty in her appearance. Her parasol lay across her knees, and was resolvedly grasped at the extremities, while her countenance indicated both fortitude and intrepidity.

"We have come, sir," said she, "having considered the proposal ye made to my sister yesterday——"

The "ye maun tak her yoursell," of Mrs Soorocks still ringing in my ears, I exclaimed: "Proposal, ma'am! I made no proposal!"

"Sister!" cried Miss Girzie, "sister, is it possible that you could be mistaen?—but I told you that it was ower gude a godsend to come to our door, especially as Auldbiggings has done sae lang without a wife."

This speech relieved me in one respect, that is, in as far as I thought myself implicated; but, considering what Mrs Soorocks had told me of the alteration in the Laird's views, I began to feel as if I had only got out of the frying pan into the fire; nevertheless, I mustered self-possession enough to say with some show of gaiety—

"Well, ladies, and what is the result of your deliberation?"

"I told my sister," resumed Miss Girzie, "that there could be no objection to Mr Mailings as a man, which was quite her opinion; but I thocht it wouldna be prudent of her to give her consent to an acceptance of his hand until we both knew what sort o' settlement he was disposed to make upon her."

"Settlement! Miss Girzie," cried I, glad to find any loophole. "Settlement! surely, ladies, you must have long known the embarrassed state of Mr Mailings' affairs. Were times to mend, as we hope they will do, doubtless he may have it in his power to make a settlement; but really, under existing circumstances, anything like a regular settlement ought not to be expected."

"Is't possible," replied Miss Girzie, "that you cou'd suppose my sister wou'd marry ony man without a provision for a family? I'm sure she shou'd ne'er hae my consent to such indiscreetness."

Glad to find the venerable spinster in so sturdy a humour, I grew a little bolder, and said—

"Whatever your sentiments, Miss Girzie, may be, I have always had a very high opinion of the disinterestedness of your sister, and will say so before herself, there where she sits; but if I thought that in an affair of the heart, after the great tenderness and affection shown by my friend Mr Mailings, she could be so mercenary as to make any such sordid stipulation, I would advise him to have nothing further to say to her."

Here Miss Shoosie said, with a plaintive accent: "I'm no o' a mercenary disposition, and so I told my sister when she first spoke o' settlements."

This was alarming, and I was completely perplexed when Miss Girzie subjoined—

"It's vera true, Shoosie, but when a thoughtless young couple's coming thegether, it behoves their friens to see that the solid temporalities are no neglected in the delusions o' love."

"Indeed, Miss Girzie, you are quite right, and you would be wanting in sisterly affection if you did not see a proper jointure secured. At the same time I will be plain with you: as the friend of Mr Mailings I will set myself against everything of the kind. I am very sorry, ladies, that so unsurmountable a bar should have arisen to the completion of a union every way desirable."

Miss Shoosie moved as if she would interpose to prevent me from proceeding, but I was so apprehensive of a more frank avowal of her willingness to accept the Laird that I raised my voice, and continued—

"It cannot, however, be helped. I cannot see a gentleman's affections treated as no better than saleable commodities. You will excuse me, ladies, but my feelings are strong on the occasion. I do not blame you, however, Miss Girzie: you are but doing your duty, as I am doing mine. I will tell Mr Mailings of what has passed; and as a lady is waiting for me on particular business in another room, you will pardon me for so abruptly wishing you a good afternoon."

Miss Girzie at these words started up and said, " Sir, sir, just a minute."

" I can hear no more," cried I ; " it is plain you intend to make a bargain with my friend. No abatement of expectation, no retraction of opinion on the subject, can change my mind. I may seem to you warm, ladies, and I am so. Who can help it when one hears of a gentleman's heart and hand regarded as of no value unless the hand be filled with glittering trash ! "

The tone in which I expressed myself had so sounded through all the house that Mrs Soorocks came rushing into the room, crying : " Gudeness me ! have they flown upon you too ? "

At the sight of that lady the two sisters rose, and, making a formal courtly courtesy, moved towards the door, while she returned the recognition by another so profound that she seemed to have fairly seated herself on the floor, setting up at the same time a guffaw that made them tottle out of the room with short nimble steps, supporting each other, as if some horrid monster was bellowing at their heels.

CHAPTER XXVI

W**HEN** I had told Mrs Soorocks of what had
passed with the ladies, and related to her the
conversation I had held with Mr Coball; when
we had mingled our opinions respecting the demand which was likely to come so suddenly on
the Nabob; and when I saw the interest which
the doubtful situation of that gorgeous personage
had excited in the eager sympathy of my visitor,
I ordered tea for her, that we might discuss at
leisure the course we ought to adopt in a case so
singular and important; but before the kitchen,
anglice tea-urn, was brought in, the Laird made
his appearance, evidently dressed for some occasion of ceremony.

His coat and waistcoat were of the same snuff
colour — the latter with flaps after the manner
of, but of greater amplitude than the style of, the
court dress; his breeches of black silk, rather
short and scanty, were adorned at the knees with
heirloom buckles of Bristol stones set in silver;
his stockings were also silk, of a bluish tinge, and
a cottonial dimness, the effect of many lavations;
his shoes, cleaned by his man Jock, though jet

M

black, yet were more of a lack-lustre clothy appearance than of the satin-like brilliancy of Day and Martin — contrasting finely, however, with the radiance of his richly-chased massive Patagonian silver buckles; he wore his best wig well powdered—a demi-forensic structure of a middle and anomalous architecture, between the prim tye-wig, with Ionic volutes over the ears of a snug and debonair citizen, and the wig of wisdom, luxuriant with Corinthian curl, which distinguishes the upper end of a Lord of Council and Session. In the one hand he carried his Sunday hat, a fabrication of the last century, silky and sable,—the sides half looped up towards the crown indicated that it had been formed in that equivocal epoch when the aristocratic cock, yielding to the progress of taste and the march of intellect, was gradually relaxing into the philosophical fashion which ornaments the craniological organisation of the present enlightened age; the other hand grasped his tall malacca cane, crowned with gold and shod with brass. A tassel of black silk, which dangled from the whole above his hand, by its centrifugal force swept the air with magnificent oscillations as he came staffing his way into the centre of the room.

The first impression of this ceremonious appearance led me to think that the old gentleman had so adorned himself for the purpose of paying a visit of gratitude to the Nabob; and Mrs Soorocks, it would seem, had formed the same opinion, for before even the common salutations were exchanged she said—

"Dear me, Mr Mailings, ye can never be going to Nawaubpore's at this time o' the day? He'll be at his dinner—eating his dishes gude for the liver complaint; to be sure, he may excuse the intrusion of an auld-fashion'd man, a hame'art gentleman who has never seen the world, nor gallanted, like him, wi' the yellow ladies in yon palaces o' delight in Indy."

"Dinna lift me before I fa', Mrs Soorocks," replied the Laird, evidently not entirely pleased with her observation; adding, "I am not going to Nawaubpore, but to pay my respects to Grey Stane."

"Grey Stane, Laird? I didna ken that you and the family were on visiting terms," said Mrs Soorocks. "Mrs Luggie is certainly a pleasant woman, and they say Miss Jenny, who cam last week frae the boarding-school at Edinbro', is grown a perfec beauty, and can play on the spinet, and paint red cabbages and kail blades upon paper. It was a better world when a laird's daughter learned to play on the spinnin' wheel, and kent the wholesome use o' kail blades; but nae dou't your visit's a curiosity to see the beauty?"

"Ye're a woman o' sagacity," replied the Laird, "and I'll no deny the truth among frien's; for ever since ye pointed out to me the discon-solateness o' my situation, without a helpmeet,

I hae been seriously thinking that I wou'd be the better o' a wife."

Here I interposed, exclaiming : " My gracious ! Mr Mailings, did you not authorise me to carry a proposal to the ladies of Barenbraes ? "

" And," cried Mrs Soorocks, " when I showed the need that ye stood in o' somebody to take care o' you, did I not tell you that Miss Shoosie was the fittest woman in a' this country-side for that purpose ? "

" But ye ken," said the Laird, addressing himself to us both, " that my heart grewed at the thocht o' ony ane o' the twa reisted [1] auld frights —crined [2] in the flesh, wi' hides like the skin o' a pouket [3] guse, and hues like——denty lions I mean."

" But, Mr Mailings," said I, " I have done my duty, and fulfilled the sacred trust which you confided to me. Miss Shoosie has consented to accept your hand and share your fortune ; and although her sister has some scruples of a mercenary nature, yet your faith and troth are pledged, and to retract now would be most dishonourable."

" Dishonourable ! " exclaimed Mrs Soorocks ; " it wad be even-doon perfec perjuration. If Dr Lounlans were at hame, and siccan a sinfu' abomination to be committed within the bounds o' the parish, he wad set the session wi' its seven heads

---

[1] *Reisted.* Withered.   [2] *Crined.* Dried up.
[3] *Pouket.* Plucked.

and ten horns upon you, and ye hae had some experience o' what it can do. O Mr Mailings, ye havena the heart within ye to betray the love o' a young woman. Whare div ye think ye'll gang when ye dee?"

The Laird, raked by this cross fire, fell into confusion, and, instead of parrying the attack, replied with humility—

" I aye thocht that a man had a richt, at least for ance in his life, to please himsell."

" Please yoursell to be sure," said Mrs Soorocks, " but wi' a discretion. And what discretion wou'd there be in a feckless auld man to marry a gallopin', gallantin', gigglin' Miss in her teens, and to forsake a sober, douce, sensible, agreeable, judicious woman? I may weel say to you as Mause, in *Patie and Roger*, says to Bauldy—

' Vow and loup back ! was e'er the like heard tell ?
Swith tak him, Deil, he's ower lang out o'——'

I'll no attempt to metre't, but it means the ill place. Deed, Auldbiggings, ye had better repent and sin no more, or ye'll maybe hae Miss Shoosie's death laid to your door, for she's a kind gentle creatur, and canna miss but to die o' a broken heart ; and what'll come o' ye then, when, like a ghost in *William and Margett*, her spirit appears at your bed-fit, with a lily hand and a sable shroud ? "

" But," rejoined I, " it is not to the session only he shall answer—it is not only before the injured spectre o' Miss Shoosie that he will lie

quaking at the dead of night. He must answer
to me. I will not submit, after having been so
entreated to negotiate the marriage, to see it so
lightly broken off, and for what?—a young girl
that has nothing but flesh and blood to recommend her! Mr Mailings, I consider myself exceedingly ill used."

"Na!" cried Mrs Soorocks; "I canna see hoo
ye can be aff fechtin a duel wi' him—and a bonnie
sicht it would be to see him brocht hame on a
barn-door, after getting his head shot aff, and
Jock, poor creatur, greetin', and following the
mournfu' procession, carrying the head by the
lug, as if it was no better than a sheep's gaun to
the smiddy to be sing't."

The consternation of the Laird was continuing
to increase, and looking first at me and then at
his ruthless tormentor, he exclaimed—

"Have I fallen into the hands o' the Philistines?"

"Philistines!" cried Mrs Soorocks. "Surely
ye're an uncircumceesed as weel as a man-sworn
deceiver. Had I no mollified Nawaubpore, there
would hae been less daffin in your head the night;
for instead of dressing yoursell out like a squire
o' high degree, and singing, 'I kiss'd and I prattled
with fifty fair maids,' to mak conquests o' bits o'
lasses, ye would hae been sitting in your forlorn
chair, confabbing wi' Jock about whether by rope
or gun was the easiest way o' deeing. But I'll
go to the Nabob this precious minute—I'll let

him ken what a false deluding man ye are—I'll tell him o' the plague ye were to the kirk-session, before Mr Firlot got ye to right that amiable ill-used woman your first wife, and the wrongeous mischief ye would noo do to the sweet girl whom Providence has made me an instrument to choose for your second."

This last threat finished the Laird; he lay back in his chair with his eyes fixed on one of the bell-cranks, his arms hanging as it were powerless by his sides, and every feature of his face relaxed with helplessness.

"I canna," said he in soliloquy, "warstle wi' this—I hae lang thole't the consperacy that has sookit my rents—I hae endur't the loss o' my first love, Annie Daisie—I quietly submitted to my first wife till it pleased Providence to quench her—I hae seen the lands o' my forefathers mouldering awa—I hae known the terrors o' the law, and the judgment o' a wadset—I hae had sickness o' heart, and the rheumatics, and the toothache—weel may I say wi' the playactor in the show that I allowit in our barn—

'But it's this too solid flesh which makes the calamity of life,
For who would bear the pangs of despised love—
The oppressor's wrong—the insolence of law?'

The deevil take Hugh Caption, and all the other ills that flesh is heir to—I'm ruin't beyond redemption—Mrs Soorocks and sir, I gie myself up into your hands—be pitiful, if ye can."

CHAPTER XXVII

AFTER the departure of the Laird and Mrs Soorocks, I set myself quietly down to read the newspapers of the morning. Lugged as it were forth from my accustomed privacy, I felt myself involved within the influence of a vortex, pregnant with events to the worthies of my immediate neighbourhood. Changes, at least for a while, are lightsome; and really I confess that I was not a little tickled with the surrounding aspect of affairs: Miss Shoosie, Miss Girzie, and Mrs Soorocks on one side, threatening matrimony against the Laird, and his man standing "in defence," on the other; while the Nabob, Dominie Tansie, and myself put now and then a finger in the pie; keeping ever and anon a watchful eye on trig Leezie, that Abigail, running blackfoot between the skirmishing parties.

Half abstracted in these picturesque ruminations, I had just commenced an immeasurable leading article, the first sentences of which were redolent of Mavrocordato, Ulysses, Lord Byron, and the Greek Committee, when I was roused from my reveries by the thunder of the Nabob's chariot at my door.

I was much surprised at this avatar, and no less at the friendly and familiar courtesy with which the great man addressed me.

" I have come," said he, " to talk to you about a very comical affair, in which I may stand in need of some assistance, and you are the only man of any sense in the county."

" Then you have never been in Greenock, I presume ? "

" Oh yes, I have, though !   A very good sort of a town—plenty of punch and much jaw—quite edifying to hear the excellent character every one there gives of his neighbour—they have some fun too among them—one John Esdaile has long served them instead of Joe Miller—but I have no time at present to send for my friend the Bailie ; besides, he's not very portable, and I have left all my elephants in Bengal, where I had one that could have carried him."

I was here so shocked at this personality that I almost fainted.   I entreated him to forbear, and endeavoured to recall him from the digression into which he had so much the habit of falling, although he might have excused the objection-able expression by making an apology, as is usual on such occasions.

" Why, the business," said he, " is nothing less than a claim on more than half my fortune.   I had a friend in India, one Tom Bayfield, who rose to the rank of Colonel in the Company's service.   He married one day a very pretty girl, the daughter of my old chum, Dick Campbell; they were very happy, and got three children between them. Tom was a devilish clever fellow, made upwards of ten lacs—and died suddenly. I was in Europe at the time, but in making his will he left me his executor; and, failing his own children, his heir—for I had lent him a helping hand when he was only a cadet. Somebody, however, put mischief into the widow's head against me, as if her children had been cheated by this settlement, and she wrote me such vixen letters that I told her, but in polite terms, that she might go to the d—l; although out of regard for her husband I did intend to adopt her son. Well, as ill-luck would have it, on receiving my letter, she was advised by some of her nincompoop relations in Bengal to ship herself and family for Europe, when, if she had stayed till a decent time after her husband's death, she would certainly have got married again; but the ship was lost at sea, and it was supposed that every soul on board perished, so that I administered as heir to the Colonel. But the deuce is in't, there has been with me this afternoon a confounded impostor, as I think, who says that he was in the ship with Mrs Bayfield and her family; that the vessel was not lost, but burned; and that he had saved her son Charles, whom I had intended to adopt. And what do you think? he brought a great lubberly boy, whom he called Charles, and who was no more like the babe that I saw in the arms of the ayah when I left India than an Arab is like a Caffre; but certainly, considering the time that has elapsed since I saw the child, it may have grown up to something like the size of the impostor's brat. Now, what would you advise me to do in such circumstances? I don't want such proofs as the old Humbugs and Vakeels in Edinburgh would require; but before a man parts with one half of his property just now, and makes up his mind to leave the other at his death, it is but reasonable that he should know what he's about, and to whom he either gives the one or leaves the other. My friend Dr Dewai came home with a large fortune; a writer's wife in Dundee palmed herself on him as his near relation, and got the old fool to leave her a legacy of ten thousand pounds; but when he died, and her husband had got the money, it turned out that her mother had been his mother's chambermaid, and so got acquainted with the secrets and connection of the family. How d—d foolish I should look if it were discovered after my death that I had been as silly as Dewai! I never knew such a silly fellow as Dewai. When I was resident at Lucknow, he was surgeon to the Residency——"

Apprehensive that the Nabob was again digressing from the matter in hand, I brought him back to the point by asking if he had examined the stranger as to any evidence in his possession of the facts he affected to state.

"Oh, to do the fellow justice," replied the Nabob, "his story is plausible enough; and he says he has some letters of my own to Mrs Bayfield, but which, out of regard for the boy he calls Charles, he will only show in the presence of witnesses—I like the fellow for his caution. I want, however, you and that very sensible lady, Mrs Soorocks, to come over in the morning, and tiff at Nawaubpore to-morrow, when we shall meet the fellow, and will be able to say something more about it. 'Tis a d—d hard case, however, to be plucked so unexpectedly, and that too by one whom the unconscionable sea has given up, as it would seem, for the express purpose. It puts me in mind of a story which once happened in Calcutta. An officer was going up the country, and somewhere above Cossembazar, his budgerow was upset, and the Doudies all drowned; he was himself ashore at the time and so escaped. When he found what had happened, his business being urgent, he got to the nearest village, where he procured some kind of conveyance to a station, and proceeded by Dawk. The vessel, however, was picked up; and as he had not been heard of, it was presumed he had perished with the rest. So his agents in Calcutta immediately mounted black waistcoats and entered a probate to his will. But lo and behold! they received a letter from their late friend, dated at Agra, stating that as he had lost all his *Shraub* by the upsetting of his budgerow, he would thank them to send a fresh supply."

Here I found it necessary again to interrupt the Burrah Sahib by saying that I would not fail to be with him at the time proposed—asking him at the same time if he would take something after his ride.

"Thank ye, my good sir," said he; "I'll take a glass of brandy pawney, as the evening's hot."

I immediately ordered the brandy and some spring-water fresh from the well. While preparing the beverage, he resumed—

"The would-be-genteel coxcombs of Calcutta scout brandy pawney as vulgar, but we old sportsmen of the Mofussil know better than that comes to.

"There's my worthy friend old Sir Thomas. When he came round to Calcutta, he took up his quarters with old Frank at Barrackpore. Now the old peer always kept lots of the very best wines, chiefly French, and other thin potations, that did not at all suit the tone of Sir Tom's stomach; and still, by way of kindness, Frank used to press him to drink every wine on the table. The Knight was obliged to comply from politeness; but often, while swilling the well-cooled stuff, he would sigh for this old friend the brandy-bottle. One day he got to Calcutta, and slipping quietly on board of a Drughy, he pushed off for the ship which had brought him round from Bombay, and declared to the captain that he was apprehensive of a gangrene in his bowels from the gallons of sour trash he had swallowed;

and though it was only two o'clock P.M., the brace of them sat down, and finished their gin-tumblers apiece, which the gentleman declared was the saving of his life.   Oh, it's a famous thing brandy pawney.   Dr Jock, my worthy friend, recommended it both by precept and example.   By-the-bye, Jock sent me out some of the d—d black draught he's so fond of, when I some time ago felt myself bilious and queery; but as I was well before it arrived, I thought it a pity such good stuff should be thrown to the dogs; so I ordered a dose of it for my best China pig, for it was then slightly indisposed, as a Cockney would say.   And do you know, it poisoned her !   She died within the hour—d—d lucky I did not take it myself."

Here the Nabob having finished his tumbler, rose, and requesting me not to forget my appointment, adding that he would send his carriage to fetch Mrs Soorocks, bade me good-night.

CHAPTER XXVIII

I WENT by times next morning to the residence of Mrs Soorocks; but on approaching the house, discovered many signs which indicated that the lady could not conveniently accompany me. It was washing-day, and the little grass plat within the sweetbriar hedge between her house and the highroad was covered with all manner of female and household drapery. Ropes fastened in various directions to the iron railing, the lilac-trees, and the bolts and bars of the window-shutters, were festooned with shifts, sheets, and night-gowns, fixed on by split pieces of wood feruled with tin; napkins and towels were spread upon the rose and gooseberry bushes; and the large tablecloth, so admired at her New-Year's-day festivals for its damasked views of Amsterdam in Holland, and other foreign cities, hung upon a special cord, like a mainsail, between the lime and the rowan tree across the path leading to the front door. Access at one entrance being thus shut out, I was obliged to go round to the back of the house, the great scene of the operations of the day.

In front of the wash-house, with kilted petti-coats, our old acquaintance Leezie ravishingly "lap and flang" in a washing-tub, the spray of which, enveloping her in a mist, made her appear like a tutelar goddess amidst the spouting tritons of a Parisian fountain.

Deep within the steamy shade of the wash-house, the full round physiognomy of the cook, like the moon in a mist, loomed through the rising vapours; and in the darkness beyond, Jean Japples, the hired washerwoman, stood elevated on a tripod, like another Medea over the cauldron renovating the contents of it with an ex-broom-stick.

Not seeing Mrs Soorocks, I turned round to inquire at Leezie for her mistress; but at the same moment the lady herself made her appearance, in dishevelled morning garments, with a watering-pan in her hand. On seeing me, she set it down; and coming forward, begged that I would walk into the house. I explained, however, on the spot, the object of my visit, and the wish of the Nabob that she would accompany me; "But I see," said I, "that it is a pleasure I cannot expect to-day."

"It's vera true," was the reply; "for we're thrang, and in confusion wi' oor summer washing; it's just extraordinar what a family files [1] in the course o' half a year, forbye the plague o' sma' claes atween hands—but it's a trouble you men

[1] *Files.* Fouls.

are never fash'd wi', and some of ye even laugh
at us drudging women. My dear Mr Soorocks
used to say in his jocosity, that twa washings
were equal to one whitewashing, twa whitewash-
ings to one flitting, and twa flittings to one fire.
Really, I'm fash'd that I canna go wi' you, and
I wad fain stretch a point, if it were possible, for
the Nabob's cold collations are verra nice, and
he's himsell so much o' the gentleman. But dear
me, isna that his carriage coming alang the road?
—it's no. in possibility to come up to the door,
and I hae naebody to gang to the yett to speak
to that gran fitman. Leezie, put yoursell right—
step out o' the boyne as fast as you're able, and
say I'm dressing; for I maun go noo, since he has
sent the coach on purpose."

Accordingly, while Leezie went round to the
gate, taking time to adjust her own apparel,
which was no more in a state to receive visitors
than that of her mistress, Mrs Soorocks went into
the house, and in less time than could reasonably
have been expected (she is a clever woman), returned adorned for the visit.

As soon as we were seated in the carriage, I
related with some degree of minuteness what the
Nabob had told me of the state of his feelings
towards the family of Colonel Bayfield.

"Weel," said the lady at the conclusion, "I
aye said that Nawaubpore had a generous heart,
for a' his vanity and ostentation; but it will be
a dreadfu' thing if a man like him—so kind a
N

neighbour, and who may be a blessing to the country-side—should be impoverished by an impostor. I'll no soon forget the genteel way he pardoned, at my intercession, that daized remnant Auldbiggings; and maybe in requesting me to be present this day at the precognition, it may be put in my power to return his condescension."

"But surely, Mrs Soorocks, if the case is clearly made out that the boy is the son of Colonel Bayfield, you would not think of intercepting the just intentions of Mr Rupees?"

"' If ' 's a word o' power. It's no in the course o' nature, sir, that a ship burned at sea, and all hands on board perished, should send forth a leevin' witness to contradict the fact."

"True; but it would appear that all on board had not perished."

"Now that's what I'll no credit, and I'll gie you the reason of my misdoubt. Wha's the testimony? A land-louper that naebody kens onything about. Ah! sir, if 'ye had sic experience of the devices of man that I hae had, ye wadna be sae credulous. A man coming out o' the deep like a Robinson Crusoe, wi' a white Friday, to claim awa' the biggest half o' a gentleman's fortune—it's just a thing for playactors, and the likes o' Sir Walter, to mak a clishmaclaver o'; but amang people o' understanding it will be seen through, as a contrivance begotten in sin and brought forth in iniquity."

"There are many circumstances in the story,"

said I, "singular and almost improbable, I admit. But Mr Coball, the stranger, appeared to me a man of unaffected sincerity—warm in his feelings and simple in his manners."

"Simple manners! Verily, verily, that shows how an author may be versed in books, but scant of experience respecting the multifarious crookednesses of a wicked world. Did ye no hear o' the leesin'[1] makin' that I was made the innocent victim o', nae farther gane than last year, when the ne'er-do-weel wi' a blackit face came through the kintra, makin' a wally-waeing about how he was blawn up in a bombshell by the Algerines? I had my doots o' the story when he cam to my door, though he made it be as very true-like a tale as your condisciple from the uttermost ends o' the earth tells his; but no to be thought a'thegither hard-hearted, I put doon a sixpence in his book o' beggary, wi' my name til't. And what do ye think the graceless Gehazi did? He gaed to Widow M'Plooky's public, and waur'd the sixpence on gills; so, waurin' the sixpence on gills, he forged ten shillings before my sixpence, makin' it look in the book like half-a-guinea. Then he gaed to Mrs Scuitles, and she seeing my name doon for ten shillings and sixpence, and knowing me for a woman o' moderate means, and o' a sifting and discerning spirit, she put doon hersel for a whole guinea. Syne he gaed to auld Leddy Roughills, and she, no to be behint-hand, gied

---

[1] *Leesin'.* Lying.

him another guinea; and then he ventured to
my lord's, wha wi' his dochters could do nae less
than double the example.   But as he was on his
way to the Nabob, the drink—for of course he
had been dry by the way—took his head, and he
fell on the road at the toll, where he was kent,
and there brought to light; for in dighting his
face, he dighted aff the cork coom, and stood before the toll-keeper a barefaced malefactor.   Think
what I was obliged to endure, wi' the wite o'
being such a simpleton as to gie him such a love-
gift largess!   Ye see what it is to believe stories
o' folk blawn up in the air, and what ye're like to
get for your pains."

"You have certainly assigned, Mrs Soorocks,
very good and sufficient reasons for doing nothing
rashly ; I have, however, no apprehension that Mr
Rupees will suffer himself to be easily deceived."

"He'll no be alloo'd, were he ever sae willing,
if I hae ony voice.   It wou'd be even-doon *compos
mentos* to give ear to the tale o' a Jonah frae the
whale's belly; but whisht, whisht, for here's the
house, and there's ane o' the heathens leadin' Mr
Caption's whuskey to the stables.   Weel, I'm glad
o' that; indeed, it wasna to be thocht that a
man o' judgment and sensibility like Nawaubpore
would be content on sic an occasion wi' the like
o' you, or even me, to bear witness."

CHAPTER XXIX

On being shown into the library, we found already before us Mr Coball, with a small red leather brass-nailed trunk in his hand, and the boy at his side seated on a sofa. The Nabob was at the writing-table opposite, with Mr Caption at his right hand. The reception of Mrs Soorocks was particularly gracious, nor had I cause to complain of any deficiency of heartiness in mine.

The proceedings were opened by a summary statement of the whole story from the Nabob, who on this occasion showed both his shrewdness and good sense as a man of business; he made no digressions, but concluded with requesting Mr Coball to produce his vouchers.

The red case was accordingly unclosed, and the letters laid on the table. The Nabob took them up one by one; and, having looked at them carefully, was on the point, as I thought, of acknowledging at once their authenticity, when Mr Caption said, who probably thought the same thing—

"It is not enough to be certain as to the writing —look at the paper; the seals do not appear to me as if they were exact impressions of an original seal."

The Nabob knit his brows, but made no answer.

Here Mrs Soorocks stepped forward, and lifting one of the letters, looked at the seal, and said—

"It's my opinion this is no wax at a', but fiddler's rosett, wi' gold foilzie in't, and oh! it is waff paper. Nawaubpore, ye wad never write your letters on huxtry tea-paper."

The Nabob, smiling, shook his head, and Mrs Soorocks looked to me with a triumphant countenance.

"Any dishonest servant," said Caption, "might become possessed of such papers, admitting, for the sake of argument, that they may be genuine."

"True," replied Mr Coball; "but such letters do not appear, from anything in their contents, to have been worth the stealing."

"Hoo can ye tell what a covetous-minded servant wad think worth stealing?" cried Mrs Soorocks eagerly. "I had a servant-lass that stole one of Mr Soorocks' Greek books. What use could a Greek book be to her? But she confessed that she did steal it. There's no telling what dishonest servants will do."

The Nabob interposed.

"The letters are mine," said he; and turning to the lady, added jocularly: "As to the wax, I know it well: I bought it at Hazaribaug; and the paper is Chinese I brought from India with me. Moreover, on reference to my Dawkbook now before me, I find that the dates agree."

"But," he added, addressing himself to Mr Coball, "it is strange that you should have obtained possession of these letters only. Have you nothing else? For they prove nothing as to the identity of the boy there."

"With these letters," replied Mr Coball, "were several valuable trinkets and two packets of pearls."

"And what have you done with them?" cried Caption eagerly. "'Tis easy to say so."

"He'll hae made awa' wi' them," said Mrs Soorocks, in half a whisper to me.

"No, madam," replied Mr Coball, who had overheard her, "they are here;" and he laid the packets and trinkets on the table.

Caption was evidently confounded, while the Nabob's countenance brightened.

"But I canna see," resumed Mrs Soorocks, "hoo a wheen gew-gaws can prove that black's white, or, ony mair than the letters, mak it a bit clearer that this bairn's no anither."

"Certainly not, madam," said Mr Caption firmly. "Certainly not; you are quite right."

"I thocht I wad be sae," said Mrs Soorocks, and she looked significantly.

The Nabob in the meantime was examining the trinkets; and I observed that he noticed a necklace with particular attention.

Mr Coball at this crisis took out of the trunk

a small neat pocket memorandum-book, and presented it open to the Nabob, saying—

"I think this must have been a diary which Mrs Bayfield was keeping of our voyage; the last entry is the date of the very day preceding that night on which our calamity happened."

"I acknowledge," said the Nabob, at the first glance, "that the writing appears to be Mrs Bayfield's."

"But what does that prove?" said Mr Caption.

"You will find," said the stranger calmly, "that my name, James Coball, is mentioned in a list of the passengers at the beginning."

Here Mrs Soorocks begged to look at the list.

"To be sure," said she, "there is the name of a James Coball; but whar's the proof that ye are that James Coball, or that ye are a James Coball at a'?"

The stranger looked confused.

"Yes," cried Caption, "where is the evidence of that fact?"

No immediate answer was given, but after a short pause Mr Coball answered—

"I think sufficient evidence has been produced to convince any honest man that there is truth enough in my story to induce the executor of the late Colonel Bayfield to examine the whole circumstances, although there is not enough to make the heir in possession of Colonel Bayfield's property surrender to this boy. But when I add that several of those who were saved with us in the boat, and particularly the officer to whom we were all so much indebted, are alive, and I believe are at this time in England, it would seem to me that beyond a decent investigation of the facts there would be little honour or honesty in resisting the claim."

The Nabob looked at me and said—

" He's an honest man, after all."

" Dinna be deceived, Nawaubpore," exclaimed Mrs Soorocks ; " for there's mair depends upon this matter than being beguiled wi' a blackened ne'er-do-weel, as I was, ye ken, last year."

The Nabob turned to Caption. " Ought we not immediately to institute an inquiry to find those witnesses ? "

" No, sir," replied Caption, with a professional smirk. " No, sir, the *onus probandi* lies with this gentleman, who hath spontaneously placed himself *in loco parentis* to the infant."

" Ye're a man o' observation, Mr Caption," cried Mrs Soorocks, her countenance brightening with satisfaction. " Ye're a man o' observation. I'll say naething concerning the sincerity o' lawyers' bosoms ; but I aye thocht there was something in your head, whatever ill-natured folks might say to the contrair."

The lawyer took no notice of this remark, which, like most of the good lady's compliments, cut both ways, but resumed—

" It is not to be expected that the respondent is to furnish the pursuer with evidence ; even the

Jury Court would hardly require anything so unreasonable."

"But, Mr Caption," said the Nabob, "it may turn out in this case that I am both plaintiff and defendant; and all I require is full and sufficient proof—for another heir may make his appearance. I wish I had Craigdarroch with me to set us on a proper train; but, d—n him, he's doing patriot just now, and humbugging the nincompoops of the Stewardry. If we had him even fresh from one of his election-dinners, I should be content; for I have known him after a hard drink, and before going to bed, give a clearer and sounder opinion than any of his brethren could after a light supper and a sober sleep. He once conducted a case for me——"

"Na," interrupted Mrs Soorocks, "if he's a man o' that discernment he'll do us some credit in the Parliament-house, and that's mair than can weel be said of a' 'the chosen five-and-forty.'"

The Nabob here rejoined—

"This business, my dear lady, promises no good to your friend the Laird; for, in duty to myself, it will be necessary to foreclose his mortgage immediately. Caption, you will take no notice of my note of last night, desiring you to stay the proceedings against Mr Mailings."

"Very well, sir," replied Caption; "misjudged lenity, as I said; but as your order was in writing, you will be pleased to instruct me in writing to the contrary effect."

" O Mr Roopy !—Nawaubpore, as I should
say," exclaimed Mrs Soorocks, " haud your han'
and be melted to tender mercies, or what will
become o' the puir auld man ? Work he canna,
and want he maunna—he'll be a burden upon us
all, and little do ye ken o' the woe ye may bring
upon a most excellent woman ; for he's on the
point of marriage wi' Miss Shoosie Minnigaff, ane
o' the amiable leddies o' Barenbraes. She'll dee
o' a broken heart, if she doesna lay violent hauns
on hersell."

This sad and gentle appeal, instead of producing the desired effect on the Nabob, only served
to make him burst into an immoderate fit of
laughter.

" Married ! the old guddah ! and to one of those
camelopards too ! Who the devil contrived this
hopeful union ? It must have been yourself, Mrs
Soorocks ; for it never could have entered into
the heart of man—of any man—to marry a
crane—an adjutant is corpulent compared to
her. Why, my good lady, if the worst comes to
the worst, he can only simply be starved ; but if
your benevolent scheme were accomplished, he
would be starved and pecked to boot. But this
long sederunt, as you would call it, Mr Caption,
will go well nigh to starve us all, so I shall order
dinner. Mr Coball, do you, as soon as possible,
procure the necessary evidence. You may rest
assured that there shall be no unnecessary or
vexatious delay on my part—only make good your

proofs, and I shall be delighted to do justice to
the son of my old friend."

"Na," said Mrs Soorocks aside to me, "the
man's demented. Did ye ever hear o' sic a dis-
tracted action? To give up a property—and sic
a property—without being obligated according to
law! I ken advocates in Embro, Nawaubpore,
that could keep the case in Court for a' your days.
There's my frien'—But I'll mention nae names."

Here dinner was announced, and we adjourned
to the banqueting-room.

CHAPTER XXX

NEXT morning, agreeably to an appointment which I had made with Mrs Soorocks as we came home together in the Nabob's carriage, I went over to her house to carry her with me on an expiatory visit to the ladies of Barenbraes. We had agreed that the decision of the Nabob's character, notwithstanding his vanity and foibles, was such as left no hope he would again recede from his determination to foreclose the mortgage on the lands of Auldbiggings. I had therefore urged her with all my powers of persuasion to call with me on the venerable sisters in our way home. The cares, however, of her great washing pressed heavily on her mind, and she could not at the time think of consenting; but, to do her justice, she evinced no reluctance to make an ample apology to Miss Shoosie; and in consequence, it was agreed that the ceremony thereof should be deferred till the following day.

On the day following, accordingly, I went to her house, and we walked leisurely on together.

" I'm thinkin'," said she, as we got on the footpath of the highroad,—" I'm thinkin' that the

auld man, if we were to forsake him now, would
be a perfec object ; but I feel that we are agents,
raised up, as it were, like babes and sucklings
to bring him out o' the house o' bondage, the
which in my opinion is the debtor's-hole in the
Tolbooth, if waur than captivity were not to be
his lot."

" I agree, ma'am, in all you say. It is most consolatory to think that we are both afforded an
opportunity to show how mankind are capable of
doing a disinterested action."

" I'll mak' nae rouse o' mysell," replied the
lady, " but I ken the secrets o' my own breast ;
and tho' I dinna wish to lightly your loving-kind-
ness towards Auldbiggings, I hae a notion it may
be something like a bit spunk o' curiosity that
has helped to heat the zeal o' your disinterestedness ; for I have remarked—I mean nae offence—
that ye hae a particular pleasure in lookin' into
the catastrophes o' ither folks. For my part, I am
thankfu' to walk wi' a humble heart and a contrite
spirit ; for if good come o' my sma' endeavour,
sure I am that nane o' the merit thereof can be
attributed to me."

Thus piously discoursing, we plodded onward
to the door of Barenbraes ; and, as it was agreed
between us, I entered first, and thus opened the
business—

" Ladies, I have brought with me a person
whom we have all great reason to esteem. Ever
since she had the misfortune to incur your

" Remember, Mr Mailing," interposed the lawyer . . .
  " remember you have no license to sell by public roup
  or auction "

Last of the Lairds]

displeasure, she has been the most wretched of womankind—she comes to confess a fault, to acknowledge a sin, and, if you require it, even on bended knees to kiss the hems o' your garments——"

"In a figurative sense," interrupted Mrs Soorocks.

But I waved my hand to her to be quiet, and continued—

"Miss Girzie, I have long respected your prudence, and valued your excellent sense; so I told our mutual friend here that although her offence was of very great enormity——"

"Enormity! her assurance was large," cried Miss Shoosie.

"Yes, Miss Shoosie, her imprudence was large indeed, but her repentance is without measure——"

"In a certain sense," said Mrs Soorocks.

"But," continued I, "it would be idle to waste words on ladies of your piety, were I to attempt to urge that this was a case for the exercise of the Christian grace of forgiveness. If Mrs Soorocks be hasty in temper and rash in tongue, you know, Miss Girzie, that you have the failing of sometimes giving provocation; and, Miss Shoosie, mild as ye are, which my friend Mr Mailings regards as the greatest grace of your gentle sex, yet you know that there are times when the best of us may err, and even when you yourself——"

"If," interrupted Miss Shoosie, "Mrs Soorocks

has come to beg my pardon, she'll find that I'll no be insensible to the dishonour she has brought upon hersell."

"She comes to beg your pardon, but you must not use such words as dishonour when we are treating of peace. Mrs Soorocks, do you ask pardon of the ladies? Ladies, do you on your part acknowledge that faults are on both sides? For, in the exercise of a sound discretion, reciprocal concession is what I would recommend to all."

"Weel, leddies," said Mrs Soorocks, "since it maun be sae, what can we do but submit? Tho' I think, Miss Shoosie, ye give baith the sore stroke and the loud cry; howsever, since it's a' past and we're frien's again——"

"Friends!" cried Miss Girzie, with an English accent. "Friends! We may forgive what's past, but I see no obligation for us to be friends."

"Come, come, ladies; neighbours should be neighbour-like," said I; "and, Miss Shoosie, if you knew the cause that has brought Mrs Soorocks here to-day, instead of standing so far aloof from reconciliation, you would embrace her in your arms and press her to your heart. She has been explaining to me the mournful situation of Mr Mailings."

"It's no my fault," interposed Miss Shoosie; "for if ye had waited to hear what me and my sister were going to say the other night, you would never have thocht us such mercenary women as to have broken off with a gentleman like Mr Mailings for the lucre o' gain."

" Na," said Mrs Soorocks, " considering the jeopardy that you and Miss Girzie are in o' a sudden retribution frae your sister, Leddy Chandos, like a thief in the night, ye wad hae been waur than mad had ye made a hesitation ; for oh ! it rins before me like the shadow o' a forthcoming judgment upon ye, Miss Shoosie, the terrible day that the cry o' Justice, wi' the scales in her ae hand and the sword in her ither, will be heard afore your door, and plack and bawbee to the uttermost will be required aff ye. I canna imagine, leddies, what makes you swither."

" We dinna swither ; but we would act prudently."

" Ca' ye't acting prudently, in your situation, to risk the loss of a most estimable man's affections for what canna be modesty, Miss Shoosie ? You surely hae lived ower lang in the world to ken what modesty means between fifty and threescore. Leddies, leddies, I maun use the freedom o' an auld frien' wi' ye—ye're tyning [1] your time. Just come ower the night, and tak your tea wi' me, and I'll send for Mr Mailings ; and as Nawaubpore's a Justice o' the Peace, I dinna misdout his coming, and we'll get the marriage put out o' haun——"

Miss Shoosie cast down her eyes, as she replied—

---

[1] *Tyning.* Losing

O

"I could never think of such a rash step."

"O Mrs Soorocks!" exclaimed Miss Girzie, "it's what I never could alloo—twa clandestine marriages in my father's family—oh no!"

"You are quite right, Miss Girzie; it would make folk expect a third."

"But," said Mrs Soorocks, "noo when I think o't, it might occasion malicious insinuations to the great damage and detriment of Miss Shoosie's fair fame, considering the well-known and long-tried affection subsisting between her and the Laird—so I'll no insist; but come to your tea, and I'll hae Mr Mailings o' the party, when we can arrange a' about the booking and the buying o' your bridal braws, since ye will hae a regular marriage."

Having thus established peace, and arranged, as I had supposed, the business of the evening, and being regaled with the ladies' home-made wine, Mrs Soorocks and I bade them adieu and bent our steps towards Auldbiggings. Before we had, however, reached the bottom of the avenue, we observed Jock coming from the house like an ostrich at full speed—his arms swinging in the air and his skirts streaming behind. As he drew near, horror and consternation were legible in his countenance; and in one hand he held a letter which he gave to me before he could collect breath to explain the burden of his haste. As the shortest means of discovering the motive of his speed, I opened the letter and read as follows :—

" To MALACHI MAILINGS, Esquire, of Auldbiggings.

" SIR,—I am instructed by my client, Mr Walter
Rupees of Nawaubpore, to beg your attention to
my last, dated 3rd current; and further to state,
that if satisfaction is not rendered thereto *quam
primum*, diligence will immediately issue.

" I am further instructed with respect to the
matter of the interest due last money, and *toties
quoties* called for, to request an answer *quam primum*.
I am, sir, your obedient servant,

" HUGH CAPTION."

By this time Jock had recovered his breath,
and said—

" Weel, ye see the last trumpet's now blawn—
what's to be done ? Is't no possible to get a re-
spite till the lottery be drawn ? The Laird's just
gane by himsell—he's toddlin' but and toddlin'
ben the house, whiles wringin' his hauns, and
whiles makin' murgeons as if he was speakin'.
It was a better world when gentlemen werena
fash'd wi' law. I'm sure the ten commandments
are worth a' the King's statutes, and ye'll no fin'
a word in them about payin' o' debts, e'en an ye
were able. I'm just wud to think o' the mischief
that this law—law—law has brocht upon poor
Scotland ! But oh ! I'm glad to see you and Mrs
Soorocks—ye'll be a great cordial to him under
his calamity ; and oh ! mem, dinna mak' your

charity on the present occasion a bit and a buffet
wi't, but speak him kindly ; for oh ! he's helpless,
and far past the power o' Jenny Clatterpans and
me to gie him ony comfort, even though we baith
fleeched him and clapped him on the shoothers,
yin at every side, to tak anither tumbler o'
toddy ; for hath not Solomon said, in the words
of Robbie Burns,—

> ' Gie him strong drink until he wink,
>   That's sinkin' in despair ' ?

Blyth was I when I saw you comin', but when ye
gang to the house, dinna let wot that ye hae
seen me, or ken onything about what's gaun to
happen ; for our Laird was aye proud, and this
misfortune has made him a perfect turkey-cock
for pride. He storm'd at Jenny Clatterpans and
me for our kindness, and push'd us awa, and
wonder'd hoo we daured to be sae familiar wi' our
master ; crying out—a wee deleerit as I thocht—
that had it no been for the poortith come upon
him, we would never hae been sae upsetting ; and
he wyted[1] it a' on the liberty and equality speerit
o' the times, and the taxes, and the high wages,
that were grindin' the rightfu' gentry frae aff the
face o' the earth. Noo, dear sir and mem, I beg
and beseech that ye'll speak him kindly, and mak'
much o' him ; for oh ! he's grown thin-skinned !—
Mrs Soorocks, he canna thole a taunt noo ! "

---

[1] *Wyted.* Blamed.

This sad account of the Laird's condition had the effect of embarrassing us both ; and on leaving the simple and faithful creature, we proceeded towards "The Place," without exchanging a word, or making a single comment on what we had heard.

CHAPTER XXXI

ON approaching the door, Jenny Clatterpans was standing there, and from time to time she looked towards the garden; the other maid was also visible behind her, and every now and then took a peep in the same direction. The aspect of Jenny was visibly troubled, nor did her companion's wear a more tranquil expression; but still the countenances of both betokened something which commanded deference to their feelings.

Whether Mrs Soorocks felt exactly as I did, it were impossible to determine by anything in her voice or gestures; but she abruptly left me and went towards the maids. At the same moment I happened to turn round, and discovered the Laird walking to and fro in the garden, with his hands behind, his eyes perusing the grass of the walks, and his whole figure, by the bend and by the solemnity of his air, indicating the perplexity of his spirit.

I went immediately towards him, none displeased at that moment to be relieved from the presence of Mrs Soorocks. I put on the blithest face I could assume, and tuned my voice to cheerfulness as I drew near to the dejected old man. But although he saw me coming, and nodded in his wonted familiar manner as I approached the walk which he was pacing, he soon relapsed into his reverie and moved along unconscious of being so observed.

I stopped some ten or fifteen yards from him ; I looked forward, and the distress of his mind, though visibly mingled with a strong ingredient of absurdity, was yet such as could not be seen without sympathy.

As he walked along the dark unmowed grass he paused suddenly, and stooping forward he pulled a rose.

" It's my ain yet," said he with a smile, as he turned round, and smelling it, held it out towards me.

" It has grown in my forefathers' land," he added ; "I set it mysell—I made the hole for't wi' my ain very fingers—I watered it wi' the china jug that was my father's punch-porringer, as I hae heard my kind mother say—and what can be a man's ain if that bush and bud be na mine ? "

Then he moved some four or five paces, and tearing the flower into pieces, he scattered the petals around ; and knitting his brows and clenching his hands, he rushed with his left hand extended, as if he entreated and deprecated some afflicting power revealed in form only to himself. It is the peculiar characteristic of all grief-ful emotions to move and gesticulate with the left arm, as in like manner it is for those of power and exertion to indicate their predominance by the energy and emphasis of the right.

When that brief paroxysm had subsided, he returned leisurely and sedately towards the spot where I was standing.

" Is there no a possible o' ony kind by the which this may be eschewed ? "

He seemed to think (by the expression) that I must of course be acquainted with the cause and sources of his trouble, and had his perturbation been less obviously painful, perhaps I might have played a little with his perplexities ; but his look was so vacant and infantine that it was impossible to regard him with any other sentiment than pity.

" I understand," said I, " that the Nabob has resolved to follow out his determination. I am sorry for it, but his own condition half pleads in extenuation of his rigour."

" It was a luckless day," was the answer, " when the thread of my life was ravelled wi' his knotty thrums—my lot and station, though lanerly, was lown [1]—I had nae law fashin' me, but only an uncertainty about a bit heritable bond that in a sense wasna worth the speaking about. Noo, I'm driven to desperation. There's that limb o' Satan, Caption, greetin' in the king's name ; there's John Angle, the surveyor, demanding a compensation ; and there's that goolden

[1] *Lanerly . . . lown.* Lonely . . . serene.

image o' Nebuchadnedzor, Rupees. Oh, oh, and
alas! if I wasna preserved, I wud droon mysell.
My book I canna write—to work I'm no able—
the curse o' Gilbert, when he was a beggar-man,
has overtaken me; for when the three pound in
the desk-head is spent and gone, I'll no hae a
penny left for a morsel—I'm a destitute creature
—I'm a forlorn auld man—I'm a verra object—
Oh, I'm an object!"

I endeavoured to console him as well as I could,
but the sense of desolation was so strong upon
him that the endeavour was ineffectual.

"It's a terrible thing," cried he, "for a man
to be miserable. O Adam and Eve! ye hae
muckle to answer for. If I was young, I would
be a sodger. Were my mind composed, I could
write an instructin' book. Had I been bred a
tailor, I could have made claes; but I canna even
sing ballats, for Heaven in its displeasure made
me wi' a timmer tune. I can do naething but
beg. I'll no can lang even gang frae door to door,
for I'm auld, and I hae an income in my leg. I'll
hae to sit on a stane on the roadside, wi' a ragged
hat on my knee and my bare grey head in the
shower — Heaven preserve me, will I be sittin'
beggin' at my ain yett!"

The last sentence was uttered with a tone of
horror that made me shudder, and I said—

"Mr Mailings, do not give way to such fright-
ful presentiments; I beseech you to be more
composed."

"I'll be put in a prison," cried he. "I'll be fastened doon wi' an airn chain in the debtor's-hole—but what will they mak by that? for I hae naething—the dyvor's bill can do nae gude to a failed and broken-hearted auld beggar-man. To be sure, I might steal cocks and hens and be sent to Botany Bay; but what could I do there. O dear! I wish I was in another world, for my use and part in this world is done now."

He then walked away from me, and continued for several minutes pacing another part of the garden. Sometimes he halted and raised his hand, as if he were arguing with himself; anon he quickened his pace; and at last he turned briskly round, and came rushing towards me with exultation in his countenance.

"I hae found a redemption," he exclaimed. "I'll marry Miss Shoosie Minnigaff. She has goold in goupens. I hae heard my mither say there wasna sic a plenished napery-kist as the ane at Barenbraes in a' the west o' Scotland; and if I dinna like her, ye ken, she'll hae the means of providing hersell wi' a separate maintenance."

So intense had been the distress of the old man that I really felt as it were relieved when he proposed to adopt this sinister and sordid expedient; and in consequence—it may be not in a spirit of the purest morality—I applauded his resolution, and began to commend the merits and qualities of the lady with many a magnifying augmentative.

At this juncture, Mrs Soorocks joined us; it was evident by her manner as she approached that the servants had very sensibly affected her compassion, and her exhilaration was at least equal to mine when I told her that the Laird had resolved to marry Miss Shoosie.

"It's a wark—" said he, however, with a sigh.

"And of mercy to yoursell, Laird, that ye'll alloo. But no to mak mair clishmaclaver about it, I expect my friend Bailie Waft frae Paisley in the afternoon; so ye'll come ower and tak your tea and a crack wi' him, and I'll send for the leddies, and we'll soon get a' settled."

"It's a soor drogue,[1] mem," replied the Laird; "but the ill and the ail need the dose. I canna but say that it's a most extraordinar thing that a man hasna a choice o' his ain in choosin' the wife of his bosom. That weddings are made in Heaven it's ill to believe, if I'm ordained to be brocht to sic a puir pass as this comes to! To think that ever I should hae been brocht to marry such a grey gull as Shoosie Minnigaff! It's an iniquity—it's a cryin' sin—it's a sellin' o' me to the Ismaelites. D—l tak baith law and gospel, I'll no marry her yet."

"But consider," cried Mrs Soorocks, "there's Mr Caption——"

"Whare?" cried the Laird, starting and looking round.

"And Mr Angle," resumed the lady, "demanding,

[1] *Soor drogue.*   Sour drug.

as I am told, twenty golden guineas for his curiosity."

"He may thank the Government," replied the Laird, "that it's an impossibility to get them. Wasna the guineas put doon and hidden frae the light o' day and the sight and reach o' man in the bottomless dungeons o' the Bank o' England, like prisoners doomed to everlasting captivity; a' to let the King raise money by a Stamp Act on bank-notes, by the which——"

Here the old man was getting on his hobby, when Mrs Soorocks interfered——

"Hoot toot, Laird, we dinna want to hear o' your standard unit the noo, when we're speakin' o' marriage—so ye'll just come to your tea and meet your blooming bride. Leave a' the lave o' the trouble to folk that understand thae matters better than yoursell."

CHAPTER XXXII

At the time appointed, and punctual to the hour, I was at the door of Mrs Soorocks. My friend Leezie admitted me with a pleasant and significant smile. I was desirous of saying something to her on the occasion, but the parlour door being open, I could only smile in return and walk forward.

On entering the room, I was delighted to see the Laird in full dress, and the two ladies of Barenbraes all there before me. Miss Shoosie was sitting far aloof with downcast eyes, and looking interestingly bridal to the best of her ability. The air of Miss Girzie was more disengaged; and she was seated beside the Laird, seemingly on terms of easy conversation. Mrs Soorocks herself was busy spreading and cutting down the greater part of a large loaf.

As the entertainment was of a pre-nuptial character, it was of course of more than wonted ceremony; and accordingly the tea-table displayed a more than usual show of shortbread, puffs, and seed-cake, to which were added the delicacies of jellies and marmalades.

A little behind Mrs Soorocks, and not observable on first entering the room, her cousin Bailie Waft was seated, refreshing himself after his walk with a glass of whisky and water sweetened with Muscovado sugar.

"Dear me, Bailie," exclaimed Mrs Soorocks, looking round after I was seated, "what have I been about no to gie you a lime, when I hae got five left o' the half-a-dizzen that was sent to me by the carrier frae our frien' Mrs Puncheons? What dainties thae West India folk in Glasgow enjoy! They weel ken hoo to mak' turtle-soup wi' Madeira wine, and no like the lady o' their Port, that boiled a whole turtle-fish wi' barley, and was feared to eat it, thinkin' it wasna wholesome because it didna turn red in the shell like a partan."

So saying she rose, and opening her cupboard door, took out a lime from five lying in a small china plate, shrivelled on the skin, and as brown as walnuts.

By-the-bye, Mrs Soorocks' cupboard was what in Renfrewshire is called a dining-room press, being one of those domestic museums peculiar to the royal county, and as hers was an example of the kind, it well deserves to be particularly described.

The folding-doors disclosed an arched niche, with pilasters on each side. The shelves were scolloped in the edges, the whole painted of a bright green, and the edges of the shelves and the capitals of the pilasters were gaudily tricked and gilded.

On the bulging centre of the first shelf lay inverted a large punch-bowl, on the bottom of which stood one of lesser dimensions, out of which rose a curious cordial-bottle with two necks. The bowl was flanked with a row of long-shanked wine-glasses, with white spiral ornaments in the stalks, and at the extremity of each wing stood a tall urn-like china pot with a lid. In the obscurity behind the glasses you might discover a row of china plates on their edges; and above each, on a brass-nail, hung as many custard-glasses by their handles.

On the second floor the curiosities were somewhat reversed. The shelf receded in the middle, and sweeping forward on both sides, projected over the trays, which below were adorned with the tall spiral-stalked glasses already described; on each of these projections two middle-sized punch-bowls were inverted, the bottom of each surmounted with a china teapot of an antic and fantastical form; in the centre was a vacant place, generally occupied by the silver teapot then upon the table; at each side of it usually stood a lofty porcelain tower of teacups and saucers—but one of them was at this time demolished, and placed on the tray for the use of the company. A variety of minor bijoutry and wine-glasses filled up the interstices.

The centre of the third shelf again projected,

and on it stood a stately crystalline structure, consisting of several stories of syllabub-glasses, crowned with a large and lofty shallow goblet, which at the New-Year festival of Mrs Soorocks, when the whole power and splendour of her cupboard were made effective, was usually occupied with a venerable preserved orange—a gift of some years' antiquity from one of her nieces, confected *a priori* to her own wedding. On each side of this glittering and fragile pile stood a miscellaneous assemblage of marrowless cups, cracked creampots, and ale-glasses, flanked by two enormous goblets with the initials of the late Mr Soorocks engraved thereon. Like many of the other things, they were never used, save on the great annual banquet so often referred to; on which occasion the one was filled with ale and the other with porter after dinner.

The tea-urn having been brought in, Mrs Soorocks said—

"As ye're the young leddy, Miss Girzie, ye'll mak the tea;" and so saying she rose from her chair at the tea-table, and then came and seated herself beside the Laird, while I drew my chair close to the left of Miss Girzie; her sister also moved in echelon upon her right.

Miss Girzie having lifted one of the little silver tea-canisters, began to take out the orthodox quantity with a spoon, by one spoonful for the teapot, and one for each guest. During this process I heard the intended bride whisperingly say, " Girzie, dinna be wasterfu' ; shake the spoon, and no heap every ane as if it were a cart o' hay."

Tea being made, the task of handing it round was imposed upon the Laird ; he being, as Mrs Soorocks observed, the young man of the company. though this chronologically was not exactly the fact.

During the time the entertainment was being served, our conversation was of a general and ordinary description.   Bailie Waft talked political economy, and argued with the Laird against the corn laws ; Mrs Soorocks expatiated on the felicity of the married state ; while I said agreeable things to Miss Girzie, interspersed with exhilarative allusions in parenthesis to her sister.

So passed the time till tea was finished, and when the equipage was removed by Leezie and the door shut, Mrs Soorocks thus began the prologue to the matrimonial theme :—

"I have long wished to see such a meeting as the present.   Time wears out all things, and lairds and ladies are like the flowers that bloom and plants that perish—creatures of a day, and butterflies o' the sunshine.   It has often been a wonder to me how year after year should have passed away, and the affection so long nourished in secret atween—I'll no say wha—should never hae come to an issue."

The Laird hemmed sceptically, and Miss Shoosie looked for her pocket-hole, no doubt

P

that she might be ready with her handkerchief.

"But," continued Mrs Soorocks, "whatever is ordained will sooner or later come to pass; and seldom hae I ever had in my life a pleasanter reflection than in seeing here twa young persons made for one another."

The Laird looked with the tail of his eye towards Miss Shoosie, and seemed as if he smelt senna or mandragora; while she drew her hand over her face bashfully, as if to conceal the depth of her emotions.

The Bailie interposed—

"There's nae need, cousin, to mak thrown-up warp o' the web we hae in han': the young couple understand one another, and if the yarn has been ravelled for a time, it's weel redd noo. The only thing that I would object to is the delay, and for twa sound and substantial reasons: first, it's an auld byword and a true, that delays are dangerous; and under the second head, I would speak o' economy, and anent the expense o' what extravagant wasterfu' women ca' bridal braws."

"In that," said I, interrupting him, "I agree with you, Mr Waft; on this occasion such expenditure is quite unnecessary."

"But," rejoined Miss Girzie, "wouldna my sister, Mrs Soorocks, don't you think, require a riding-habit for the wedding-jaunt?"

"It's verra true," was the answer, "that mony

a young leddy that ne'er was on a horse's back, nor expects to be, gets a riding-habit at her marriage, the which is put to nae ither use after than to be made up into claes for some o' the bairns ; and in that respect there might be something to be said for your sister getting ane ; but all things considered——"

Here the Laird groaned from the depth of his spirit, and the Bailie quietly interposed—

"But if there is no marriage-jaunt, and I see no need of such a thing, where is the need to mak an outlay for a riding-habit at all ? 'Deed, my friends, if you'll be ruled by me, you'll mak up for your lost time and declare a marriage at once, without further summering or wintering about the matter."

"Oh," cried Miss Girzie, lifting her hands and spreading her fingers, "is't a possibility !"

Miss Shoosie heaved a sigh. The Laird rose from his seat, and walking with his hands behind his back to the window, raised another in responsive echo ; while Mrs Soorocks, before commencing operations, gave me a sly nod, as much as to intimate her ability and readiness to carry on the attack.

"Laird," said she, "I'm no ane that is for hurrying on a solemn business in a rash manner. Before we come to speak of the wedding seriously —tho' we're only joking yet——"

The Laird interrupted her tartly, and looking round with a particularly sinister expression of

countenance, concluded the sentence by adding:
" And I houp ye'll be lang sae."

"Weel, weel, Laird," replied the lady, "ye
know it's all your ain doing; tak your wull o't;
it depends entirely on yoursell."

"On me?" cried the Laird. "My gracious!
wha ever heard the equal o' that?" Then he
muttered in an under-tone, "If ever there was a
lee, that's ane."

" Lee!" said Mrs Soorocks, catching the Laird's
aside. "Every joke's a lee o' its kind. But
come, help yoursell to a glass o' my old wine; for
ye seem to be in an unco low key, Laird. Ye see
the Bailie requires neither precept nor example
wi' his tumbler when the mercy's [1] afore him."

For some time after this, there was a visible
embarrassment in the manner of all present.
Mrs Soorocks, however, was the ruling spirit of
the hour, and she presided with undismayed
equanimity.

After taking off his first glass, the Laird was
persuaded by his active hostess to a second, and
to a third; but still matters looked, to use her
own expression, "unco dowie." She then tried
him on a new tack.

"Ye believe, Laird," she said, "that whatever
is destined to come in at ane's door 'ill no gang
by them?"

"Doubtless," answered the Laird, "there is
nae arguing against that."

[1] *Mercy.* A dram.

"Weel, if ye come that length, I maun just tell ye my mind, that for mony and mony a lang year it has aye struck me, somehow or ither, that Providence, Laird, destined Miss Shoosie there and you for ane anither. I'm persuaded you're mair than half o' that opinion yoursell?"

"Doubtless strange wheemsies will enter intil leddies' heads," replied the Laird, turning his face half away from the speaker, like one half-unwilling to listen to unwelcome intelligence. "It's neither your duty nor mine to dive sae deep into the hidden secrets o' nature."

"Na, but, Laird, just hear me a moment," said Mrs Soorocks, lifting up nuts from a china plate on the side-table; "seeing is believing all the world over. Now, ye see, if I was to take a pair of these nuts, and say to mysell, 'There's me and there's Mr Roopy' as I throwed them into the fire, ye wad see the ane fizz and flee away frae the ither up the lum, or out at the ribs like a bomb-shell; for, ye observe, it's no in the course o' nature that the like o' him and me should ever come thegither; but on the contrair—sae deeply am I impressed wi' the truth o' what I am saying—I could wager my life maistly that were I to put in these twa, and say as I do noo, 'There goes you, Laird, and there goes Miss Shoosie'"—all the time Mrs Soorocks was suiting the action to the word—"ye wad observe them burn to a white aizle lovingly together."

The two nuts, according to Mrs Soorocks' prediction, burned together lovingly.

"It's gey curious, I allow," said the Laird; "but dinna expect to throw cantrips in my een wi' ony o' your glaumrie. Whether I take or rejec, it maun be a free-will gift."

"Maist certainly," was the reply of Bailie Waft; "and from what I've seen and heard aboot ye, Laird, I aye jealoused where your guid taste wad land ye."

Mrs Soorocks, though sorely put to her mettle by the Laird's obduracy, yet was determined not to leave the well-foughten field without gaining her point; so with Mr Mailings' consent she mixed for him a tumbler of punch, "the rum of which," as she told him, "having been procured from Cornel Archy of Greenock, was of a suavity as mild as its vendor."

The general jocularity was meanwhile on the increase, Mrs Soorocks from time to time urging the gentlemen to use their freedoms with her bottles, and do a little for the good of the house; and, though tardy to relax, the Laird's features at length brightened up with congenial sympathy. The Bailie became garrulous, and hinted away from time to time to Miss Shoosie on the pleasures of housekeeping. Miss Girzie argued briskly with Mrs Soorocks for and against the propriety of irregular and clandestine marriages, but with a tone of concession gradually softening into conciliation; while the Laird, continuing to wax still more cheerful and bold, boasted of his youthful sprees, and as he snapped his thumbs, sang aloud a verse of the old ballad—

> " The carle he came ower the craft
>   Wi' his beard new shaven."

" Na," cried Mrs Soorocks, " if it's come to that wi' ye, Laird, it's time we should bring ye afore a magistrate, and hae your vows honourably ratified. Bailie Waft, I tell ye to put him to the question."

Here the Bailie rose, and endeavouring to wipe the flush from his brow with his handkerchief, looked as grave as the occasion would let him, and said : " Mr Mailings, is this lady "—pointing to Miss Shoosie—" your wife ? "

" Ony lady's my wife," said the Laird, " that will condescend to tak me."

The Bailie then turned to Miss Shoosie. " Do you, madam, acknowledge this gentleman for your husband ? "

" Confess, confess," cried Mrs Soorocks, " and dinna spoil our ploy."

Miss Shoosie simpered, and said, " Sister, I canna refuse ony langer."

Here there was a general clapping of hands, and the health of Mr and Mrs Mailings was drank in bumpers by all but themselves. The bride acknowledged the courtesy with solemn propriety, and the Laird answered with a loud laugh ; but there was a ring in its sound wild and sardonic. Another tumbler, however, soon restored the hilarity; and in a few minutes after, supper, which Mrs Soorocks had prospectively prepared for the occasion, was announced.

The fête passed over with all due humour and conviviality. The Laird warmed more and more towards his bride, and said many sweet things across the table, as much to the amazement as the amusement of the company. Bailie Waft waxed eloquent in Glasgow stories, and forgot himself at length so far as to lose the solemnity of his official situation in jocose song-singing.

At a late or rather an early hour, the happy party arose from table, and under a moon—

> " Ploughing the azure depths, and looking down
>   With sanctified benignity on man,"

sallied forth for The Place, the bride hanging tenderly on the bridegroom's arm.

After taking off a glass of the Laird's Canary to the future felicities of the enamoured couple, we at length wished them a good-night. The Bailie and myself, talking of matrimonial comforts, conveyed Miss Girzie, weeping, to her now solitary home.

CHAPTER XXXIII

Early next morning I went over to Mrs Soo-rocks, to assist her in the reveille of the young couple; but on approaching the door, she chanced to observe me from the parlour window, and let me in herself.

"Oh!" said she, in a voice of serious alarm, "what have I no got to tell you!"

I was thunderstruck at the earnestness of her exclamation, and cried—

"My gracious! has the bridegroom run away?"

"Waur than that, waur than that; meikle hae ye to answer for. Nawaubpore yestreen, when we were at our daffin'—blind mortals we are, and little ken the perils o' our situation—Nawaubpore, as I was saying, sent ower his London newspaper to read; but I was so taen up that I neglecket it till this morning, and what do you think was the first thing that met my consternated eye?— the marriage o' Dr Lounlans—and to whom?— guess."

"I hope your suspicions have not been verified?"

"Verified! they have been dumfounder'd. He's married, and married to Miss Clawrissy Chandos, the great heiress, and, failing her mother, the rightfu' leddy o' Barenbraes. Now think o' that and weep."

"This is indeed extraordinary news!"

"It's a thunderclap," said Mrs Soorocks. "It's an earthquake—I think I fin' the world shooglin [1] beneath my verra feet. We thocht the Nabob wad be an oppressor, but what has the puir Laird to expect frae the hauns o' Dr Lounlans, on his mother's account! Na, I canna think at a' about Mrs Mailings. Na, it was never ordained that she shou'd hae been married! O sir, what have ye no to answer for!"

"Upon my word, Mrs Soorocks," replied I gravely, "it has been all your own work; I have been but an innocent spectator. I took no particular part in the business. You first suggested it to me; I remember very well the time and the place. It was in the avenue of Auldbiggings. Me, Mrs Soorocks! no one can impute any blame to me."

"Weel! after that," cried the lady, "I'll be surprised at nothing that man may say. But hoosever, I shake myself free o' them, and let you and them settle it as ye may; for I hae lang promised Mrs Puncheons a visit, and I'll be aff to Blythswood Place this blessed day. I declare I dinna ken whether I'm standing on my head or my heels; surely it's all a dream and a vision o' the night-season! Shoosie Minnigaff married!

[1] *Shooglin.* Rocking.

the thing's no possible, tho' it has taen place afore
my ain een."

"But, my dear ma'am, let us be calm—let us
consider what is the next best to be done."

"Consider yoursell; what have I to consider?"
exclaimed the lady; "I wash my hands—I have
had nothing to do with it from the beginning
to the end. They'll be a cess upon us baith—
they'll be on the parish—Oh, oh, oh!"

At this moment a knock was heard at the door,
and Mrs Soorocks giving a hasty glance out,
cried—

"Whare shall I hide mysell?—here's puir misfortunate Girzie."

And she immediately began to compose herself,
so that by the time that dejected maiden was
admitted, she had mustered fortitude enough to
break the doleful tidings to her thus with gravity,
composure, and decorum,—

"Have you had any letters by the post, Miss
Girzie, for I have gotten the newspapers?"

"No," said Miss Girzie, "not *this* morning;"
dwelling, as I thought, rather emphatically on
this, which excited my attention.

"Your sister is a lucky woman," rejoined Mrs
Soorocks, "a most lucky woman indeed—she has
just been married in the verra nick o' time."

"I hope she'll be happy," replied Miss Girzie
composedly.

"But do you ken what has happen'd? Dr
Lounlans is married."

" We expected that some time ago, you ken."

" But wha has he married?" cried Mrs Soorocks. " No less than your niece and deadly enemy, Miss Clawrissy."

" So we have been informed."

" Informed!" exclaimed Mrs Soorocks; " and whan were ye informed?"

" Yesterday morning by the post, in a most kind letter from Dr Lounlans himself."

" And did you know of that last night? Girzie Minnigaff, you and your sister have long been known as twa sordid wretches; but such deception, ye deceevers, to practise on a worthy gentleman! I think it's reason enough for a divorce; at ony rate, it canna fail to bring a judgment upon you. And what's to become o' you, Miss Girzie?"

" It was agreed between my sister and me that I shou'd live with her."

" What did ye say, Girzie Minnigaff?"

" It was agreed between me and my sister that I shou'd bide wi' her at Auldbiggings."

" It's a confess'd plot," cried Mrs Soorocks, turning to me; adding, " So, sir, a bonnie haun ye hae made o't; the laird's to be burthen'd wi' the twa; but bide a wee till I get my hat and shawl, and I'll gang ower wi' ye, were it for nae mair than to bid the misfortunate couple fareweel before I leave hame."

In a little time we had rung the Laird's doorbell, and Jenny ushered us into the parlour, till she had informed her master of our arrival. I was afraid from the bickering which was recommencing between my two female wards that some mortal rupture was threatening to take place. But at this critical juncture the young couple came into the room, seemingly on much better terms with one another than I had ventured to expect. The lady had herself informed him of the event, at which, instead of expressing any feeling of apprehension for the consequences, he was only confirmed in stronger feelings of dislike against the reverend doctor; vituperating the whole body of the clergy, and considering the ambition of his adversary as dictated by insolence, to mortify himself.

Mrs Soorocks, who had anticipated neither the felicity of the new pair, nor the complacency with which the Laird appeared to regard his lot, said: "But, Mr Mailings, tak thocht, remember ye're a ruin'd man. Ye hadna left yoursell the means to maintean you alone; how do ye think that ye can maintean other two?"

"I have made my calculation," said he; "I'm going into Edinburgh. I'll publish my book in numbers, and mak a monthly income by that. Miss Girzie's to bide wi' us, for, as my dawty here says" (chucking Mrs Mailings under the chin), "the house that can haud twa can haud three; the fire that can warm four feet can warm six; the same pot that boils for two can boil for three; so that, you see, no to be entering into particulars,

Miss Girzie can leeve wi' us at no expense, and she'll be company to her sister when I'm in my study concern'd wi' my work."

Mrs Soorocks clapped her hands together, and turning up her eyes, said with an ejaculatory accent: "Who cou'd have thocht o' this!"

Breakfast was then announced, which, considering the calibre of the respective parties, passed off with so much propriety that my conscience began to be a little appeased. It really appeared to me that the part which I had taken in the business (for I no longer now affected to deny, even to myself, that I had been instrumental to the completion of the marriage) was rather commendable—so much are we prone to judge of the rectitude and propriety of even our own actions by their results; and the same sentiment seemed to strike Mrs Soorocks, for when we were returning from Auldbiggings after breakfast, she whispered to me—

"Weel, sir, I think we haena made sae verra bad a job o't after a', only what's to become o' them? We maun try what can be done by working on the tender mercies o' Dr Lounlans; and I hope Mrs Lounlans will be found to hae bowels o' compassion; and if she has, I'm sure she'll be the first o' her kin, by the mother's side o' the house, that ever had ony. Cou'd ye hae ever imagined that the twa deceitfu' creatures would hae had the sense to do as they did yestreen? I'll ne'er put trust in the countenance o' womankind again."

Much more of the same sort on both sides passed between us till we separated, having previously arranged that we should watch the return of the Doctor, and endeavour to complete our good work by soliciting him to allow the three Graces, as Mrs Soorocks called the Laird, the bride, and bride's sister, to enjoy the remainder of their days at Barenbraes.

CHAPTER XXXIV

ON returning to my own house, I was somewhat surprised to find that during my short absence Mr Loopy, of the respectable house of Loopy and Hypothec, writers in Glasgow, had been calling, urgent to see me, and had mentioned to my housekeeper that he had several places in the neighbourhood to visit—among others Auldbiggings.

As there had been for some time a rumour through the country of an expected dissolution of Parliament, I was at no loss to guess, from the connections of my old friend Loopy, the probable motive of his civility in calling upon me, with whom he had no particular ostensible business; but I could not account for the circumstance of his intended visit to the Laird, who in his political predilections had ever been opposed to those of the present ministry.

Having given up the day to idleness, it occurred to me that perhaps I might be able to intercept the worthy man of business, either on his way to or from The Place, and induce him to take a quiet dinner with me, for I have ever found his shrewd conversation particularly racy

and relishing. Accordingly, after giving orders
for the leg of my last killed five-year-old to be
dressed, I sauntered along the highway towards
Auldbiggings, seeing nothing of the lawyer till
I was at the bottom of the avenue, where his
post-chaise was waiting—the approach to the
house being in such a state with ruts and stones
that the postillion did not venture to take his
carriage and horses to the door.

I went up to the house ; but long before I
reached the entrance, everything indicated that
there was indeed a change of administration
within.

Jenny Clatterpans, bare-footed and bare-legged,
with her petticoats kilted, and her hair falling in
masses from under her cap, was standing on a
stool whitewashing the lintels of the lower windows with an old hearth-brush ; her whitening-
pot was a handless and cripple tureen. The cook,
ghastly and piebald with soot and whitening, was
rattling with the remnant of an old blanket in
her hand, in the midst of a numerous assemblage
of all manner of kitchen utensils—brazen sconces,
pewter trenchers that might for magnitude have
been shields to Ajax, copper lids of departed fish-
kettles ; a warming-pan, damasked with holes in
the lid, and the handle of which had been lost
beyond the memory of man ; a brass basting ladle,
a superannuated tormentor, a bright copper tea-
kettle, the spout of which had long become loose
by many scourings, but still it was the pride and

Q

glory of the shelf on which it was wont to stand, flanking a long array of various sorts of brass candlesticks which were lying on the grass around it. Beyond her, at a picturesque distance, lay a mound of feather-beds, pillows and bolsters, which Jock, without his coat, was manfully thrashing with a flail, raising such a dust that he could only be seen at intervals like a demon in the clouds of a whirlwind.

As it was impossible to think of interrupting so many indications of a radical reform, I walked into the house, intending to go up to the old gentleman's study ; but the lobby was so crowded with old casks, tubs and firkins, empty bottles and boxes, that I with great difficulty made my way to the foot of the stair, on which the bride and her sister were endeavouring to bring down a large worsted wheel, which, from the death of the first Mrs Mailings, had been removed from the kitchen and placed upon the great napery ark that stood at the stairhead, being the first stage on its way to the lumber garret.

Having assisted the ladies to bring this woollen mill round the turn of the stair, I at last reached the room where the Laird and the lawyer were seated, engaged so earnestly in conversation that neither of them hardly observed me enter. Their topic was the impending general election, and it soon appeared that Mr Loopy was not canvassing for the vote, but for the purchase of the superiority of Auldbiggings.

"Three hundred pounds," Mr Loopy was saying as I came in, "and of money down too, no trouble but to count it—it is a very large sum for my client to give."

"But your client, Mr Loopy, is a capitalist, and kens hoo to mak his outlay productive," rejoined the Laird. "When he bade you offer me three hundred pounds, he was thinking o' my agricultural distress; but this is no sic a rainy day as to cause me to sell my hen below her marketable value. It's but the second, ye maun ken, o' my honeymoon—and when will a man be croose if he's no then? And isna my wife yin o' the heirs-portioners, as ye wad ca't, in law, o' the estate o' Barenbraes? But noo when I think o't, Mr Loopy, I'll no sell at a'; for it may be a mean hereafter to help me to get a post in the government, or a cadetcy to Indy for one of our younger sons. Three hunder poun', Mr Loopy! I wadna tak three thousan': the superiority is 120 pun' Scots, auld valuation, and it wadna be kittle to mak a piecing, as ye weel ken hoo, that wad gie ye the poore and capacity o' twa votes instead o' ane."

"But, Laird, how could I be aware of that circumstance?" replied Mr Loopy. "However, that it does make a difference I admit, yet you should consider that votes are falling in value; for you know," and the lawyer appealed to me in verification of the fact, "the great landholders in this county are splitting their superiorities to the utmost extremity, and actually giving them away for nothing ; they are a drug in the market, that is to say, in a manner."

I now began to see the drift of Mr Loopy's visit to the Laird, and with the more satisfaction, as it never had occurred to any of the helpless man's friends to think of the value of his vote for the county as a means to lighten, if not to avert, the misfortune with which he was immediately threatened ; nor probably had it ever before occurred to himself, for such was the improvidence and slackness in all his affairs that nothing was ever done in them until it became absolutely necessary or inevitable.

The Laird was touched on his weak side by reference to the multiplication of votes tending to reduce their value, and being evidently at a loss for an answer, I thought it my duty to interpose, saying : "That the making of so many new votes was only a proof that the ensuing contest was expected to be a hot one, and that those who kept aloof from either party till the proper time could not fail to realise the full value of their influence."

"Oh !" exclaimed Mr Loopy, "it would be most abominable, and what no honest man like Mr Mailings could think of doing, to sell himself to the highest bidder ; and besides, the general election is not expected before the fall, and a vote made at this time will in that case be of no use, for the infeftment must run year and day.   But, Laird, to mak short work o't, notwithstanding all these disadvantages, I think I could almost promise— for my client is a liberal as well as a wealthy man—I could almost promise that he might be brought to go the length of five hundred pounds.''

" I can say nae mair about it," replied the old man, " without consulting my amiable spouse, Mrs Mailings ; " and he vociferated, " Dawty, come ben the house, dawty, and help me to mak a bargain wi' Mr Loopy."

The lady, however, did not immediately answer to the summons; her labours had dishevelled her dress and discomposed her temperature ; but when she had somewhat arranged the former, and cooled herself with a towel or handkerchief, after being again called, she came into the room, followed by Miss Girzie, whose complexion was equally heightened by her share in the toil, and her dress even still more disarranged.

The Laird briefly stated that Mr Loopy had come to buy, if he would sell, the superiority of Auldbiggings, and had offered five hundred pounds.

" If he would speak about fifteen, it would be mair wiselike," said the leddy, looking askance at the lawyer, who pushed his chair back and regarded her with the utmost astonishment of features, gradually relaxing into a smile expressive of incredulous wonder.

" Mr Mailings," he exclaimed, "oh, ye are a happy man to have such a wife ; and when you come to have your children round your table like olive plants, she will indeed be a fruitful vine!"

"Dawty," said the Laird, quite delighted to hear such commendations bestowed on the lady of his love,—"Dawty, let us be reasonable, and not rigorous."

"Be just before you're generous," said his spouse.

"Think o' wha's to come after you," rejoined Miss Girzie.

"Consider your small family," cried I, "and your young son that you intend tc send to India."

"Mony a laird's daughter has been waur tochered than wi' her father's vote at a contested election, Mr Loopy," interposed the Laird firmly; "your client may tak his five hunder pound and mak a playock wi' a whistle in its tail or he'll either get heft or blade o' my vote for sic a trifle. Five hundred pound! talk o' a thoosan', and I'll maybe hearken wi' the hearing side o' my head."

"A thousand!" exclaimed Mr Loopy, starting up and affecting to move towards the door, "I never heard anything so unreasonable."

"Weel, weel," cried the Laird, "will ye split the——"

"Hold your tongue, Auldbiggings," exclaimed Mrs Mailings, "and dinna mak yoursell a prodigal son; an ye wad part wi' your patrimony in that gait, ye wad weel deserve to eat draff wi' the swine; na, na, a thousand pound is ower little!"

"I wonder," said Mr Loopy, still standing on the floor—"I wonder, Mrs Mailings, that ye wadna say guineas, when ye think there's such fools in the world as wad gie a thousand pound, and for what?——"

"For a vote," said Miss Girzie sedately, "and ye ken the full value o't, Mr Loopy."

The leddy shook her head significantly. "I thank you for your gentle hint, Mr Loopy," cried she, "and we'll no take ae farthing less than a thousan' guineas."

The lawyer turned round with a well-affected huff, and at that moment Mrs Soorocks made her appearance, puffing and blowing, crying out—

"I hope I'm in time—I hope ye haena concluded the bargain—I hope, Mrs Mailings, ye'll protect your gudeman. Mr Loopy, Mr Loopy, hoo could ye think, after wheedling, as I hae heard this morning, auld Peter Kethcart out o' his bit laun, for little mair than the half o' its value, to say naething o' the superiority, to come fleeching here to beguile Auldbiggings; knowing as ye do, Mr Loopy, that it's a' the residue left o' his patrimony; but, leddies, when I heard he was here, I came running like a maukin to snatch you as brands out o' the burning; for he has a tongue that wad wile the bird aff the tree!"

"I'm no safe here," rejoined Mr Loopy, with

a smile, and turning to the Laird, he added:
" As I was instructed by my client to go a certain
length, if you are willing to treat with me I shall
be liberal ; you shall have a thousand pounds for
the superiority down, if you choose to take it ;
and further I am not empowered to go."

The Laird was evidently on the point of
accepting the offer, when Mrs Soorocks exclaimed—

" The superiority o' Auldbiggings sell't for a
thousand pounds, that is sae weel worth double
the money ! O Miss Shoosie—Mrs Mailings, as I
should ca' ye—tak that man o' yours into your
bedroom and gie him admonition—it's no for a
sma' profit that my friend Mr Loopy's scamperin'
frae Dan to Beersheba——"

" I certainly think," rejoined I, " that Mr
Mailings ought to have some time to consider
of the marketable value of his only remaining
property."

Here Mrs Mailings cried—

" It would be cheatrie to bargain away a right
and property that Mr Loopy's sae ready to gie
a thousan' and fifty pounds for—na, a thousan'
guineas ! "

With that she turned round to the lawyer,
and said with a mim mouth and a dulcet
accent—

" If ye'll call the morn, Mr Loopy, maybe
ye'll hae an answer."

" 'Deed," rejoined the Laird, " it's my solid

opinion that if the qualification o' Auldbiggings
be worth a thousan' guineas at this time, it
ought, wi' discreet management, to be soon
worth a great deal more; because you see all
trade is in a state o' panic and calamity, and
folk will have nae other way o' making their
bread than by gettin' posts in the government;
so that if a vote noo be worth sae mickle, what
will it no be worth when mair customers for
posts come to deal in the market; for you know,
Mr Loopy, that there's a standard o' value by
which the price of everything may be measured,
and all we want to know is, what this natural
standard is."

"I doot, Mr Mailings," replied the lawyer,
"that, like the other political economists, ye
run some risk o' mistaking the ell-wand for the
cloth; but I observe you are not in a humour to
deal with me to-day, so I will take Mrs Mailings'
hint."

Accordingly he left the room, and I followed to beg his company at dinner, which,
however, he declined at first; but seeing the
confusion in which the house of Auldbiggings
was, he said at the time, "Perhaps the Laird
might be induced to join me;" and he would
look in upon us in the afternoon, on his return
to Glasgow.

CHAPTER XXXV

ON returning into the room, I found the Laird
alone. The ladies had retired to an inner apartment, to determine, as he informed me, in what
manner he should deal with Mr Loopy.

"Isna my wife," said he, "a clever wife?
Weel does she ken how many blue beans it
taks to mak five. Had I married her twenty
years ago, I wouldna hae needed this day to
stand in awe o' lawyers and naubobs, and sic
like o' the clanjamphry. And she's sic a pleasant
young creature that she blithens my verra blood;
I couldna hae thought it possible for matrimony
to mak a man sae happy. It's true, I had an
experience before; but then my first was a
forced marriage, whereas this, my second, has
been a free-will offering, a' o' my ain instigation,
the which maks an unco difference. I didna
think when I tell't you in the garden that I
would fain marry Miss Shoosie Minnigaff, that
I had sic a sincerity o' sound affection for her,
as a' my friends had sae lang discovered; but
you know it is written in the Word that we do
not know ourselves; and behold, I am a living

illustration of the text. However, anent the
thoosan' pounds for the superiority, what's your
opinion ? "

I told him that I considered it a great godsend ; but remarked that, as it was not sufficient
to procure for him any effectual relief from his
mortgages, it would be much better to give
up the estate at once to the Nabob, and buy
an annuity with the money on the joint lives of
himself and Mrs Mailings.

" Had we no a prospect of a family, what ye
counsel would be worth hearkening to."

" I doubt, Laird, that's but a barren prospect ;
and besides, you ought to consider the great
wickedness of augmenting our national distress
by increasing the population of the country,
already so redundant. I beseech you, Mr Mailings, to respect the admonitions of economical
philosophy."

" Hoots, hoots ! dinna talk sic Malthusian
havers to me. The cause o' our national decay and
agricultural distress, broken merchants, ravelled
manufacturers, and brittle bankers, come a'thegither frae another well-ee. Were sic calamities
ever heard o' in this reawlm before the turnip
farming came into vogue ? Answer me that. Weel
do I mind that it was in the ha'rst o' that verra
year, when the first peck o' turnips was sawn in
the shire, that the sough came through the
kintra o' the Ayr bank gaun to pigs and whistles.
My auntie, wha was then in the lan' o' the livin',

and has since been sleeping in Abraham's bosom,
wi' the rest o' the patriarchs, said on that melancholious occasion—and she was a judicious woman
—that to gar sheep and kye crunch turnips was
contrary to nature, their teeth being made for
grass and kail-blades; and that it would be seen
that the making o' turnip-pastures would prove a
sign o' something.   Never did I forget her words
o' warning, though I was then but a bairn, a very
babe and suckling, in a sense; and I hae noted,
year by year, that her prophecy has been mair
and mair coming to pass; for, with the ingrowth o'
turnip-farming, there has aye been a correspond-
ing smasherie amang the looms and sugar-hoggits.
Last year, I was in a terror for what was to happen
when I saw sae mony braw parks that used to be
ploughed for vittle to man sawn for fodder to
beasts."

"Your story, Laird," said I, "well deserves
the attention of his Majesty's Ministers; for
some of them, in my opinion, have been finding
similar effects, as legitimately descended from
causes equally proximate.   But if turnip-fields
were sown with corn, would the distress be
abated?"

"How can ye misdoot it?—and the redundant
population would be abated too, for as they
baith came in wi' the turnips, wouldna they
gang out wi' them?   Isna that a truth o' political
economy?"

At this crisis the ladies returned into the room,

and the Laird addressing himself to his wife, said—

"Weel, dawty, hoo hae ye settled the government anent the price o' the superiority?"

"We hae disposed o' it a' to the best advantage," interposed Mrs Soorocks; "and ye needna trouble your head about it. We'll get Mr Loopy to lay out the money—for he's a clever man in his line—on a life-rent for you and Mrs Mailings; and ye'll gang intil Enbro' and live comfortable, like twa patriarchs. There, Laird, ye may spend the evening o' your days in lown felicity; and hammergaw frae morning to night wi' the advocates about corn-laws and circulating middims; and my frien' Bailie Blackwood, he has a great respec for me—he'll, on my account, let you write in the *Magazine* for your amusement."

"Devil's in that woman," muttered the Laird aside. "She's a torment to me and to every other body. But, dawty," he subjoined aloud to his lady, "I hae a plan far better than the veesions o' life-rents that Mrs Soorocks would beglammar us a' wi'—this godsend o' the thousan' pounds——"

"Thousan' pounds!" exclaimed all the ladies with one voice. "Ye'll surely never tak a farding less than twa thousan'?"

"For which," continued Mrs Mailings sola, "Mrs Soorocks tells me we may get mair than two hunner and fifty pounds a year, paid down in bank-notes, without ony stress o' law, — and wouldna that be a grand thing ? "

" But if the banks break," cried the Laird.

" If the lift fa's it'll smoor the laverocks," [1] retorted Mrs Soorocks ; at which the Laird bounced from his seat, and giving a stamp with his foot, exclaimed—

" I'll be master in my own house—I'll be ruled by naebody—I'll hae a will o' my own ; and I will. The devil's in't if a man o' my substance is to be snuled [2] in this gait."

He then turned round to his wife, and said in a softened accent—

" Dinna be frightened, dawty—I'm no in a pashon wi' you, but ye'll let me hae my ain way."

" And what's that way ? " inquired dawty, in a tone which did not indicate an entire acquiescence in the doctrine of passive obedience.

" I've had a notion," said the Laird, addressing himself to me, " that there's a mine o' copper ore aneath the whinny-knowes ; and don't you think it would be very advisable for me to work it, and pay off the wadsets wi' the profits ? "

I participated in the alarm and consternation of the ladies at the propounding of such a scheme. Miss Girzie clasped her hands in agony, and sat in a supplicating posture. Her sister stood erect, many inches taller than her wont, with her arms extended, and her fingers spread out like the leaves of the palmetto ; while Mrs Soorocks burst

---

[1] Smother the larks.   [2] *Snuled.* Snubbed.

into an immoderate fit of laughing, exclaiming :
" Did ye ever hear sic a goose wi' a golden egg ?
A copper mine ! I wonder, when ye were at it,
that ye didna dream o' a Potosi."

" Weel, weel," said the Laird, nettled at the
effect he had produced, " mak a kirk and a mill
o't ; but my plans will get justice some day."

At this juncture, a rattling voice on the stair
drew off our attention from the matter in debate ;
and Jock, with his flail over his shoulder, and
covered with feathers, as if he had been in a
snowstorm, rushed into the room, crying—

" Odsake, odsake, here's ane o' the minister's
lasses, wi' news that'll freeze your verra marrow.
The minister's come hame wi' his bridal-wife ;
and they're awa in a cotch o' their ain—set a
minister up wi' his ain cotch !—to had the infare
at Barenbraes. Leddies—leddies—oh, my leddy
madam mistress, he'll tak possession o' the house
and heritage—and what's far waur, here's likewise
the Nawbob in a' his glory, comin' nae doot to
drive you and the Laird, like Adam and Eve, out
o' this pleasant paradise and garden o' Eden, that
it might be, for the sma' cost o' a little reparation."

Mrs Soorocks was the first who broke silence
after this portentous announcement. Addressing
herself to the ladies, she said—

" Weel, cousins, havena ye found at last the
true prophecy o' my words ? "

" Cousins ! " said I to Mrs Soorocks ; " you told
me they were only distant connections ? "

" But near aneugh," replied she actively, " to hae been a cess upon me, had I no got them otherwise provided for ; and I thank you, sir, for the helping-hand ye hae been to me in the work."

I felt much inclined to exclaim with the Laird, " Devil's in that woman, she's a torment to me and to every other body ; " but the sound of the Nabob's voice, as he forced his way up through the chaos of chattels, with which the staircase was encumbered, arrested the imprecation.

CHAPTER XXXVI

THE Nabob came in with well-acted jocularity, and, totally regardless of his sulky reception, began to rally the Laird on his spirit in choosing so young and so blooming a bride. Nor was he less lavish of his compliments on the lady. On Mrs Soorocks, to whom he justly ascribed the entire merit of having designed and accomplished the match, his commendations were without end; nevertheless, in all this bustle of boisterous gesticulation, it was soon evident that he had come for some other purpose than to felicitate the happy pair.

After the first rush and froth of his merriment had subsided or run to waste, he began with his characteristic straightforwardness, seemingly unconscious of the abruptness of the transaction, to state that he had been informed that Mr Loopy was buying up the superiorities of sundry small parcels of land, with the design, as it was conjectured, of uniting them together; so as to enable him to dispose of qualifications for the county election. "And I hear, Mr Mailings," said he, "that the snaky rascal has been with you. Have you sold yours? If you have, recollect the purchase-money is mine."

"We'll hae twa words about that," replied the Laird dryly.

"Is not my security over all the estate?"

"'Deed is't; it's o'er the whole tot o' the lan' —but I may say, in the words of a reform in Parliament—'the whole land and nothing but the land.'"

"If that be the case," cried the Nabob, piqued, "and that the superiority may be sold by itself, I think you ought to have given me the first offer. A man has but the half of his estate, when he has not all the rights belonging to it."

"And for what should we hae gi'en you the first offer?" exclaimed Jock with indignation, as he still stood in the middle of the room, feathered, cap-a-pie, and with his flail shouldered.

The Nabob looked with a tiger-like scowl, and going sedately towards him, seized him calmly by the collar, and walking him to the door, pushed him headlong out, tartly applying his foot at the same moment to the seat of Jock's honour. But Jock was not to be so touched with impunity. In the instant of his expulsion, he ran after Mr Loopy, and catching him just as he was stepping into the chaise, which was waiting at the avenue gate, he worked upon him to return.

"I take you a' to witness, leddies and gentlemen," cried Jock, as he returned with his man of business, "I take every ane o' you to witness anent my bottomrie. There's the panel that did the deed, Mr Loopy—deal with him, as he has written on the brod at the corner o' his planting —' according to the utmost rigour of law.' I'll be even wi' you noo, Nawaubpore, for a' the dule and sorrow that you and cleipy Caption would sigh and wallywae about, for the bit clink I gi'ed wi' a harmless fishing-rod to John Angle's brazen whirligig."

Whether Jock had informed Mr Loopy of the immediate cause of quarrel, as he brought him back to the house, did not appear by anything in the manner of the lawyer; but after some alter-cation, partly in good-humour and partly spar-ringly, the assault which poor Jock had suffered was forgotten, and the man of business, with an equivocal deviation from the fact, reminded the Laird that he promised to sell the superiority to him, warning him to beware of dealing with any other.

"Hooly, hooly," cried the Laird; "ye ken, Mr Loopy, that if for ceeveelity, I maunna in my ain house ca' that a lee, it would be the next thing till't to say it wasna like ane. But since we hae gotten twa candidates on the leet, I'll play even-down justice wi' you baith. A thoosan' pounds sterling for the superiority o' Auldbiggings—wha bids mair?"

"Eleven hundred," cried Mrs Soorocks.

Mr Loopy looked at her, and raising his out-spread hands in mirthful amazement, said with more sincerity, however, than he intended should be discovered, " And what would Mrs Soorocks do with a superiority ? "

" Sell't to you for an advantage," replied the lady with a significant nod, and a smile to me.

" Eleven hundred pounds sterling for the superiority of Auldbiggings," resumed the Laird— " wha bids mair ? "

" Twelve hundred," said the Nabob with a perplexed and embarrassed look, as if he was not quite aware of the consequences of the bidding.

" Mr Rupees, are ye really in earnest ? " said the lawyer, with a slight inflection of the voice, almost in the key of alarm.

" I'll bid thirteen hundred," said Miss Girzie, with a giggle ; " for I hae heard o' a vote sell't for more than seventeen hundred pounds."

" Thirteen hundred pounds for the superiority of Auldbiggings — going for thirteen hundred pounds," resumed the Laird, drawing his chair towards the table and striking it with his snuff-box for a hammer.

" Nay, if ye're making a diversion o't," said the lawyer, " I may as well give a bode too ; so I say fourteen hundred, Mr Mailings—but mind I have no intention of standing to the bargain."

" The devil ! " exclaimed the Nabob ; " then I say fifteen hundred, Mr Mailings, and I intend to stand by the offer."

" Do as you like, Nawaubpore," interposed Mrs Soorocks ; " but, Laird, if ye get a better, ye're

free to take it ; so I say saxteen hundred, Mr
Mailings, and I intend to stand to the offer."

Mr Loopy was every moment plainly becoming more and more excited ; he endeavoured to
appear calm and to smile, but his eyes were
eager and restless, and his nether lip quivered.
"This," said he, "is the most extraordinary proceeding I ever witnessed. Surely, Mrs Soorocks,
you can have no intention of buying ; and, Mr
Rupees, you could never think of giving any such
money ?"

"Sixteen hundred pounds sterling for the superiority of Auldbiggings ! once—" shouted the
Laird, chuckling with delight.

"I beg, Mr Mailings," cried the lawyer, "that
you would allow me to say one word."

"Sixteen hundred pounds sterling for the
superiority of Auldbiggings—mind, Mr Loopy,
it's pounds sterling," was, however, all the
answer he got.

"Seventeen hundred, and be damned to it !"
roared the Nabob.

"Remember, Mr Mailings," interposed the
lawyer in professional expostulation, "remember,
you have no license to sell by public roup or
auction."

"Seventeen hundred pounds sterling, Mr
Loopy, for the superiority o' Auldbiggings—will
ye gie me another bode ?" was the Laird's
reply ; and rubbing his hands in ecstasy, he
added, "Seventeen hundred pounds, once—

seventeen hundred pounds, twice — going, Mr Loopy—going."

"I know this is all but a joke," rejoined the lawyer, "and to humour you, I'll go the length of eighteen hundred."

"And just for the joke too," said Mrs Soorocks, "I'll bid nineteen hundred, Mr Loopy."

"I think," cried Jock, with a guffaw like a cataract, "that it's cheap at twa thoosan'."

"I'll give the money for it, Laird," growled the Nabob, "and end this foolish competition."

"Many a droll sight and sale have I seen," said Mr Loopy, "but never one like this. Mr Rupees, are you in your senses?"

"If you are," was the emphatic answer.

The lawyer made no further observations, but turning to the Laird, said in an accent which could not be misunderstood, "Then I bid another hundred."

From that the contest lay between him and the Nabob, till their respective offers reached six-and-twenty hundred pounds.

"Going, once—going twice!" shouted the Laird.

"Another fifty," said Mrs Soorocks quietly, but slyly.

"We're all mad," said the lawyer.

"Twa thoosan' sax hun'er and fifty pounds sterling," said the Laird. "Mak it guineas, Mr Loopy, and the bargain's yours."

"Guineas be't," exclaimed the lawyer; and in

the same moment the Laird struck the table and
roared out, "Thrice." The ladies all screamed
and rushed upon him, while the Nabob made the
house quake with his stump; but Jock, flourish-
ing the flail in triumph, smashed a looking-glass
into a hundred pieces and fled.

CHAPTER XXXVII

WHEN order was restored, the lawyer took out his pocket-book, and drew from it a ready prepared minute of an agreement for the purchase, with a blank in it for the money. He then went to the mantelpiece, where an inkstand with pens stood, and taking one of the pens, looked at it between him and the light, and afterwards touched it with the tip of his tongue.

"You are a noble hand at auctioneering, Laird," said he, as he spread the paper on the table. When he had filled up the blank, he laid it before the Laird, who, in taking the pen, turned and addressed his wife, " Isna this, dawty, a gran' hansell to our marriage ? "

"Nawaubpore," said Mrs Soorocks, " ye hae lost a gude bargain."

The great man made her, however, no answer, but inquired, with more energy than the question required, if I thought the sale valid.

I excused myself from giving any opinion by reminding him that I was no lawyer, upon which he wheeled abruptly, and without the courtesy of leave-taking quitted the room ; and the lawyer

soon after, having finished his contract, also retired; and although I had come on purpose, I
neglected to ask him to dinner as I had intended.
Indeed, the sudden change which had thus taken
place in the condition of the Laird was so extraordinary that it engrossed my whole mind;
nor was the good fortune which so crowned his
marriage confined that day to the successful sale
of the barren superiority. Before the lawyer had
left us many minutes, and while Mrs Soorocks
was with indisputable justice lauding herself for
the part she had played in the biddings, the
arrival of Dr and Mrs Lounlans was announced.

The Laird's complexion changed at the name
to the ashy paleness of fear and aversion.

"What's brought them here," cried he, "the
cheatrie dominie! Is't no aneugh that he has
rookit my wife and my gude-sister out o' their
father's heritage, but he maun come in triumph-
ing chariots to trample us in the mire? It's a
bonnie pass the world's come to—the heiress of
a house like Barenbraes and the dochter o' a
bauronet to marry a dominie! No wonder that
our auncient gentry are so fast weedit awa like
cumberers o' the ground."

"Wheesht, wheesht, Laird," said Mrs Soorocks.
"Hearken! they're on the stair."

"I'll gar ding the door in their faces," exclaimed the indignant Malachi; but before he
had time to put his threat in force, the doctor
entered with his lady leaning on his arm.

The effect of this apparition—for, by its immediate impression, it may as such be described—was instantaneous. Miss Girzie sat with her hands elevated, and her elbows pressing against her sides. Mrs Mailings, with more self-possession, went forward to receive the strangers; Mrs Soorocks, who was seated beyond Miss Girzie, stretched forth her neck, and inspected the young lady with sharp and jealous eyes, her most peculiar and characteristic features; and the Laird sat twirling his thumbs, as if resolved to take no heed whatever of his visitors. Every moment, however, he stole a glance at them; and in so doing, slackened his twirling, and then as often resumed it with redoubled vigour. But the appearance of Mrs Lounlans was calculated to conciliate a kinder reception.

She was one of those unaffected and prepossessing young ladies, who, without any particular personal endowment, wear an air of so much good sense and natural gracefulness about them, as to attract confidence and esteem at the first sight. When she withdrew her arm from her husband's and came forward to meet her aunt, Miss Girzie rose, and Mrs Soorocks put on a countenance of ineffable benignity.

Dr Lounlans having introduced the ladies to one another, turned to the Laird and said, " Our next friend here is Mr Mailings."

" They're a' friens that arena faes," was the answer; the sullen respondent endeavouring to sit erectly dignified, twirling his thumbs with accelerated velocity. Mrs Lounlans had evidently, however, been prepared for an uncouth reception; and being none dismayed by his ungracious mood and repulsive manner, lifted one of his hands, and with much conciliation of accent felicitated herself on being numbered among his relations.

"My mother too," she added, "whom we have set down at my aunt's—for we expected to have found them at home—was happy to hear of what has taken place, for she recollects you as one of her early friends."

The Laird was subdued by the gentleness of this address, and looked up with a smile, half indicative of pleasure and of incredulity, while Mrs Soorocks said to the doctor—

"And is't possible that Leddy Chandos has ta'en actual possession?"—and she added with a significant sigh, "O Miss Girzie!"

The doctor replied, with more archness than belonged to his grave and habitual equanimity, "You know, Mrs Soorocks, that the estate is entailed, and that Lady Chandos is the elder sister." But observing that the sisters misunderstood him, he addressed himself to them, saying—

"Her ladyship waits impatiently to see you. Tired with her journey, and deeply affected with the many tender reminiscences of youth and childhood, which every object in the scene of the early pleasures has revived, she found herself unable to come with us."

By this time, Mrs Lounlans had so far ingratiated herself with the Laird that he drew a chair towards his own, and requested her to sit down beside him.

" Dawty," said he to his wife, " I think she has a cast o' thee; but it will be late in the day before she'll can compare."

Mrs Soorocks here again addressed the doctor, inquiring if Lady Chandos was come "to spend her auld days among her forefathers?" adding, " But I needna be surprised at it, for she was aye a sweet, sentimental lassie, a perfect Clarissy Harlowe, though I maun say it's no verra like a heroine in a novel to come and take possession. 'Deed, Miss Girzie, I feel for you. It's just like the cuckoo dabbing a wallydraigle out o' the nest; but I'll reason wi' her."

" Give yourself no uneasiness on that head," replied the doctor; " for, to remove all anxiety from her sisters, she has settled the house and property on them during her life. She could do no more."

" But when she dies?" said the anxious and affectionate lady. The doctor smiled, and then told her that Mrs Lounlans had, before their marriage, confirmed and extended the settlement for her life also.

" Noo, that's Christianity, doctor"—and she justly commended the delicacy with which the settlement had been made, ascribing it all to his influence and advice.

CHAPTER XXXVIII

THE Nabob, though a vain and ambitious, was by no means an unprincipled man, and when the identity of his ward was fully made out, he set himself seriously to render him all due restitution and fair play. The expense, however, in which he had unfortunately allowed himself to indulge since his return from the East, did not admit of his doing this with any comfort to himself, without unavoidably trenching on the comforts of the poor Laird. In a short time notice was conveyed to Malachi, in as delicate a manner as might be, that he must prepare, as speedily as possible, to leave the home of his ancestors.

Perhaps none of the human feelings are more extensive or powerful in their operation than local associations ; for early remembrances of the fields wherein we roamed—the school wherein we were tutored, and maybe flogged—the river wherein we bathed, waded, or fished—the cherry-trees whose unripe fruit we plundered — the "old familiar faces," that frequented parlour or hall—the dog which we were wont to caress—and the room wherein we slept, form in process of time almost a part of our very existence, and find a chord that answers to their thrill, alike in the bosom of the cultivated and philosophic as in the simple and untutored.

That to the Laird nature had not been prodigal of her intellectual favours, it were vain to deny; and that a long course of indulgence in the caprices which his station permitted him to exercise had blunted moral perceptions which never were particularly vivid, admits not of a doubt; yet even with his inveterate selfishness was occasionally mixed up a spice of the more ennobling ingredients of the human constitution. Though prepared by the storm which he had long felt brewing around him, for its some day, and that not far distant, breaking on his head; yet the tidings that he must leave Auldbiggings came to him like a sentence of death to the criminal, who through the investigation of his crimes still perceives a loophole or two, by which the sunshine of mercy may possibly descend on his fated head.

But we must to action—and a truce to sentimentality and "the influence of local attachment," which we leave in the competent hands of the Reverend Mr Polwhele.

The Laird and I were taking a saunter about his premises; and, observing the downcast peevish melancholy of the old man, I lent in a word or two by way of soothing encouragement.

"As Mrs Soorocks justly observed——" said I.

"Hang Mrs Soorocks!" interrupted the Laird pettishly; "I dinna want to hear onything about her, or ony o' the like ten-fingered intermeddlers. What signifies a' that Mrs Soorocks has said or done, or can say or do, when I maun leave my auncient inheritance of Auldbiggings, and be driven out—an auld broken-doun man wi' grey hair — into a wicked warld, without kenning where I am to find a hame, or where, I should rather say, I am to look for a grave to lay my banes in—for that date will no be lang!"

"You take a black view of matters, Laird," said I, throwing as much cheerfulness into my voice as my really touched feelings would permit. "What signifies it, if we have a snug roof to cover us, where we lodge? We have no abiding-place here, Laird."

"Abiding-place here, or abiding-place there, noo can ye deave me wi' sic havers, as trying to convince me that ane shuldna have a regard for the place where they were born, and bred, and brought up! Do ye see that saugh-tree at the corner o' the avenue? I planted that fifty year ago wi' my ain hand; I dibbled the yearth, and stappit it in there, a thing no half as lang as this walking-staff; and now it towers ower our heads by a hunder feet, and the birds o' heevan bigg their nests amang its branches. I wadna touch that tree, come o't what wad, tho' it was to buy a coat to my back; but feint a hair will strangers ken or care about the like o' that; and it will maybe be sawn down next week, to gie the new-comers a veesy in that airt, towards that cursed Nawaubpore house o' theirs."

Trying to divert his mind from the train of feelings which had taken possession of it with more than ordinary force, I asked him "if he intended that forenoon returning the visit of Dr and Mrs Lounlans."

"'Deed wad I," answered he, "for I freely confess he has behaved in a way I wad hae given him little credit for acting in towards Mrs Mailings and her sister. Yes, yes, I'll no be sae thrawn as to deny his having been kinder to me and mine than we had ony reason to expect; but woe's the day for Auldbiggings, and a puir pass has the like o' a house such as ours come to—which in its time had feasted half the lords and leddies in the land—when we are reduced to accept of a god-send from the like o' sic hands as those of auld Jock Lounlans' son, that I was ance obliged to roup out o' house and hall for not having left the needful to pay his just and lawful debts."

"Oh, but, Laird," said I, glad of any way by which I might break in upon his heavy thoughts, "ye surely cannot be displeased with him for repaying evil with good?"

"Evil wi' good!" exclaimed the Laird, stand-ing still and looking me in the face, leaning forward on his staff as he propped his back with his left hand, "and have ye turned against me in my hour of adversity like all the rest, or hoo

come ye to affront an auld man like me in the
very whirlpool o' my calamities. I dinna gie a
curse for Dr Lounlans, as they ca' him—set him
up wi' doctor !—nor ony o' his kith, kin, or
generation ; bodies that wad have been glad of
a nievefu' out o' my faither's kitchen meal-ark.
But them that were glad to find a way into Auldbiggings by the back-door lang ago now venture
proudly up its front steps in broad daylight, and
ring our door-bell as if they had been born and
bred gentlemen. But what are we standing
palavering here for ? Let us away into the house
—for it will no be lang that I'll hae a house, so
to speak."

When we entered the lobby, the Laird took off
his hat—the unique article of dress already described—and as he hung it up on one of a range
of wooden pins, the extremities of which were
quaintly carved into something grotesquely re-
sembling cats' faces, he seized hold of me by the
sleeve, and said : " Hech-how, for sixty year—
ay, sixty year, and mair siller, I have hung up my
hat on that 'dividual same pin. That was aye
called my pin—naebody that kent it wad hae
been sae forrit-some and impudent as to have
made use of that piece o' wood for their hats,
kenning that I reserved it for my ain peculiar use.
If, whan I cam in, I fand anither hinging there—
let it have been headpiece o' gentle or semple,
nae matter—I just scuffed it doun wi' the head o'
my staff, and left Jock to lift it up at his leisure,

s

as he liket. Naebody daured to have used such liberty in Jock's presence. But ye'll stop and tak a check o' dinner with me, as it's now wearing on to dining hours?"

I endeavoured to make the best excuse I could, and pleaded an engagement at home.

"'Deed and ye'll no stir a fit the day out o' this place, without tasting o' the hospitality o' Auldbiggings; I'll likely never can ask ye again, and though I'm pressing ye the day, it's maybe we'll no have ony great thing to offer ye."

Jock here appeared with a towel below his arm, threading a transverse passage. "Hollo, Jock, I say," cried the Laird, "can we gie a stranger his dinner wi' us the day?"

"Brawly," answered Jock, rubbing down his towsy head with the flat of his hand; "that is a question to be after speering, maister—no only this day, but ony day of the year, from June to Januar, I houp."

"I'm glad to hear't, Jock," said Auldbiggings, with a smile half natural and half sardonic, in which pride and regret seemed equally mingled; "have ye killed the auld bubbly-jock, as ye threatened this morning?"

"Killed him, ay, and wad have killed him an he had twenty lives, afore I wad have left him to gang snoitering away wi' his coulter and his big umbrella of a tail, parading afore the window of ony stranger that wad hae impudence eneuch to set fit within bounds, that have descended to us from of auld, and that are ours yet, stick and stane, by all the rules o' law and gospel."

"Aha, Jock," cried the Laird, acting the hero in his valet's presence, "right now-a-days is might, and 'tramp' is the word; we maun bow before our betters. Our betters!—the thing mostly sticks in my throat—but it's a' ae woo—'tramp's' the word, Jock. "But what for," added he, turning to me, "are we standing here, condescending to hold a confab wi' a jackanapes of a servant? Haiste ye're ways, Jock, but the house to the scullery, and get ye're knives cleaned. We canna take them wi' us to sican a braw toun as Edinburgh all spatted with red rust. But holt, Jock, look up to the clock in the stair, and tell me exactly what a'clock it is."

Jock ran up a few steps, and shading his eyes with his hand, answered, not without a scrutiny of the horologe, which showed he was not particularly an adept at noting the recorded flight of time, "It wants, I think, maister, only nine minutes of three—nine, did I say? troth, I daursay it only wants seven."

The Laird had at the same instant drawn from his fob a massy structure of embossed gold, whose face, chequered with Saxon figuring, proclaimed it a work not of this age, but probably the descended heirloom of some long deceased progenitor, which had come to the Laird in the regular line of inheritance.

"Now isn't a curious thing," said he to me,

"and Jock there can bear witness to the fact, that this watch has gane like a regulawter for thirty year, without ever needing a touch in the handles? Nine minutes, did ye say, Jock? troth, wi' me it wants only seven. Where will ye find a piece of warkmanship like that now-a-days? But haiste ye're ways to the parlour, for dawtie will be wondering we are sae lang in coming in from our pleasant out-o'-doors excursion."

On coming away early in the evening, as Jock was chaperoning me downstairs, he gave a sly look first up to the clock, and then in my face. I perceived there was something in the creature's noddle, so, as he was handing me my hat in the lobby, I said to him, "Jock, yon is surely a capital old watch of your maister's. He tells me you wind it up for him regularl . Has it never gone wrong for thirty years?"

"Thirty years," said Jock with a loud guffaw, as he gave his hand a slap on his thigh. "Thirty years, say ye? That beats cock-feighting; the auld turnip wadna gang thirty hours without losing a quarter, less or mair. But I aye tak it out cannily frae aneath his head every morning, and set it to a moment. I wish ye a good-night, sir; tak care o' your feet on the outer staps."

CHAPTER XXXIX

PERHAPS if the faithful Jock had heard repeated the thousand-and-one appellations of his Majesty of the Celestial Empire, he might have been for a moment disturbed in the calm assurance of those thoughts which reposed in his master as indisputably the greatest of mankind; but certainly none other could have had the smallest chance in the competitorship, as we before have taken occasion to observe. Jock's ideas of terrestrial pomp, pride, and ambition were grievously hampered within the bounds of his native parish, in which the family of Auldbiggings, as he had heard his father and his grandfather asseverate, were in the old times a sort of petty despots in their day, "ruling the country from Dan to Beersheba," as Jock expressed it, "like a wheen Solomons, and suffering for the cause, sword in hand, in the bluidy days of the martyrs."

It was very evident however, now, that change of times had brought change of circumstances, and that the baronial power of Auldbiggings was so circumscribed as to deny of its extending any protecting banner over the last of its adherents.

As I pondered on this, the thought of what was to become of poor Jock pressed on my mind; for the state of the Laird's circumstances rendered the possibility of Jock's transference with him to Edinburgh a matter wholly out of the question. I spoke of this to Mrs Soorocks, and begged her opinion as to the best political move for the faithful creature during the present distressing crisis.

"Silly body," said Mrs Soorocks, "what earthly thing is he good for or capable of? He has been so long accustomed to his ain jog-trot that it's a matter o' moonshine to him how the world wags, provided he be able to keep himself snug and easy. As to recommending him to a flunky's place in Renthrew, Greenock, or Glasgow, or to mount guard wi' the spicy mushroom-bonneted heathens of Nawaubpore, is totally and entirely out of the question. I wish the poor cratur mayna dee in a ditch yet; for, like the auld rebel Jacobeets, he has stucken ower lang to a falling house; or the best that can come o't is his landing on the parish, or begging his way (for Jock is weel liket) frae door to door through the world."

"Could the man not find a remedy in matrimony like his master, Mrs Soorocks? It is a miserable thing to see the poor fellow cast on society utterly destitute. He is a feasible enough looking dog, and I dare say some widow's comfortable open door may be found for him."

"Weel," replied the lady, "isn't it strange that

a body hasna at all times their wits about them?
Ye have just hit the nail on the head. Bless
me! and did such a thing never enter into my
stupid head? Cast him on the world when we
have such a market for disposing of him! I
really canna see yet how you and me have over-
lookit this business till this time o' day. Widow,
did ye say? Na, there is nae need of his ganging
even that length by way of sacrifeese. There's
Jenny Clatterpans, that has had a lang snug time
o't, and has a pose in her kist-nook, or I'm a
mistaken woman. She'll be out o' place, too;
and I doutna will grup like a drowning creature
at ony comfortable down-sitting. I'll have her
sent for this very blessed afternoon—for there's
no time to be lost; and I daur to say that Jenny
has mair gude sense than stand in the way of
such a godsend of good fortune."

"Well, Mrs Soorocks," said I, "I leave the
matter in your excellent hands, and have the
strongest hopes that you will be able to bring
the business to a speedy bearing; for, when Mrs
Mailings is gone, I am afraid Jock's slender funds
would speedily show themselves 'like the morning dew, that soon vanisheth away.'"

Mrs Soorocks was not worse than her word,
for the mercurial activity of the lady's constitution seemed expressly to have been given her
to counterbalance and remedy the listlessness of
more saturnine neighbours; the same call, which
served as a parting one to the Laird and his lady,

being appropriated at its conclusion to brightening up the promises and prospects of Jock's future life. Contrary, however, to expectation, Jenny at first rode refractory, and resented her being evened[1] to Jock as a high insult; but calming down before the strong and subtle reasoning of Mrs Soorocks, she began at length to view the matter in another aspect.

"Weel, weel," said Jenny, as Mrs Soorocks afterwards told me, "what is ordeened for ane will never gang past them; but onybody that wad, ance in a day, have telled me that our man Jock and me was to be buckled thegither, I should hae thocht had nae ither intention than of making a fule o' me. But, for a' that, I'm no denying that he is a good-natured soul; and, in gude keeping, might through time come to be a civileezed creature. A brokener ship nor that has come to land."

Not long after parting with Mrs Soorocks, on that same day, I encountered Jock on the road, with a band-box in his hand, containing probably some article of female finery; for which, as he told me unsolicited, his mistress had sent him in to Renfrew. On questioning him on his future prospects, and what he intended doing after leaving the Laird's service, he informed me "that he was just thinking of taking a stap ower bye to me, to see if I kent ony gentleman or nobleman in the neibourhood in need of an active steady

[1] *Evened* in marriage.

butler, for he wasna fond o' travelling far frae hame ; and a place o' the kind of the Laird's getting for him in Embrough might lead him gude kens where—maybe up to Lonon, which he had nae brew o'."

I could not help smiling both at the humility of Jock's choice, and the confidence he seemed to express of the Laird's interest being able to procure for him any settlement of this sort ; but one minute's attention to the tones of Jock's voice, and a single glance at the poor fellow's uncouth and undrawing-room-like gestures, carried manifest testimony with them of the absurdity of such a proposition.

" Upon my word, Jock," said I, " it strikes me that, from the experience you have had in the world in the capacity of factotum to the Laird, you are well entitled to shy for evermore the trammels of servantship, and commence head of a house on your own account."

" Me the head of a house !" cried Jock.   " Na, na, that will never sowther.   I'm neither able in the capacity of purse or person for ony such upsetting, to say naething aboot being yedicated ; but I can baith read and vrite, for a' that."

" I'm sure, Jock, you have long had a sweetheart somewhere or other, that is the apple of your eye, and whom you long to make the wife of your bosom ?   It is nonsense denying the fact."

" As sure as death," said Jock, with his utmost attempt at gravity and earnestness, " I never had

ony sweethearts in my life—deil a yane—except
a bit wench, Matty Primrose, that gied me the
slip whan I least expected it, and followed a
dragoon regiment that lay in Hamilton.   She
gaed away to the wars wi' her gudeman, and
doubtless baith him and her are doun amang the
dead men lang ago."

"I've heard, Jock, that Leezie and you have
been drawing up of late.   Is that true?"

"Whae?   Leezie, Mrs Soorocks' maid!   No a
word o' truth in't, as I'm a leeving sinner.   Na,
na, she's ower young for the like o' me.   I wad
like a canny an' sedat housekeeper.   I wadna
tak Leezie."

"Well, Jock, perhaps Leezie has other fish to
fry; but I'm sure you can have no earthly objec-
tions to Jenny Clatterpans?   If you and she were
to come together, you would just find yourself as
much at home as at Auldbiggings.   How long
have you been in the house together?"

"Let me see," answered Jock.   "Jenny—let
me see—has been aboot us, ae way and anither,
aboot aughteen year.   She was a gude while the
errand lassie, but I spoke to the Laird to promote
her to the charge of the kail-pat.   Jenny and me
aye gree very weel, but it wad be condescending
in the like o' me to have onything to say to the
like o' her—me that's been upper servant at The
Place ever sin' I was the height o' ye're walking-
stick.   But I'll do whatever's thocht best; I'm no
doure in the constitution, like some fo'k."

"Perfectly right, Jock.   If I were in your place,
I would at once see what could be done.   Maybe,
if you are not good at the courting, we may get
somebody to help you a bit."

"I'll be obleeged to ye, but really, as I maistly
never tried, there's nae saying hoo I might come
on—'faint heart never wan fair leddy,' as the
spaewife ance vrote doun to me, when the leeing
fief tell't me I wad hae three wives."

I could not help smiling at Jock's earnestness,
as he deprecated the latitude to which the tether
of the fortune-teller allowed him to range; and
as he added—

"But for a' that, I daur say your advice is
wholesome.   Jenny'll be packing up bag and
baggage immediately, to gang away as soon as
the Laird and his leddy take the mail-coach,
to her native, somewhere awa doun aboot Paisley.
She's weel connectit, as I've heard her say mysell; and though its stooping doun, I maun confess, for the like o' me to lift up sae little as her,
yet folk are obligated to bow their back to the
times, and it's a great chance but my lottery-
ticket may come out a blank."

"Keep up your heart, Jock," I said to him;
"but whenever you get home, see what you can
make of Jenny."

"I'll do that, sir, but it's time for me to be
moving; for if I dinna jealouse wrang, Geordie
Joug, o' the Tanker and Tappit-Hen public, has
a sheep's-ee after her; but I daursay she wad

never be siccan a fule as pit the like o' me and
Geordie Joug, wi' his ringle-ee, into a balance."

As Jock moved on with his pavior-like steps
and uncouth habiliments, "whistling as he went
for want of thought," his hat turned up behind,
and the band-box of his mistress suspended from
his left hand by a blue ribbon, I could not help
more than once turning to look after him on the
road, as I thought to myself, "There goes a
veritable picture of Adonis—the beau-ideal of
a lover."

CHAPTER XL

LITTLE remains to be added to this brief domestic tale, which we now hurry on to its conclusion, premising, however, that the united eloquence of Jock and his able advocate Mrs Soorocks eventually succeeded wonderfully with Jenny Clatterpans; and after being three times regularly proclaimed in church—an acquiescence with propriety and church-laws which was more than his Laird and Leddy could boast of—Dr Lounlans joined them together as man and wife. To such as are interested in their welfare we have the felicity of saying that, assisted by Jenny, who is of a managing turn, Jock is now in a thriving way, their united funds having been sufficient to buy a cow or two, and a myriad of cocks and hens —the produce of which in the shape of milk, eggs, butter, chickens, and cheese, enables them to enjoy all the necessaries, and a few of the luxuries of life. To add to their connubial bliss, we have the greatest satisfaction in adding that Jenny has lately presented Jock with a fine boy, the very image of his father.

Stimulated by disappointment, yet under the

pretext of doing justice to his ward, the Nabob
prosecuted with ardour the claim which he had
on the lands of Auldbiggings, till the old Laird,
like a bird hovering round its desolated nest
and loath to take his leave, fairly finding himself
driven to his wit's-end and unable longer to
retain possession, abandoned the home which for
many a generation had been the pride and sanc-
tuary of his ancestors, and moved with his leddy
and her sister to Edinburgh. By the purchase-
money of the superiority, together with the
income and gatherings of the two ladies, he is
enabled to live in great comparative respectability ;
yet he is said to have been at first much annoyed
at finding himself only one of an immense crowd,
thoughtless of him and busy with their own concerns, instead of the West Country Laird, " the
admired of all admirers," and the sovereign of
his own petty domain.

Regularly, whenever the season is over, the
Laird and his leddy revisit Barenbraes, reducing
their establishment, and haining[1] for the winter ;
for, like the other Athenian gentry, they make a
point of returning to town when the Courts open.
The Laird still talks of publishing his Memoirs,
though we have not lately had opportunity of
learning what progress he is making in that
elaborate, curious, and erudite work, consistency
having obliged him to cancel some parts and re-
model others, on account of his alteration of

[1] *Haining.* Saving.

opinion, having become a strenuous advocate for
free trade in corn since he ceased to be interested
in the fluctuations of agriculture.   When the
weather is calm and fair, he is sometimes met with
in Princes Street, with one of the ladies on each
arm. They seem particularly fond of the windows
of the picture-shops, opposite which they may be
frequently observed pausing ; nor do they disdain
taking a view of the " Hydras, Gorgons, and
Chimæras dire" plastered up in front of the
menageries on the Mound, when the newspapers
announce any fresh importation of natural curiosities.   In general, however, he prefers to sit at
home watching the mutations of the clouds from
his window, or the shapes of Saracens and sala-
manders in the fire.   In this pensive guise and
solitary occupation he is allowed to spend many
an unmolested hour ; for the ladies are great forenoon visitors, talking much of their sister Lady
Chandos, and but rarely alluding to their niece
Mrs Lounlans, of whom when they do chance to
make mention, one of them makes a point of
sighing, as it were to indicate how much they
feel for her imprudence in having marred their
pedigree by marrying so far below her own
station.

We had almost overlooked the amiable dominie,
Mr Tansie : so fares it often with unobtrusive
merit in this busy and bustling world ; but the
reader may not find it unpleasant to be told that,
with the equanimity of one of Plato's disciples, he

keeps the silent tenor of his way, " teaching the young idea how to shoot" for his livelihood, contented with a situation whose privacy enables him to indulge in his philosophical day-dreams, with but few wants to supply, and having these amply satisfied.

A pleasant time for him it is during his Christmas vacation—the season of long starry nights and wintry devastation—to pay his annual visit to the metropolis, when he never fails, as in duty bound, to pay his respects to the Laird and the ladies; constantly carrying with him, from the faithful Jock to his master, some little token of his grateful remembrance, in the shape of a seasonable goose, or a pair of well-fed ducks, in the corner of his portmanteau.

I was much pleased with Mr Tansie's description of the Laird's town residence, and the remarks to which it gave rise in his unsophisticated mind.

" They dwell," said he, " in a fine double house, with two entrances. One opens to a common-stair that leads to the upper flat and attics, which certain of the lower orders inhabit. The other is a genteel door with pillars and architraves, such as befit the porch of a house for a family of rank and pedigree.

" You cannot go amiss in looking for the house, for it has a brass plate on the door, with ' Malachi Mailings, Esq., of Auldbiggings,' on't at full length; the which to observe caused me much perplexity, for I could not divine what

the Laird had to do with a sign. That doctors,
advocates, and writers to the signet, should
have recourse to such brazen devices to make
themselves notorious and to bring custom, seems
not unreasonable; but for landless lairds, and
freeholders of parchment, to set themselves up
as a titular nobility, and expect fame and renown by inscribing their 'teetles,' as they call
them, on brass, is, to say the least o't, not the
way that Horace took to raise himself a monu-
ment; but I daresay it is done by the quondam
Laird, our friend, in a spirit of bravery, for I
was told that he still refuses to sign or assent
to any legal surrender of Auldbiggings to the
Nabob, though he may be brought to trouble
for his contumacity."

NOTES

NOTES

Note A.—AUTHOR'S REMARKS

The Last of the Lairds.—During the same interval I wrote the sketch of *The Last of the Lairds.* I meant it to belong to that series of fictions of manners of which the *Annals of the Parish* is the beginning; but owing to some cause, which I no longer remember, instead of an autobiography, I was induced to make it a narrative, and in this respect it lost that appearance of truth of nature which is, in my opinion, the great charm of such works. I have no recollection how this happened, nor what caused me to write it as it is, but the experiment was a very unwise one, and some day I will try to supply what is wanted, namely, the autobiography of one of the last race of lairds.

But although the work lacks essentially in being a story, it ought to have been more amusing than it is, and yet it is not deficient in that kind of caricature which is at once laughable and true.

The character I had in view was a Laird of Smithstown, who was alive in my boyhood. His first leddy was the first corpse that I saw, and the scene, though it must have been contemplated when I could not have been above three or four years old, is still very vivid in my recollection, and so exceedingly ludicrous, that no effort of reason can oblige gossip memory to describe it with becoming seriousness. My grandmother took me to see the spectacle, and as it is one of those old Scottish exhibitions which no longer can anywhere now be seen, I may be excused for introducing some account of it here, moderating as much as possible with decorum the unaccountable propensity I feel to laugh whenever I think of that death-chamber.

It was, of course, a bedroom, and the windows admitted a dim funereal light, the panes being covered with napkins in the most melancholious manner. The looking-glass was also covered; indeed, as I have said in the Dirgie, one of my excellent songs in the vernacular of my beloved country,—

> "A damask servit co'er the glass,
> And a' was very decent."

The bottom of every chair was also dressed with white towels. The laird himself sat in a solemn elbow-chair at the bed-head, and some three or four old women opposite to it, all in the most mournful postures. But the bed itself was "the observed of all observers." On it lay the mortal remains, at full length, of the leddy in her shroud of white crape, most ingeniously ornamented with bows and scalloping (as I must call it, not knowing the technical name), and on her bosom was a white mystical plate of mingled earth and salt.

What was deficient in the funereal paraphernalia cannot now be called to mind; but something so tickled

> "The wond'ring innocence of my young fancy,"

that I began to laugh and ask questions, which obliged my grandmother, as I stood at her knee, to roughly shake me into silence. I noticed one thing, however, which no intimidation could awe me from inquiring what it meant.

The laird was well stricken in years, and not being, of course, the wisest of men, had an unseemly custom of making his lips go as if talking to himself; and I hearing no sound issuing from the "country gentleman," became very importunate to know if he were conversing with the dead leddy, as his words were so like nothing; but the answer vouchsafed to my inquisition at the time has accidentally fallen into the pit of oblivion. The question, however, afterwards gave rise to a very philosophical controversy among the matrons when we retired, in which one of them stated it as her opinion that he was praying. In that pious notion the others were on the point of concurring. I happened to hear her hypothesis, and inquired, with all the sagacity becoming my years, how he could expect to be heard so far up as the skies ; for although I had said my prayers every night with all my birr, I was not sure of having yet been heard.

Here I may once for all state, that the cherishing of a preference myself for some of my compositions, which are not well thought of by "my public," is owing to no feeling of disrespect towards the opinion of my readers. It is a pardonable egotism to suppose that some of them may not have excited as much attention as they deserve. —*Literary Life*, i. 270-274.

Note B.—"DELTA" AND *THE LAST OF THE LAIRDS*

The share which "Delta" had in *The Last of the Lairds*, and the circumstances which led to his having anv, are most fully explained in Dr Moir's own *Memoir* of Galt, prefixed to the *Annals* in the edition of Blackwood's Standard Novels :—

Whfle yet in suspense about the time of again leaving England for Canada, and shortly after finishing the *Omen*, Mr Galt commenced another Scottish tale, which in its progress received the name of *The Last of the Lairds*.

In a letter dated London, 23rd January 1826, I find that it was then in progress. He says, "I am still very much harassed with the Canadian concerns. They are as yet undetermined ; but I have been doing a little to the 'Laird,' and hope to be able to send a quantity of it by the next monthly parcel." In such intervals of leisure as Mr Galt could command during the summer, portions of the manuscript were regularly sent down for press to Edinburgh ; but unfortunately, some suggestions of Mr Blackwood happening to prove unpalatable, the composition was for some time suspended. The coolness thus engendered required something like friendly arbitration to do away with, and happening to stand in the same amicable relation to both author and publisher, the manuscript was put into my hands for an opinion. From the tenor of the following letter, it would appear that I had tendered one. Shortly

after that had been received, and while the work was yet
barely finished, Mr Galt was obliged to take his departure for
America.

"LONDON, 1st October 1826.

"MY DEAR SIR,—I consider myself as having been fortunate
in making your acquaintance ; for although my inclinations
have always been literary, yet my pursuits, and the class of
persons among whom I have been thrown, have not favoured
the predilection. I do not know a single person to whom I
could have applied to do for me what you have done, to say
nothing of the manner in which the favour was granted. But
I shall not offend you by saying more on this head.

"I shall be glad, indeed, if the 'Laird' gives any satisfaction. . . . The character of Mrs Soorocks, to which I attached no
small importance, Mr Blackwood expressed himself so offended
with, that I could not help laughing at his energy on the
occasion, for he spoke of her as if she had been an actual being
—I wanted no better proof of having succeeded in my con-
ception. What you say of the Nabob is perhaps just ; but
then he is requisite. Some such vigorous personage was necessary to be opposed to the 'Laird ;' and we find but few men
of business with individuality enough to make a character of.
At one time, I had an idea of introducing in his stead a successful Glasgow manufacturer ; but the Oriental seemed to
me more picturesque, and moreover there is such a person
in R——shire, so I could not resist the temptation. Beings
like Jock and the Laird will not stand bringing out. There is
something in imbecility that will not suffer it to endure much
handling. The Laird's character has cost me more pains and
reflection than anything I ever attempted. I began the work
as an autobiography, and, after having made considerable progress, threw it into the fire. The station of the Laird in society
affords but few incidents, and the selfish stupidity of the person
is too offensive in itself to interest. To avoid disgusting is as
much as one can hope for in delineating such a being. I know
not if I make myself understood ; but I have said enough to
explain why there is so little of the Laird and Jock. My
object in the work was to delineate a set of persons, of his own
rank, that such an obsolete character as a West Country Laird
was likely, about twenty years ago, to have had for acquaint-

ance and neighbours ; and I hope so far it will be found not altogether a failure.

"With regard to those blemishes to which you advert, do with them as you think fit : I give you full liberty to act ; carve and change as you please ; and I am sure whatever you do in either way will be improvements. . . .—I remain, my dear Sir, yours truly,   J. GALT."

"I think the title of the 'Laird' should be simply, *The Last of the Lairds*, by the author of, &c. By the way, I wish you would write a page or two of deprecatory preface, stating under what circumstances the editorship came to you. It would oblige me if you would put Δ to it. . . . I leave town on Wednesday to embark. I should have been off this evening ; but I have business to transact with the Chancellor of the Exchequer on Tuesday, on which day he comes to town, so that I am actually running the risk of losing my passage.

' Perhaps a sentence or two may be wanting at the conclusion of the 'Laird.' If you think so, supply it."

Mr Galt again set out for America, although, from several circumstances which had occurred, he had great doubts as to whether his sojourn there was to be altogether a pleasant one. . . .

At this time, I received from Mr Galt the following pleasing and characteristic letter :—

"QUEBEC, 22nd *February* 1827.

"MY DEAR SIR,—I am really under very great obligations to you. A copy of the 'Laird' having come to the castle from the New York publisher, Lady Dalhousie lent it to me. I observe what you have done with Jock and Jenny Clatterpans, which improves the dramatic effect. If the work come to a second edition, I will avail myself of the improvement, and write a courtship scene for the pair. I see you have put in Blackwood's story of the watch, but I am not sure of the effect ; and I wish the Renfrew uproar had been retained. However, I can trace various points of minor improvement ; and I am persuaded that the character of Mrs Soorocks will tell. It would seem by the New York papers that the work has taken there. I have several hints for Canadian tales that

U

may help your muse, which, if my mission is not prolonged, I will bring home ; otherwise, I shall send them. . . ."

[New and interesting light is thrown upon the origin and progress of the book in Mrs Oliphant's *William Blackwood and His Sons*, i. 456-461. Edinburgh : 1897. Cf. the present writer's article, "The Last of the Lairds : A Centenary Tribute," in *The Juridical Review*, December 1926.—W.R.]

PRINTED BY WILLIAM BLACKWOOD & SONS LTD.